YEARS
SIMON &
SCHUSTER

SET FOR LIFE

a novel

ANDREW EWELL

SIMON & SCHUSTER
New York   London   Toronto   Sydney   New Delhi

YEARS
SIMON &
SCHUSTER

1230 Avenue of the Americas
New York, NY 10020

First Simon & Schuster hardcover edition February 2024

SIMON & SCHUSTER and colophon are registered trademarks of Simon & Schuster, LLC

Simon & Schuster: Celebrating 100 Years of Publishing in 2024

For information about special discounts for bulk purchases, please contact Simon & Schuster Special Sales at 1-866-506-1949 or business@simonandschuster.com.

The Simon & Schuster Speakers Bureau can bring authors to your live event. For more information or to book an event, contact the Simon & Schuster Speakers Bureau at 1-866-248-3049 or visit our website at www.simonspeakers.com.

Interior design by Carly Loman

Manufactured in the United States of America

10 9 8 7 6 5 4 3 2 1

Library of Congress Cataloging-in-Publication Data is available on file.

ISBN 978-1-6680-1142-3
ISBN 978-1-6680-1144-7 (ebook)

SET FOR LIFE

part one

DEAD ART

1

I WOKE TO THE PING OF THE OVERHEAD ALERT SYSTEM, HOV-
ering somewhere between the Fifty-Second Parallel and Queens,
New York. The drink cart rattled down the aisle, soda tabs hissing in the thrumming pressurized air, and the world slowly returned to form around me. I was on an Air France flight from
Bordeaux to JFK, headed home from a three-month fellowship
abroad, with nothing to show for my time but a high tolerance
for brandy and a few new French curse words. I was supposed
to have written a book in that time, but I was a total blank. My
job was depending on it. My marriage, too, as it turned out. But
I couldn't come up with anything. Whenever Debra asked how
the work was going, I told her it was great, I couldn't wait to
show her some pages. After all, this was my wife we're talking
about. A writer herself, and a professor, too. Not to mention the
director of creative writing at the college where I was employed,
and therefore my de facto boss. She'd acted encouraging the
couple of times we'd talked over the summer. "Don't overthink
it," she'd said. "Something will come." But her blandishments
never stuck. Instead of turning out a novel like I was supposed
to, I spent my days walking listlessly around Bordeaux, squeezing the breads, sniffing the cheeses, partaking of the wines and
spirits, and then returning home at night to get drunk on Ar-
magnac with the ceramicist and the composer who were in residence with me. Not the sort of stuff that gets you tenure.

My only succor was dinner in the city that night with our best friends from graduate school, John Reams and his wife, Sophie Schiller. We'd known one another almost twenty years, since long before anyone expected anything of us, when the future was still abstract with possibility. John had been a poet with a taste for bathos and sexual innuendo. Sophie had written short stories that combined the vernacular of her native Ohio with the gothic imagery of Flannery O'Connor. John now practiced law, and Sophie worked for a marketing firm. I still knew them as the misfits and casual alcoholics they'd been in their twenties, though, and I looked forward to one last plunder before my humble homecoming.

The plane touched down at six. I took a cab into Brooklyn and caught up on voice mail messages. My father had called to tell me the roof of the shabby seaside motel of which he and my mother were the proprietors probably wouldn't make it through another hurricane season. I deleted the message before the part where he asked for money.

Debra had called, too, to say she was stuck upstate in Halbrook, where we'd been living the last four years, and couldn't make it down to the city for dinner. Something to do with an event at the dean's house. "It's a great opportunity for me," she said. "Almost nobody else in the department was invited." She was quiet for a moment. "Except for the chair, of course. So, you know, it's not something I can miss." That was the extent of the details.

The cab expelled me twenty minutes later on the corner of Withers and Lorimer, the BQE rumbling overhead. I grabbed my bag, threw it over my shoulder, and headed toward Bamonte's, the marquee looming down the block like a storefront church.

The dining room was crowded, seats full, the light dim and crimson-hued, the air dense with conversation. Some priests in flowing black cassocks were sipping wine at a table across the way. I spied John and Sophie near them in the back, waiting with martinis, John looking rose-cheeked, like a drunken country lawyer, in his white dinner jacket and silk tie, Sophie sitting across from him, impatiently tapping an unlit cigarette on the table like she used to do when she was bored in workshop.

I sat down between them, ordered myself a martini, and as soon as it arrived I began confessing my failure with the relief of a serial killer who's finally been caught. It felt so good admitting to the colossal goose egg that was my summer, telling my oldest, closest friends about all the blunders and misfires I'd been keeping secret from Debra. Afterward, I sat back and let out a deep sigh. I sensed forgiveness in the air. Atonement. Absolution.

But Sophie was having none of it. She leaned forward, laced her fingers above her cocktail glass, and stared at me with that dark, serious glare of hers. "You didn't write at all?" she said. "Not even a word?"

"Nothing worth keeping," I told her, perhaps a little too self-satisfied.

"And you're gloating?"

In fact, I was miserable. "Don't mistake my unbosoming for happiness," I said.

John set his glass down and put his hand on my shoulder. "Let me tell you something, friend. There's no sense beating yourself up about it. What's happened has happened. Nothing to do but move forward." He raised his glass. "And besides, no one reads fiction anymore. You shouldn't take it personally."

Sophie curled up her lip. "Do you even think before you speak?"

"Not if I can help it," he said. "But on this matter, I do happen to be something of an expert." Once upon a time John had enjoyed real success as a poet, with poems in the *New Yorker* and *Poetry* and a collection put out by Yale Press. Then he abandoned it all and enrolled in law school. The closest he ever came to poetry these days was to get drunk and recite Philip Larkin to strangers at a bar. For comic effect, poetry apparently retained some value. Otherwise, it was a dead art. "Fiction's headed in the same direction," he said. "And I ought to know."

Sophie ignored him. This was a diatribe she had obviously heard before and was tired of listening to.

"At least you got to travel," she said. "Do you know what some people would give for three months alone in France? And all that time to write?" She worked for a digital marketing company in SoHo these days, writing white papers, blog posts, and advertising copy. I assumed she'd given up on fiction.

"Why, are you working on something?" I said.

"That isn't the point," she said. "But I could be."

I remembered her short stories from graduate school, stories about her childhood in Ohio, about her father's death from cancer when she was nine, about the asylum where she and her brothers would visit their mother in the years that followed. They were stark, arresting, and would be easily published, everyone agreed at the time. But Sophie didn't care whether they were published or not. Even when she caught the attention of a major agent who wanted to help her turn her vignettes into a novel, she refused. "Then why write at all?" Debra had asked, incredulous. "Because it's how I think," I remembered Sophie saying.

The entrées soon arrived, and after a few forkfuls of spaghetti Bolognese John turned to me and said, "What are you trying to write about anyway? That same old stuff about boatyards and boardinghouses? Fishing trawlers and whatnot?"

I grew up in Big Pine Key, Florida, in a dilapidated two-story motel called the Last Resort, which my father won in a poker game and spent the rest of his life failing to make profitable. Though I hadn't been back in more than fifteen years, the place was crystalized in my mind: the steel-blue travelift hauling sail-boats back and forth across the asphalt lot, the curdled odor of bilge waste and diesel smoke in the salt air, the piggish grunt of cormorants taking flight from the bollards each morning, my father's white panel van parked forever by the lobby door, its sides painted over with the names of aborted business ventures like a palimpsest of failed ambitions. It was all I'd written about in graduate school—that place, those people. I had even penned a novel by that name. But over the years I grew embarrassed of the place, and probably it showed in my work. When my agent tried to sell the novel, the editors mostly agreed it was too parochial, not relatable enough. So I took a cue from Debra's playbook and went to France in search of something—anything—else to write about.

"Nobody wants to read that stuff anymore," I told John. "And besides, a guy like me, relating his sad life's story? It's unbecoming. Like wearing the band's T-shirt at the concert, there are some things you just don't do."

"Perhaps you should set your sights on something more topical then," John suggested. He reached across the table for the bread and tore off a piece, dipping it in the sauce on his plate. "Have you considered right-wing extremism?" he offered, chewing. "Or global warming?"

I stabbed a piece of osso buco and pushed it around the plate. "I don't think I'm qualified to tackle those subjects."

"Something to do with a cult, then. Or a young person with supernatural powers. Or perhaps an apocalypse."

Sophie sipped her martini. "What does Debra say you should do?" she asked.

"She says to write a book. It doesn't matter what it's about, as long as it sells."

"Typical," she said. "And I suppose you agree with her?"

I couldn't help admitting it was an effective strategy. Debra

7

had published three books in the last six years, turning them out as coolly as quarterly statements, and although her process struck me as chaotic and a little faithless, it worked shockingly well for her. Sometimes I'd come downstairs to the living room and see her typing on her laptop while the TV was showing reruns of *Law & Order* and her sister was jabbering on speakerphone and Ernie, the dog, was licking his haunches at her feet, and I'd think, *How is this possible?* It was unsettling to witness. But I knew she was onto something. She had tenure, job security, a respectable readership. Even the dog seemed to favor her.

Sophie shot me a glacial deadpan over the lip of her cocktail glass, then looked away, rolling her eyes.

"What?"

"It's nothing."

"Then why the daggers?"

"I guess I just thought you still wanted to make something good," she said. "Great even. But I suppose that's too much to ask anymore."

John wiped his mouth, laid his napkin over his empty plate, and turned his palms out like a Pentecostalist. "As the great Dolly Parton reminds us," he declaimed, "it's hard to be a diamond in a rhinestone world."

Sophie pushed her seat back and stood up. Our plates were mostly empty now, our cocktails were down to the last sips. She pulled a soft pack of Camels from her purse. She had the lighter poised in her other hand. "I suppose one of you two can figure out how to get the check?" she said, then headed for the door. I pulled out my wallet. Outside, through the front window, I could see her lighting a cigarette, pacing up and down the sidewalk, blowing smoke out in huffs.

"She all right?" I said to John.

"Don't worry about it," he said.

John and I drank a couple of quick postprandial whiskies,

settled the bill, and then joined Sophie outside about five minutes later. The three of us walked together up Union. John kept going on about how I might hack into the publishing business. "Have you considered a pseudonym?" he said as we walked. "Or perhaps a fictional persona?" Sophie was ten paces ahead of us. I thought about jogging to catch up to her, but what was there to say? I knew what she meant. We had changed—all of us had, in our way. When we met in graduate school, the world still seemed like a place that could accommodate the peculiar kind of person who wanted to spend their life around books, who wanted to talk about ideas in bars, squandering their money on drinks and conversation. I remembered that John and Sophie used to keep a photo of John Berryman on their refrigerator door, his hair wild, his shirt collar open, an unmade bed out of focus in the background. Back then we thought that picture was the essential portrait of the artist, and we all saw some aspect of ourselves and the places we'd come from in Berryman's drunken, rueful countenance. It was an emblem of John's parents divorcing when he was five, of his mother's stealing his college savings and blasting through Europe with it. Of Sophie's insane mother being picked up by the police for howling, barefoot, inside a Walmart one afternoon. Of my own father surviving nineteen days lost at sea merely to wind up broke, managing a cheap motel in the Keys, which was notable only for possessing the lowest Tripadvisor rating in all of Florida. The photo had even been a touchstone for Debra, too, who'd spent her twenties renouncing her father's ill-gotten wealth before deciding, in her thirties, to start keeping all the gifts he sent her—the leather boots and jackets and purses—in exchange for publicly acknowledging his existence. But everyone finally grew up and cast away their romanticism. Sophie became a marketing director. John became a lawyer. Debra became a "professional author." And me, I was a failed writer, teaching future failed writers at a third-tier college in a Podunk town upstate.

"What about a sprawling family saga?" John continued as we walked. "Set on a Texas ranch. Spanning four or five generations. Or an astronaut story."

I watched Sophie up ahead as John went on, curlicues of cigarette smoke spiraling over her shoulder, her arms bare in the summer night, her blazer folded over the opening of her tote bag, the sleeves flapping behind her as she strode ahead.

"Ever thought about a massive chemical spill?" John said. "Or a traveling circus?"

Sophie took a right at Richardson, and John and I followed after her.

"What about a legal thriller?" he said. "I could offer myself as a resource. At a rate of three hundred dollars an hour, of course."

Eventually we stopped at a bar on the corner of Richardson and Lorimer. A crowd was gathered outside on the sidewalk. In the window there were string lights and concert posters. We squeezed through and made our way inside. Sophie and I waited by the back wall while John snaked through the throngs to get us a round of drinks. She was right, I thought. Right about Debra. Right about me, too.

"You know," I said, "about earlier . . ."

"Forget it," she said. "It's none of my business. Write whatever you want. You and Debra both."

John came back from the bar and passed around three Budweiser longnecks and three whiskey shots. We hoisted our drinks. "To friendship," he announced. "*Ad finem esto fidelis!*"

The three of us clanked glasses and drank. Then my phone buzzed. It was Debra, wanting to know whether she could expect me on the eleven o'clock train. *Fine if you miss it, though,* she wrote. *I'll be at this party till late. Probably won't see you tonight regardless.*

"Mind if I stay over?" I asked.

It was Sophie who answered. "I already made up the futon, just in case."

Outside, a group of young people—younger than us anyway—were drinking beers on the sidewalk. John caught sight of them through the window. His eyes flashed.

"Now if you'll excuse me," he said, "I've got a date with fortune," and walked out the door with his beer. Through the window I could see him launch into his Chaplin routine, limping comically up and down the sidewalk, doffing an invisible cap, leaning on an imaginary cane. I was surprised to see he could still pull off this stunt. He would be turning forty soon, only a couple of months after me. Yet there he was on his knees, kissing the back of a woman's hand, doing his impersonation of the lovable tramp. I looked at Sophie.

"At this point," she said, "we basically live separate lives."

"To better times," I said, raising my beer to toast.

"To lost convictions."

For a few minutes I watched Sophie watch her husband through the window. Her eyes looked briefly moist. From Debra I got periodic reports on Sophie's life, and John's, but I was starting to think they were watered down, diluted and bowdlerized. How much had I missed, letting Debra play reporter all these years? Sophie seemed suddenly so much more alone than I'd imagined, so cloistered inside her cigarettes and whiskey.

Finally she turned away, spotting a free booth across the room, and went to sit down in it, facing away from the window outside of which John could still be seen gamboling around like Grimaldi. I slipped in beside her, feeling woozy and jet-lagged. For something to say, I offered my own self-deprecation:

"I shouldn't have hit it so hard last night," I said, settling down with a thud.

"Or the night before that," she said. "Or the night before

that, I'm guessing." She sipped her beer. "Trust me, I can sympathize."

"Yeah, what's your excuse?" I said.

She took her Camels out and laid the pack on the table for later. "I'm trying to kill myself. Hadn't you noticed?" This was her kind of humor. You couldn't always tell when she was joking.

"And how's that going?"

"It's taking too long."

"I can't say I blame you," I said. "Life's barely interesting anymore."

She put her hand on my thigh. It was warm. When she leaned in so she could speak above the din of music and chatter, I could feel her breath.

"You know what I think?" she said. "I think you've been upstate too long. Those little American towns have a way of blunting your nerves."

"Maybe you're right. But what's the alternative?"

"You could have stayed in France."

"I'd have gone broke."

"Then you should have gone someplace else. Someplace cheaper."

"Like where?"

"I don't know," she said. "Mexico, Nicaragua, Honduras, who cares? Anywhere but home."

Last night I'd been in Bordeaux, drinking brandy with a Swedish filmmaker. This morning I had been forty thousand feet above the Atlantic, soaring at six hundred miles an hour. Tomorrow morning I would be on the Ethan Allen Express, chugging back to Halbrook. Why not catch a flight to Puerto Vallarta instead?

"It's a tempting thought," I said.

"People leave their lives all the time," she said. "Hell, maybe

I'll join you." She was only joking, but as she went on about
the low cost of living in Mexico, the rent, the food, the people, the mountains, I started to picture a hammock swaying
between two palm trees on a sandy ridge, a Corona bottle on
the ground, my old pal Sophie Schiller in a black bikini with a
white shawl draped loosely over her shoulders. I saw her heels
dragging in the sand as she rocked back and forth, her butt
cupped in the palm of her swimsuit, her thighs hash-marked by
the hammock laces. I saw a little casita in the distance where
the two of us were living. My head felt heavy. I could feel myself listing as I dreamed, watching her mouth move. The room
was loud, but it seemed to grow quieter as she talked, and soon
it seemed to darken, and I drank my whiskey and felt my head
grow light, and then I felt our thighs touching, and as she went
on about there being other ways to live, and other means of
making a living, and other places where a person could still afford to be an artist, whatever "artist" meant these days, I found
myself leaning in toward her, inching closer to the familiar gap
between her two front teeth, like an open window, until finally
the space around us went silent and black, and our lips were
touching.

I pulled back suddenly. The noise returned, and the bass
thumped through the floorboards, and the clatter and the ringing of the old-fashioned register behind the bar came back, and
the clink of glasses and the rattle of ice. Sophie was staring at
me, touching her lower lip with her index finger, as if feeling
for a wound. I reached for my whiskey glass but it was empty.

"What are you doing?" she said. "Why did you do that?"

"I'm drunk, that's all," I said. "It was nothing. Forget about it."

"You're not that drunk," she said. "I've seen you worse."

"I'm jet-lagged. It's late. We should go. *I* should be going."

Finally John came back inside, stopping for a moment near the
door, assaying the scene. Sophie turned and looked over her shoul-

der at him. He lunged forward into a sort of dance move. Then he started swaying and jostling like Falstaff, falling over himself, putting on the next act of his show. And then he began reciting lines of Keats to anyone who would listen: "'Souls of Poets dead and gone, / What Elysium have ye known, / Happy field or mossy cavern, / Choicer than the Mermaid Tavern!'" And I thought, *By day this person sues technology companies? This person has a law degree?* Sophie gazed gloomily across the room at him, looking tired and weary. People were clamoring all around us, pressing in, pushing past, sweating, dazed, smelling of cigarettes and hot air. We looked at each other, the two of us, lingering for a moment. It was clear that John would be there till last call, maybe longer. Either way, it would be hours before we saw him again.

We left together, heading up Lorimer, past shuttered delis and formstone apartment fronts. Sophie lit a cigarette and the gold tip brightened as she drew on it. We walked several blocks in silence, bumping into each other every once in a while, ambling languidly in the general direction of her and John's apartment, saying nothing, neither of us in any particular hurry to get home. She looked over at me. Our eyes caught. Then I looked away, toward the sidewalk, tracking the dots of smattered chewing gum and cigarette butts and dog shit. I could hear her drawing on her cigarette, and when I looked over again I could see her lips making a wet mark on the filter. At some point our hands were touching, the backs of our knuckles, our fingers twining as we headed into McCarren Park. A few blocks later my fingers were on the underside of her wrist, as soft as belly skin. Now I was holding her hand, our shoulders were touching, our forearms grazing. We passed under streetlamps, stealing furtive looks at each other, hiding our glances when our eyes connected, tucking our chins into our collars, continuing quietly up into Greenpoint.

The park was empty that time of night, and almost silent. A

car turned from Lorimer onto Driggs, slapping its headlights against the dark, casting a sudden hardness on the moment. Then the car disappeared down the block and we were alone again. We were just past the gates to the track. Our hands were clasped between us. We both looked down at them swaying in the space between our bodies, as if in awe of some natural phenomenon. Minutes passed that way. We might have kept going across the park—we might have made it back to the apartment, where I might have passed out, alone, on the futon in the front room—but I knew it was already too late. Soon we were stumbling as one down the sidewalk, kissing, tumbling together onto a park bench, lying down upon it, fumbling. My hand was on the back of her neck, I could feel the damp knuckles of her spine beneath my palm, I could taste cigarette smoke on her tongue. When I opened my eyes, I saw the blurry closeness of her eyes looking back at me. Had she always had such dark irises? How long had she been wearing her hair up like that, in a bun, which I loosened now between my fingers? I felt her bare shoulders, strong and elegant as a line of calligraphy. Then everything went loose, and I reeled back, standing again. "We shouldn't," I heard myself saying. "We already did," she said. And I put my arm around her waist and pulled her toward me, and thirty minutes later we were back at her apartment, making love on the futon in the front room, her and John's empty bed visible through the crack in the doorway.

2

THE NEXT MORNING I WAS ON THE 8:50 A.M. OUT OF PENN Station, trying to remember what Freud or Hugh Hefner said about sex—that it was the most civilizing force in society, or something to that effect.

As soon as the café car opened, I got a coffee and an airplane bottle of Bailey's Irish Cream. My head hurt. My thoughts were diffuse. It was going to be strange enough coming home after three months away, but after last night it was going to be torture. My head was throbbing now—really banging around. I sat at one of the tables watching the Hudson roll by, alternating dots of shanties and steel mills and grain elevators and Victorian mansions flashing on the ridge. *You should have stayed in France*, Sophie had said last night. If not, then I should have gone to Mexico, or Honduras, or anyplace but home.

I laid my head against the cool glass. I was traveling in the opposite way of the morning commute. Most of the seats were empty. There was no one else in the café car. I couldn't shake the idea that I was going in the wrong direction.

The train got in about ten thirty. There were no cabs at the station when I arrived—I was the only passenger who got off at Halbrook—so I had to order an Uber. There was a backup on Main Street as we drove into town. A school bus kept pulling over ahead of us. Every three blocks its stop sign popped out, holding up traffic. I was in no hurry to get home anyway, so I slumped down in my seat, rocked my head back, and half hoped to be taken out by a meteor shower, or a random chemical spill the likes of which John probably thought I should make the subject of my next novel. But then I saw the sign for HISTORIC DOWNTOWN HALBROOK pass by the window, and the local library flying the New York State flag, and I knew I was only minutes away.

I grabbed my bag from the trunk and started up the driveway. Thinking I might be able to sneak in through the back and make it upstairs for a nap before Debra caught me, I entered through the side. But I wasn't so lucky. She was in the kitchen when I came in, pacing back and forth, headphones in her ears, wearing exercise tights and a tank top, her long brown hair wrapped up in a polyester headband, and her cheeks flush with health.

She didn't notice me yet. I dropped my bag on the ground. Ernie ran up to me, sniffing my leg, doing figure eights at my feet, his tail wagging like a metronome. I bent down and scratched his ears and scooped his jowls up and gave him a ruffle. He dragged his tongue across my cheek. Debra kept pacing. I waved at her. "Hello to you, too," I said, but she couldn't hear me past her earbuds. I figured she was listening to music until suddenly she started speaking aloud, as if to an invisible audience.

"A fiction writer," she declared, "has to pay attention to every little detail. You have to keep an ear out for the subtlest changes in a person's speech, a shift in tone, a strange inflection, the direction of the wind. Everything a person does can help you create a character. Me, I write down what I hear—sometimes verbatim. Does that make me a copycat? A thief? Well, isn't every writer?"

Finally she looked up and saw me. She waved, pointed to the microphone on her headset, mouthed the letters *N-P-R*.

An interview!

I plunked myself down at the counter as she went on detailing the method behind her craft. My back was sore from travel. The Uber ride hadn't helped either. And neither had last night's contortions on the futon, which had thankfully concluded before John's stumble through the front door at five in the morning. At which point I got up, dressed, went to the station, and caught the first train out before anyone had a chance to sober up and confront last night's muddled iniquities.

I clutched my side now. I must have been wincing, too, because Debra grabbed an ice pack from the freezer and silently tossed it over the kitchen island at me. Then she went on with her interview, simultaneously stretching and bending in a complicated cool-down routine.

"I write on a computer, mostly," she said as she twisted her arm above her head and behind her back, her neck craned in a painful-looking way. "But then I print everything out and read it aloud. That's one thing I'd tell any young writer"—now she was on the floor, her legs crossed elaborately—"is read your work out loud."

My head throbbed. I opened the cupboard to see whether there was anything to drink in there that might help ease the pain. I found a bottle of Dewar's with four or five fingers left in the bottom. I pulled it down. If I could swallow enough to kill my headache and maybe fall asleep for a couple of hours, then I might wake up refreshed and realize last night—everything, the whole summer—had been one bad dream. But I could already hear Debra's rebuke. It wasn't even noon. I put the bottle back and shut the cabinet.

I sat down and started going through the mail that was left for me on the counter. Credit card preapprovals. Student loan refinancing offers. Bed Bath & Beyond coupons. A recycled postcard from my parents. *Greetings from the Sunshine State*, it said.

There was no other message. Underneath the stamp was the faded ink from someone else's previously posted dispatch.

Finally the interview ended and Debra came over and pressed her sweaty self to my back and threw her arms around me in a bear hug like you'd get from a bullying older brother. I tensed up.

"What?" she said, teasing. "You're too good to take a hug from your sweaty wife? How was New York?" She returned to stretching.

"Fine," I said. I was too hungover to go into detail. Plus, the obvious reasons.

"One of *those* nights, huh."

"Appears so," I said, rubbing my temple.

"Well, I thought we'd go to Cafferty's tonight, have a little welcome-home dinner. But if you're not up for it."

"No," I said, "it's fine. I'm tired, that's all. It's been a long couple of months."

"You've been working hard," she said, bending sideways at the waist, her arm over her head. She shook her limbs loose and came over and took my hands in hers. "But maybe you can buck up by dinner?" Her hands felt strange, cold, clammy. My breath drew short. I felt guilty letting her touch me.

"I'll be all right by tonight," I told her. "I promise."

"Good," she said. "Because I'm sick of going there alone. I want everyone to see I still have a husband. So go get some rest. Take a shower. Meet me at the restaurant at six." She scooped up her water bottle and her phone and earbuds and headed for the stairs. At the threshold, she turned back. "Oh, and welcome home, if I didn't say so before."

As soon as she was out of the room I reached up for the Dewar's and downed the rest of it and tossed the empty bottle in the recycling. I lay down on the sofa in the living room with my shoes on and fell into a fitful sleep, awakening every once in a while to a frightful awareness of my surroundings—Debra's sports bra hanging on the banister, Ernie's leash slung across the back of a dining room chair—uncertain, for several seconds, of where I was, or what time of day it was, or what I was doing there.

3

HALBROOK IS A SLEEPY HAMLET TWENTY MILES SOUTH OF Albany, glazed in the soot and ash of a foundering steel plant, and home to the so-so liberal arts college where Debra and I both taught. There were no ivy-clad dormitories or white-columned buildings on the Eastern College campus. The name alone should give you some indication of the school's lack of grandeur. Not *Eastern College of New York*, or *Eastern New York College*, just *Eastern*. In four years there I never saw a tweed jacket or a corduroy blazer. I never smelled tobacco smoke wafting from beneath an office door, or witnessed a roaring fireplace surrounded by bearded academics thoughtfully discussing Proust. If you didn't know better, you might mistake the place for a city government complex. The campus was comprised of a central quad flanked by four identical Soviet-style office towers, each in its own shade of gray. The English Department was located on the first floor of one of these buildings. History, Economics, Political Science, Communications, and Identity Studies ranked above us in that exact order. This slate obelisk was known affectionately as the Humanities Bloc.

Debra got other offers the year we accepted positions at Eastern, but no one else could offer me work as well. At best I might have entered the adjunct pool and pulled in a class or two a semester at one of the other schools that had tried to court her, but it would have paid less than a graduate stipend.

Eastern, however, was putting their chips on Debra Crawford, and they were prepared to do whatever was necessary to secure her, which meant offering me a consolation job. Her first novel had been on the *New York Times* year-end list. Her second was about to come out the fall she was to start at Eastern, which meant the college would get a citation on the book jacket—"and teaches English at Eastern College" and so forth. So when Chet Bland, the chair of the department, asked whether Debra had any questions about the offer he'd just made her (this was all over speakerphone while I listened from across the room at our old apartment in Chicago), she said, "Well, actually, I do," and he said, "Uh-oh," and Debra said, "Well, I guess it's time I tell you I have a husband," and Chet said, "Let me guess"— dramatic pause—"he's a writer, too?"

Two days later I was on a flight to Halbrook to teach a sample class and tour the campus. By the time I returned to Chicago, there was an offer in my inbox. An assistant professorship, just like Debra's, at nearly as much pay. We thought we'd hit the jackpot. We had reason to rejoice.

The next six weeks were a heady mix of trepidation and excitement. We were on Zillow every day, talking on the phone to real estate agents, reading online about restaurants in Halbrook, checking Google Maps to see how close we'd be to New York, texting with John and Sophie about how often we'd see them, how we could be in Brooklyn in less than two hours anytime we wanted. I remember falling asleep those nights with my cheeks sore from laughing.

But of course nothing went as planned. Debra and I didn't end up going into the city very often after we moved. At the end of our first year there, I realized we'd only been to New York once that whole spring semester. Life in Halbrook was not *life near New York*, or *life along the Hudson*, or *life back on the East Coast*; it was simply *life in Halbrook*.

Over time—and without my noticing exactly how it happened—Debra came to actually *like* the place. The town grew on her quickly, and right under my nose. She enjoyed being a big fish in a small pond. Me, I was a small fish in a small pond in which Debra Crawford was the circling shark, and I didn't take to the role. She earned tenure at the end of her first year, making her the youngest woman in Arts and Sciences ever to do so. But it wasn't just that. She liked Halbrook's humility, its quiet fortitude, the way people earnestly backed their cars into parking spaces on Main Street to protect their fenders, the way they savored their crullers at the Sunday farmer's market, the rubber boots they wore when it rained. She liked that the only coffee shop in town wouldn't make a cappuccino (they called it "coffee with milk"). She liked that it was a place where people just kept on going, no matter what. They didn't complain, they put their heads down and they worked at whatever it was they were working at—the Dairy Queen, the flower shop–cum–hardware store, the public library that also served as the town's only art gallery—and it made her appear, by contrast, like a beacon of ambition and success. But I couldn't understand it. What did those people want? What moved them? That was the mystery I couldn't figure out. I'd be standing there at the front of the class dispensing another half-throated bromide—"Fiction isn't about generalities, it's about particulars" or whatever—and the students would all take out their laptops and dutifully copy down my remarks with guileless obedience. Once, when I said "the only subject of fiction is life itself," I noticed Lena March—engaged to be married that spring to the red-lipped young man sitting next to her—mouth the words *life itself* as she gazed longingly into the sleepy eyes of her nineteen-year-old bridegroom. *Life itself?* It was enough to turn your stomach. But Debra loved their earnestness. Plus, she couldn't resist the allure of being the town's biggest and only celebrity, nor the satisfaction of knowing that she was unlikely to face any contenders for the title anytime soon—least of all her husband.

At first I tried my best to get on board with Halbrook. We went to a student theater production of *King Lear*, but the teenage actor's voice cracked playing blind, raving Gloucester, and all the drama went out the window. We went to a women's volleyball match, but the game ended early when one of the players took a spike to the face. We even joined a softball club, but the season was canceled when the fields were dozed to build a Walmart. And of course none of it worked to allay my misery. I wound up going online at night and reading about restaurant openings back in Chicago. (Once upon a time we had talked about how often we'd travel, saving so much money living in Halbrook.) I'd read about the Caravaggio exhibit at the Art Institute. I'd see how much tickets were to the new Steppenwolf play. I'd study the cocktail list at the newest bar in Logan Square. Sometimes I'd bring up an event to Debra, saying, "The MCA's doing a thing on refugee art next month. We should go." "Do you mean the MCA, as in the Museum of Contemporary Art, as in the Museum of Contemporary Art in Chicago?" And I'd say, "Yeah, why not?" and she'd go, "Because we don't live in Illinois," and I'd go, "There's such a thing as planes." But nothing would come of it. By the end of our second year, even taking the train into Manhattan had become too big a trek for her. "What if it's late?" she'd say, worried. "What if it's booked? What if it's crowded? Let's just go to Cafferty's instead."

The lucky news was that Cafferty's was a bar I could actually tolerate. It was located in a residential area of Halbrook, on a pleasant tree-lined street, with an ample parking lot that was covered by a canopy of mature elm trees. From outside, the building looked like a giant gingerbread house, with baby-blue latticework and white shingles and a gabled roof, none of which inspired confidence. Inside, it was festooned with ruffle and lace tablecloths and still life watercolors, which were hardly an improvement. But once you turned a corner into the barroom, you found sanctuary at a bar with a good bourbon selection and a knowledgeable bartender, with a good sight line to a working brick fireplace. The food was excellent, as well. And because there were no windows in the barroom, you could make believe for a time that you were somewhere else. You had to be careful not to look too closely at the decorations, though. In addition to the doilies and lace, someone had seen fit to decorate the walls with wooden placards that had inane aphorisms printed on them. IN DOG BEERS, I'VE ONLY HAD TWO, read one. IT ISN'T A HANGOVER, IT'S WINE FLU, read another one. THE UNEXAMINED WIFE IS NOT WORTH LEAVING was posted like one of Luther's 95 Theses above the exit. I DRINK THEREFORE I AM hung behind the beer taps. It would have been enough to make you run away screaming if it weren't for the fact that the bartender always had your drink on the bar before you'd gotten your coat off.

I sat down that evening—my first night back—and Charlie, the bartender, dressed in a white collared shirt with a black bow tie, sleeves rolled up, poured my martini before my butt hit the seat. No questions about my book, the fellowship, my months abroad—just the satisfaction of present needs. I dipped my lips to the icy surface and took the first cool sip.

Debra came in a few minutes later. She had that professional glow about her. She'd just had a call with her agent or her editor, I guessed, which would explain what had taken her so long to show up.

"Who was it this time?"

"Miriam," she said. Her publicist. "Apparently the NPR thing was a hit. Lots of emails from people in the business. She says I'm kinda hot right now."

Charlie placed a glass of prosecco down in front of Debra and we raised glasses in a toast.

"Don't worry," she said. "Your time will come soon, I can feel it." She gave me a wink. "Speaking of which, Chet stopped by my office."

"Oh?"

"He seemed concerned."

Chet Bland, Chair of English, who always introduced himself this way even if you knew him, was often stopping by Debra's office. She always left her door open, so it was an easy thing to do. She liked for people to see how much time she spent at work. She would sit at her desk, rocked back slightly in her ergonomic chair, legs crossed at the ankle, as she edited student short stories. She had the same ten-by-twelve-foot cell we all did, but hers was outfitted with a Tiffany lamp, a recliner, and a Persian rug. She never turned the overheads on. It was always the color of evening in there. More than once I'd discovered Chet Bland standing outside in the hallway, gazing wistfully at her through the doorway like he was studying a work of art.

"And what, pray tell, did Dr. Bland want from you?"

"He was asking about you."

"He was concerned, you said."

"Yes."

"And what does concern look like on Herr Professor's face?"

"Oh, you know. Furrowed brow, tight lips, dewy eyes."

"You're painting quite a scene. Detail, gesture, objective correlative. I'm seeing a whole character come to life."

"Well, you know, we spent a lot of time together this summer," she said. "Working on the department bylaws and all," she hurried to explain. "I told you about that, didn't I?"

"It comes vaguely to mind."

"Anyway," she said, steering us back on track, "he seemed

to think the writing didn't go as well as you'd hoped. I assured him that wasn't true. Was I right to assure him of that?"

I took a belt of my martini and ordered another one from Charlie, who started working with the mixing tins as soon as I slid my empty glass across the bar. Debra's bubbly was down to the bottom now, too, and I made it known she'd have another one. We were moving fast tonight.

"Of course it went well," I lied. "But why didn't he come see me himself, if he was so concerned?"

The next round of drinks was set down. I lowered my lips to the glass.

Debra said, "That's what I told him myself. He'll be coming by your office tomorrow."

"Uh-oh," I said. "I'd better get a haircut, have my nails done. Press the old blazer."

"Don't be an ass. He just wants to check up on you. He is your chair, after all."

"He's an academic," I told her. "He doesn't understand the creative process. Projects change. Ideas develop. They need time. They can't be rushed."

Debra was quiet as she contemplated this truism. After a minute she said:

"You *did* come up with *something* while you were gone, though, didn't you? Please tell me you didn't just fart the whole summer away."

"Well, you see, there was a lot of cassoulet on the menu down there. A fella could be forgiven for at least a couple bouts of flatus."

Just then another couple from Eastern came in and took seats down the bar from us. They were about our age, hired last year from Michigan to teach in the History Department. The wife got a glass of red wine. The husband got a tumbler of whiskey and held it in both hands like a child's sippy cup. He had the slumped shoulders and dour mien of a fellow spousal hire. He raised his glass in my direction. We nodded knowingly at each other.

In a lowered tone, Debra said, "Forgive me for being concerned, but is it so wrong of me to want my husband to enjoy some success?"

I reached for my martini glass and found it suddenly empty again. These things were going down like battleships. Had I really gone through two already? My hands were sweating. Over Debra's shoulder I could see my colleague in History sadly sipping his whiskey, glancing up at a baseball game on the tiny TV behind the bar as his wife studied the dinner menu. In my mind I could feel the damp small of Sophie Schiller's back under my palms last night. I could see her irises glinting beneath the streetlamps in McCarren Park. My breath felt short, my chest thickened.

Finally I waved Charlie over and got him to pour me another martini. "Skip the olives this time," I told him. "And the vermouth."

"I see how it is," said Debra.

"I'm still jet-lagged," I told her. "What do you expect?"

The drink came and it was cold and bracing. When I looked back at Debra, she was staring in slack-jawed awe at my rate of consumption. I realized I was sort of chugging the thing, perhaps even gurgling a bit.

"Are you on drugs or something?"

"Define drugs," I said. "Alcohol's a drug, if that's what you mean. How about nonsteroidal anti-inflammatories? I took two Advil this morning on the train. Or what about Klonopin?"— which Debra took every time she had to board a plane or speak in public—"That's a drug, too, I'll remind you."

She was silent—which was how she always won these things. When I looked at her, she turned away. I gazed past her toward the foyer, where there was another one of those ridiculous placards.

IF LIFE HANDS YOU MELONS, YOU MIGHT BE DYSLEXIC.

I felt a wave of seasickness come on. I saw Sophie Schiller, naked beside me on the futon. I remembered lying there for several minutes afterward, staring into her eyes, her eyes staring back into mine in the dark glow of the streetlamps outside, amazed at the awesome, terrifying thing we'd done together.

"I'll be right back," I said.

In the bathroom I managed to catch my breath after retching drily over the sink. I splashed some cold water on my face. I thought of texting Sophie. I held my phone in my hand and stared at her name on the screen. Just thinking of her brought relief. Her name alone sent a quiver of excitement and fear through my guts. Just feeling my teeth against my lower lip as I silently formed the breathy second syllable was a tiny thrill. I was about to start typing when someone started knocking on the door.

"Just a minute!"

I put my phone away and made a pretense of running the faucet and flushing the toilet. There was only one restroom at Cafferty's, and for all I knew it could have been Debra waiting outside, listening. I slapped my cheeks a few times to wake myself up and came out. One of the busboys was waiting to get inside and clean.

When I got back to the bar I found Debra talking to our colleagues. They were congratulating her on her interview— "Really enlightening," the man said. "I don't know how you novelists do it. So much pressure!"—which seemed to have restored her mood entirely.

We ordered dinner. Debra had the salmon. I got the beef short ribs. We ate quietly. We ordered two glasses of wine, sipping from them in between bites, letting the air thin out between us. After a while, Debra said:

"*The Last Resort* was a good book, you know. You should be proud of yourself. No one can take that away from you. But now you have to write something else. Your readers are out there somewhere, I'm sure of it. You just have to think about what they want."

After dinner, we left in two different cars, and on the way home I stopped at Walgreens for dog food and toilet paper. Ernie was asleep on his mat in the living room when I came through the door. He didn't bother getting up, just raised his snout and plopped back down in place. Debra had already gone up to bed. I saw a small light at the top of the stairs and plodded toward it.

4

THE NEXT DAY CHET BLAND, CHAIR OF ENGLISH, WAS STANDing over me in gym shorts and a polo shirt, wanting to know when he could get a look at my manuscript. I was sitting at my desk. He was apparently on his way to the tennis club but had thought this meeting urgent enough to delay his plans. I didn't have the heart to tell him there *was* no manuscript. What I told him instead was that I'd print out some pages as soon as I got around to it, though of course I had nothing to print.

"That had better be soon," he said, twirling his racket. "There's a matter of timing to consider. We'll have to gather outside readers, and that can take a minute. I'd also like to know what I'm sending out before I make that ask. Surely you can understand my position."

When did the word ask *become a noun?* I wondered.

"Could you at least tell me a little something about it?" he said. "What's the subject? The genre."

"What if I told you my new book was a fiction," I said.

His eyes narrowed. His bald pink pate glistened in the afternoon sun. He put his finger to his brow, thinking for a moment. Then he said, "We *did* hire you as a novelist, so I should hope it's a work of fiction and not—what else would it be," he said, attempting a joke, "a science experiment?"

What I had meant was that the book was a lie, a falsehood—

it didn't exist except in my imagination, and even there it was an incoherent mess.

"It's not a science experiment," I assured him.

I looked out the window onto the quad. Students were returning from summer vacation, spreading themselves out on blankets, filling the air with their cheerful reunion. A Frisbee soared by the window in a peaceful arc. Some kids glided by on electric scooters. The groundskeeper was laying mulch beneath an oak tree. It was the annual campus portrait of rebirth and renewal, another autumn of new beginnings and fresh starts, better grades, strengthened friendships, reclaimed focus. By contrast, I felt perfunctory and frayed, like a tattered flag whapping outside an abandoned house.

I looked back at Chet, whose brow was tensed in thought. He had the somewhat frightening aspect of a dim-witted teenager on the verge of what he imagined to be a good idea.

"Listen," he said, "I understand it's a draft. But if you can just show me something—a single chapter—then maybe I can pass that around, just to start. Come on," he pleaded. "Help me help you."

I sighed. What choice did I have? "Give me a few weeks to cross the *i*'s and dot the *t*'s," I told him. "I promise I'll show you some pages." Surely I could come up with *something* in that time, even if it was just an opening chapter.

I turned back toward the early autumn tableau outside on the quad. A student with long, stringy hair and no shirt—a boy named Winston Armstrong, who for the last two years had enrolled in nearly every workshop I taught—was going by, carrying the metal railing of a bed frame over his shoulder like a crucifix. We shared uneasy grins, and I vaguely recalled a passage from Conrad about skimming over the surface of life's ocean, heading for a shallow grave.

When I looked back again, Chet was standing at the book-shelves, running his fingers idly along the spines.

"How's Debra?" he said. A beatific smile came over his face. "I heard her interview yesterday," he explained. "Is she working on anything new yet?"

"Not that I know of," I informed him. "But it's only a matter of time."

"She's really got her finger on the pulse, hasn't she?"

It was true, in a way. Her debut had been about a girl who disappears on New Year's Eve. It came out at the same time that another book about a missing girl was being released as a movie. Most recently she'd written a domestic thriller—*The Widower's Wife*—told from the point of view of a cynical, possibly murderous female narrator. Much of the plot seemed to come directly from a true crime podcast that had been popular the year before.

"She works very hard," I told Chet.

Now he was idly caressing the books on the shelf—Cather, Camus, Chekhov, Coleridge, all framed in a rhombus of yellow light. He turned to me.

"You know," he said, sort of patting the books like the head of a big dog, "it doesn't have to be a masterpiece." In the hallway I heard somebody asking the department secretary whether the donuts in the copy room were up for grabs. "It doesn't even have to be great," he said. "Or even good. It just has to be published."

I thanked him for his words of wisdom, and he left with his racket bobbing on his shoulder.

I locked up my office a few minutes later and headed away from campus, down Merchant Street, going in the general direction of Halbrook's downtown, such as it was. I walked by the business lunchers in gray and tan suits standing around outside the deli, eating their sandwiches, heads bowed to their cell phones. I passed the True Value and the Panera Bread and the abandoned storefront where there used to be a jewelry shop. My brain was heavy, my thoughts briefly perverse. I imagined Sophie's legs around my waist. Our flesh slick and sweating. A bus flew by and I jumped back onto the sidewalk just in time to avoid getting hit, and I stood panting for a minute on the street corner. Then I turned around and saw behind me the steak-house where we always took job applicants on their campus visits, and I went inside for a drink.

FOX News was playing on the TV above the bar. Several pa-trons in shirtsleeves, their blazers draped over the backs of their chairs, stared absently at the screen as they ate their cheese-burgers and French dip sandwiches. I drank a beer. I looked around at the crowd and watched them wiping their lips on linen napkins, changing their knives and forks from one hand to the other as they sliced their meats—the human animal, feed-ing itself, doing what it had to do to survive. And me, all I had to do was produce a book for Chet Bland and the dean's office. It didn't matter whether it was good or not. It just had to satisfy the requirements for tenure: *a single-author volume of no less than two hundred pages under contract with a national press by the time of promotion.* So why couldn't I do it? What was my problem? Was I that deluded by my own ego? Still cleaving to intimations of grandeur? Unwilling—or unable—to just sit and write something?

I thought of the down on Sophie's forearms, the caterpillar fur of her dark eyebrows, her hands strong and soft on my thighs and back—of the connections that were possible between two people, even as they lived inside of separate bodies. And I thought of art, and beauty, and how we'd all once believed in fiction's capacity to expand your consciousness and your ability to feel, like tearing a hole in the scrim between yourself and another, helping you to be less alone, more understanding, and better understood. To say all that aloud would have sounded callow and romantic now, but lying naked in Sophie's arms, I had felt that old florid rush of naive optimism, and I believed that she, too, felt the same inkling of renewal, that she began to remember herself as the person who'd once cared so zealously about short stories that she would stuff her classmates' cubbies with photocopies of Cheever and Mansfield and O'Connor whenever she read a story that excited her, not the person who trudged a mile to the L every morning to go write marketing copy for health apps and sports drinks. I wanted her to feel that way again—for us to test, together, the boundaries of whatever slender faith we might still share. But I worried that by coming back to Halbrook I'd ruined our shot. I could see our only chance sinking beneath the surface like a penny. I wished I could leave right then, drive down to Brooklyn, pull up at the curb outside Sophie's apartment, throw the passenger door open, and swoop her away somewhere. Start over, like all those hopeful college kids back on campus. But here I was drinking beers in the afternoon and seriously contemplating Chet Bland's admonishment to just write something, anything, it didn't matter what, as long as it could sell.

I took my phone out. I hadn't talked to Sophie since I'd left yesterday morning. Maybe I thought I'd be able to put our night together behind me, but I couldn't stop thinking about her, and about the twinge of providence she had twisted into me. I could feel it like a cramp, twitching, needing to be exercised. It would have been smart to leave her alone, but wasn't it Shakespeare who said it's only a fool who thinks he's wise? Where did that leave me? I sent her a text.

Once again, you were right, I wrote. *I never should have gone home.*

I put my phone away and tried not to think about her writing back. It was done. I'd sent it. That was all I could do. And if she didn't write back, then that was probably for the best. Maybe we'd see each other a year from now at dinner with John and Debra at some New York restaurant, and neither of us would even remember what we'd done. Or at least we'd remember our lone night together like the hazy lines of a faintly remembered song, innocuous and nonsensical, belonging to another time and place.

I finished my drink and paid the tab and stood up to go. That's when I felt my phone buzz.

Told you so, she wrote.

I felt the muscles in my face begin to rise. My cheeks felt flush. Then I laughed out loud. And for several minutes I couldn't stop smiling.

Too late to run away together? I wrote her, then stood waiting for a response, staring down at the screen. After another minute she wrote back again.

I'm busy now. Ask again later.

5

Fall classes began the next week, and the lead-up involved a flurry of emails from the dean's office alerting us to changes in registration protocols, inducing us to update our diversity statements, and reminding us that fall break was coming two weeks late this year. We received memos from the English Department secretary containing the new code for the printer (no more than fifty pages a week per faculty member, please), reminding us not to leave food out on the counters or in our offices (a rat was seen dawdling out of the communal kitchen last spring; it was said that Marianne Martone's terrified wail could still be heard haunting the stairwell from English all the way up to Women's Studies), and encouraging us all, if it was remotely possible, to please flush nothing down the toilets but paper tissue—*please.*

My first class was Intermediate Fiction, a course in which students' abilities covered virtually the entire scattershot range between Intro and Advanced. Because you could repeat the course for credit as many times as you wanted, a number of them were also more adept at *taking* fiction than *writing* it.

I arrived early with a stack of photocopies of last semester's syllabus, sat down at the head of the seminar table, and began crossing off last year's dates in Sharpie, replacing *January* with *September, February* with *October,* adjusting the calendar as needed. The students trickled in at their own pace, filling the room with the heat of the outdoors, some of them looking a little soggy from the humidity. I handed out the course materials, and one by one they took their seats around the table, each of them appearing a little more dubious and fearful, I thought, than the year before—a little more trepidatious, perhaps, about the costs and consequences of enrolling for yet another semester in a class primarily focused on discussing people and events that don't exist.

Except for Winston Armstrong, whom I'd seen the other day carting his bed frame across the quad like he was climbing Calvary. He was seated upright at the opposite head of the table, gazing at me as eagerly as an acolyte. He was not the most promising student—it had taken three workshops before he finally turned in a story that didn't end with some variation of *It was all a dream*—but he was enthusiastic. He devoured every collection I gave him—Thom Jones, Ann Beattie, Joy Williams—returning them a week later covered in marginalia. "Sorry about the underlines and stuff," he would always say. "But I couldn't help myself." *Unreliable Narrator?* he would write. *Phallic Image? Symbol of Death?*

After everyone was settled, and the syllabuses were all passed out, I got the ball rolling with a little refresher from Intro.

"So," I said, "who remembers what Aristotle said were the three basic elements of narrative?"

Winston looked searchingly into the air. Others thumbed through last semester's notes. Finally an arm shot up.

"Yes?" I said.

It was a young woman who'd written a story last year about picking out a Christmas tree with her grandmother.

"Words?" she said. "Was that one of the basic elements?"

"Well, I suppose they're pretty essential," I said. "But I was thinking more about structure. Let's take this another way. What's the *first* thing that happens in a story?"

"You're born," someone said.

"Yes, that's true, in life anyway. But not all stories start there. They start with . . ."

I looked out at a sea of wrinkled brows.

"Action?" someone said.

"Yes, that's true, too," I conceded. "But what comes *first* in the action?"

"The inciting incident," someone offered.

"Yes, which usually occurs . . ."

"When the character does something."

"In the . . ."

A quiet pall fell over the room.

"It's a synonym for *onset*," I offered.

Blank stares.

"*Commencement?*"

Bewilderment and boredom.

"*Opening?*"

Shoes squeaking, zippers zipping.

"Okay," I finally said. "I'll give you a hint. It's the third word of the Bible."

At last, a young man raised his hand.

"*Beginning*."

"Yes! Thank you. The *beginning*. A story is made of the *beginning*, the *middle*, and the *end*, said Aristotle. But let's save the rest of that lesson for another day. Now, why don't we go around the room and say what we did this summer."

After class, I strode back across campus to my office. Crossing the quad between the four gray brutalist structures that organized our academical village, I saw a squall of multicolored silken fabrics swirling toward me. As this crazy flowing gown came nearer, I recognized its owner: one Dr. Judith Stern, my ersatz therapist.

"I heard a rumor you were back in town!" she said. "I can't wait to hear how the summer went!"

Dr. Stern was a member of the Psychology Department at Eastern, as well as a practicing clinical psychologist. This meant she sometimes had a hard time making it known when she was acting as your colleague or your counselor. She also had a penchant for gossip and seemed to be as interested in hearing about her patients' misadventures as in curing them of their woes.

"When did you return?" she wanted to know.

"It's been a few days," I said.

"That's right. I saw Debra at Walgreens the other day. She mentioned you were back. Tell me everything."

Since when was Dr. Stern friendly with my wife? Perhaps I should have been seeking the treatment of a different therapist.

"Not much to tell, really," I said. "And anyway, I'm in a bit of a hurry." I made to continue down the path toward the Humanities Bloc, but she stepped in front of me with her hair and robes rippling in the breeze like so many nations' flags.

"Phooey!" she said. "I can see there's something you're not telling me."

"Well, this last week's been a doozy, that's true," I admitted.

"Ooh, sounds juicy," she said, "I'll get my appointment book," and began rifling through the enormous straw bag slung over her shoulder.

It was going to be a long semester.

The beginning of the year also meant parties, and Friday night's event was the department's official kickoff, hosted by our visiting writer for the year, Carlos Cross, who had come from Portland with his wife, Gina, and their two young children. What I knew about him was that he'd published a head-scratchingly popular novel called *We're All Gonna Die!*, which was about a league of superheroes who work by day as bond traders at a secret office complex in Pasadena. It was full of scenes set in elevator shafts and air ducts, replete with props like grappling hooks and zip lines. One reviewer compared it favorably to *Die Hard*. Words like *splat!* and *bam!* appeared in stand-alone paragraphs. Carlos was the recipient of a Guggenheim and a Whiting Award. Last spring he appeared on Jimmy Fallon wearing a T-shirt with his reading dates listed on the back as if he were promoting a concert tour.

When he opened the door to let me and Debra in that Friday night, he was wearing soccer shoes and skinny jeans and a cowboy shirt stretched tightly across his paunch. A boy, dressed the same in one-quarter scale, appeared beside him, tugging at his shirttails, as Debra and I stood in the doorway. I was awkwardly cradling the wine we'd brought as a housewarming gift. Debra was holding a tray of tartlets.

"Tell her she can't! Tell her she can't!" the boy kept screaming. "Tell her it's mine! Mine! Mine!"

Debra looked over at me without turning her head—a sideways glance of terror that said how relieved she was we'd never had children, that despite everything else, we had at least done that one thing correctly.

"We're working on sharing," Carlos explained to us, crouching down to talk to the boy. "Now go on and let your sister play with you. Be nice. Remember what we talked about? Remember about sharing?"

The boy nodded. His father patted him on the head and the kid trudged off like Linus dragging his blanket.

"Come on in then," said Carlos. "Welcome to the old abode."

He backed into the room, arms wide in welcome. There was music playing and the din of polite conversation hovered in the air. The sound of cocktail glasses and ice tinkled just above the music. The room was colored by the amber flicker of lamplight. Carlos gestured toward a bar beneath the windows across the room.

"We've got beer, wine, cocktails . . ." He raised his own glass. "I'm making Manhattans," he said, "can I interest anyone?"

"Maybe a wine in a minute," said Debra. "I'm fine for now. Where shall I—" She gestured with the platter of tartlets.

"The table is fine, thanks."

I handed Carlos the wine we'd brought and walked with him across the room toward the bar. Debra dropped the tray on the table and went to join Jill Talleggio and some other colleagues by the sofa.

The apartment, Carlos explained, was being provided gratis by the college. It was on the top floor of Seagram dormitory, and students could sometimes be heard slamming doors and carrying on downstairs. The windows were framed in mahogany molding. There were oil paintings of former college presidents in gilt frames on the walls. There were Tiffany lamps on top of walnut credenzas. This was the most collegiate-looking place I'd ever seen on the Eastern College campus, and I was almost shocked to discover its existence. My heart flashed to a time when I'd dreamed—naively—of living in such a place myself.

"Most of it's the school's," Carlos said as he shook up our drinks. He pointed out the rattan dining chairs, the oak table, the faded Persian rug. "Not the kind of stuff I'd choose for myself, but you can't argue with free." He finished our drinks, plopping a cherry on top of each, and handed me one. "Come on, I'll show you where the magic happens."

We took our drinks to Carlos's study, where there was a large executive's desk with a leather pad on top and a wall of books behind it.

"Of course, I had to bring a few things from home," he said, standing proudly before his library, which, I shuddered to realize, was organized by color, like a giant Pantone chart, spines spanning the rainbow, wall to wall, floor to ceiling.

I pulled down a copy of *We're All Gonna Die!* from a row of red covers and fanned through the pages. Carlos quickly grabbed it away like a teenager whose mother just discovered his *Penthouse* collection.

"Please, don't embarrass me," he said.

"It's too late," I said, "I already read it last year."

"Touché." He put the book back among the crimson covers. I stood, mystified, before his crazy wall of colors. I couldn't make any sense of it.

"How do you ever find what you're looking for?" I asked him. There was Joyce next to Baldwin next to Margaret Atwood. It was madness.

"What do you mean? I know what the spines look like."

"Never mind."

I ran my fingers over the curved edge of Carlos's desk, trying to occupy myself. There was a notepad on top of a stack of pages. I thumbed the edges for lack of anything else to do. Carlos took the pages and squared them up and put them away in a drawer.

"So," he said, "when can we expect something from *you*?"

"That's the million-dollar question," I said. Out in the living room I could hear Debra's laughter—a single, calculated *ha*. I tried not to believe it was directed at me.

"Getting the pressure from Bland, huh?" said Carlos.

"I guess you could say that."

"Sometimes I think I did my best work before I ever published anything," he said. "It ruins you, in a way. It makes you self-conscious. People develop expectations. It weighs on you. Sometimes I wish I could go back to the time when writing was just"—he waved the thought away—"I don't want to say *fun*. It's never *fun*. But you know what I mean. I think I miss the time when everything was ahead of me." He paused. "Publishing-wise, anyway."

This was a sentiment I'd heard from other writers, the complaint about the burden of publishing, as if there were something impure about it. I'd heard some version of this platitude at the dinner table at Yaddo, at PEN America parties, at a Robert Burns dinner I went to once in Boston. It was a stance you could take only once you'd achieved the success necessary for forming opinions about success.

"Well," I told him, "I guess I wouldn't mind seeing it from both sides before making my own judgment."

Soon some others joined us in the study. Debra was among them.

"Looks like you two are hitting it off," she said. I looked down at my glass, which was empty already. I would have gone to refill it straightaway but others soon packed into the room.

Jill, a nineteenth-century Americanist, went over to the bookshelves and started perusing the spines. She pulled down a slim blue paperback. "This one just about floored me," she said, turning the book over in her hands. "So sweet. So funny. I wish more books could be like this." It was a YA novel about two teenagers who meet in a home for kids with special powers. She thumbed the pages lovingly. I struggled to remind myself this woman got her PhD at Yale, did a postdoc at Columbia, that her book on Emerson was coming out next year from Oxford. Yet she was enthralled by a novel written for twelve-year-olds.

I finally squeezed through the throng, slithered out the doorway, and left them all poring over Carlos's books. I returned to the living room and partook of a whiskey at the little bar by the window. Night was coming on, and I tracked a lone red bicycle light tacking across campus. Downstairs, I heard students coming home to their dorm rooms, slamming doors. In the other room I heard my colleagues start chattering seriously about who would win a fight between the Val Kilmer and the George Clooney Batmen.

A moment later I felt a hand on my back. Without looking, I recognized the owner of those trembling fingers as Fletcher Mills, the oldest member of the department and the closest thing you could say I had to a friend at Eastern. I was glad to turn around and see his weathered face. He'd been at Eastern College forty years and never made it past the rank of associate, having published only one book, in 1983, about prosody in Milton. It was woefully unfashionable in its time, downright Jurassic now. I admired his ignorance of academic fashion. The friends in his mind were Shakespeare and Alexander Pope. I doubted he'd ever seen a Batman movie, let alone cared who played the lead. In the other room I could hear Carlos telling everyone about the difficult logistics involved in shipping his library from Portland. "UPS? FedEx? Don't even get me started on DHL!"

Mills put his quavering, liver-spotted hand on my bicep and squeezed. This was his way of getting your attention—and also of staying upright—and I knew by the gesture that he was about to drop some wisdom.

"I've always liked you," he said, "so I'll give you this one for free."

"Lay it on me," I said.

"So, the Devil's wandering around the halls of an English Department," he began, and I realized he was trying to tell a joke. He gripped my arm even tighter and went on in a shaky voice. "And he happens upon an open office door. The poor assistant professor is toiling away inside. 'Might I interest you in a deal?' the Devil says. And the assistant professor perks up. 'Suppose I arrange things so that for the next ten years every paper you write gets published, every grant you apply for gets funded. Yale and Stanford fight to hire you, you'll be set for life,' the Devil says. 'The Nobel people call you and invite you to Sweden. But at the end of ten years, your wife is miserable, your friends all hate you, and no one will answer your calls. What would you say to that?' the Devil says. And the assistant professor thinks about it. Then he says, 'Okay, sounds great. But what's the catch?'"

Mills looked at me and gave his forehead a little tap—*think about it,* he seemed to say—and then patted my back and shambled off.

Everyone finally returned to the living room. Gina Cross began setting out casseroles, laying out silverware and napkins. We all made our way to the table. Carlos fiddled with his iPhone, which was plugged into a small speaker on a credenza by the bar. Soft jazz came on. We all sat down. Wine bottles were opened, the plunk of corks filled the air, and we started passing around dishes. Fletcher Mills, with his ashen cheeks and white hair, looked at me across the table and nodded slowly, stone-faced, eyes cold with the secret knowledge he'd just imparted to me. We'd had a meaningful exchange, he meant to suggest. But then I realized he wasn't looking at me at all, he was just lost in milky glaucoma.

Soon everyone's plates were full and we all began eating. After a while Jill said, "Carlos, what was Jimmy Fallon like?"

Yes, yes, everyone wanted to know, was he as nice as on TV? Did he and Carlos get to talk after the segment—like, for real? Or was that stuff a bunch of baloney when they acted like they were still chatting as the band played them off to commercial?

"No, no, it's real," said Carlos. "And Jimmy's a sweetheart. The whole crew couldn't be nicer. I'd go back in a heartbeat. Of course, they'd have to invite me again!" Cue the laughter.

"And what about the dressing rooms?" someone wanted to know.

"How was the band?"

"Did you get a free mug? I heard they give you a mug."

I looked around at everyone's wagging faces. I glanced over

at Debra. Her blouse was open just enough that I could glimpse the beige border of her bra cup. Her back was arched fault-lessly, her shoulders back, palms on her thighs, just like they'd taught her at Miss Porter's. She was smiling politely, enjoying all this to no end. But she was calculating, too: *He's been on TV. How can I be as well?* I was hardly any better. I'd ridden shotgun alongside Debra's success myself. I'd gotten my job out of it, after all. But witnessing her simpering at Carlos's gossip and boasts, I felt dyspeptic, and recognized in her determined look something of my own pleading rictus.

It hadn't always been that way. Once upon a time she and I had shared the same airy and romantic ideals, editing each other's stories side by side in bed, spending the afternoons pass-ing pages back and forth, content with having made something out of nothing, happy just to move the words around on a page, then burning the evening hours at bars with John and Sophie, trading tattered copies of Rilke and Robert Lowell, Cheever and Baldwin. Then one day Debra got a story pub-lished in *Harper's*, and a book deal soon followed. Then there was money, and everything changed. I became her sidekick, adopting her successes as my own, until eventually I couldn't tell the difference between what she wanted and what I did, and, like that, I was following her from Chicago to Halbrook, to the shadowy first floor of Eastern College's Humanities Bloc, and finally to Carlos Cross's dinner table.

"Excuse me," I said. "I'm not feeling so hot."

I slid my chair out, causing the legs to squeak loudly against the floor, and headed for the bathroom. I shut the door but I could still hear everybody murmuring in the dining room like a hatch of flies. Who were these people? I couldn't understand any of them, or what I was doing in their company. If there'd been a window in the bathroom I might have climbed out of it, but instead I knew I'd return to them in just a few minutes and laugh politely at their jokes and listen courteously. My only escape was to think of Sophie. I could see her shimmering black irises like a prisoner imagines the sky. I closed my eyes and I could feel the coolness of her cheek. I could hear her hoarse, low whisper, see that little gap between her teeth.

I took out my cell phone. I wanted to call her, but the distance between us seemed as vast as memory. With every day that passed, our night together in Brooklyn was starting to seem more and more improbable. Had I made it up? Imagined it was something it wasn't? The whole affair was starting to take on the contours of a mislaid story, like an incident I'd sketched on the back of a napkin and forgotten about. It required a strenuous suspension of disbelief to think I hadn't fantasized the entire encounter.

I need to see you, I wrote.

I sat there gently rocking back and forth on the toilet seat, waiting for a response. Sooner or later I would have to go back to the table, but I needed to hear from her. I waited, wanting.

Finally my phone buzzed. *Want and need aren't the same thing*, she wrote.

I could hear laughter from the other room.

Maybe not, I wrote back. *But you didn't say no.*

You're right, I didn't say no.

Then there was a knock at the door, and I felt myself jerk nervously. I sprang to my feet and reached for the door handle to make sure it was locked. It occurred to me it might be Debra, that she'd be wondering what I'd been doing in there so long, why I hadn't come back to the party already.

"I'll be right out!" I called in a high, strange voice, shoving my phone in my pocket and gathering myself. "Just one more second!" I said in the same odd lilt that had burst out of me before.

But when I opened the door, it wasn't Debra standing outside of it but old Fletcher Mills, swaying like a sailor on shore leave, holding himself up by the molding. "Move it now, son!" he said, shoving me out into the hallway as he tumbled head-long into the loo. "I may have overserved myself!" he called out as the door shut hard behind him; an impressive stream ensued forthwith.

Back in the living room, Carlos and Debra were reaching across the table and shaking hands as others looked on in po-lite admiration. I didn't know what was going on. There was something I'd missed. "Yes! Let's do it!" Debra was saying. "It's brilliant! I'm in!"

"What's all this?" I said, sitting back down.

"We're doing a reading together," she said. "In the city. Next weekend. Carlos just invited me. A thing at Joe's Pub." Immediately I thought of Sophie, of seeing her again, of the strangeness of providence, of the whimsy of fate. I laughed out loud. Some heads turned.

"I had no idea you'd be so excited," said Debra. She was looking at me a little cockeyed.

"Of course I'm excited," I said. "It's a perfect idea. Aren't I always saying we should go to the city more? Why don't we rent a room, stay the night?"

"Yeah, sure, I suppose we could. But you seem so . . ."

"Well," I said, "you know, it's the city, that's all."

When we got home that night, Ernie greeted us at the door with his tail switching eagerly behind him. I said I'd take him out, because really I wanted to be alone so I could text Sophie about the reading, let her know Debra and I would be coming down to the city in a few days.

Ernie and I made the loop from Poplar onto Druid and around to Dexter and I texted Sophie while Ernie took a crap in front of a yard sign that read NO DOGS. I gathered his excrement in a little plastic baggie and flung it into one of the trash bins set out for pickup.

My phone buzzed. It was Sophie.

Your big news got scooped. Debra's texting me about it right now.

Somehow I'd let myself forget they were friends.

Back home with Ernie, I climbed the stairs to the bedroom. Debra was sitting up against the headboard with her bedside lamp on. She had her phone in her hands. She was smiling—still texting with Sophie, I guessed—and I lay down next to her. Ernie climbed up onto the bed and made a home for himself between the two of us. Soon Debra cut off her light and put her phone on the nightstand. Ernie squirmed, then fell asleep. I lay awake for a while, listening to the night birds chirping outside, watching the shadows on the ceiling. I remembered an article I'd read once about a man who'd kept two different families for thirty years without either one of them finding out. It was only after he died, and each family discovered that they were to inherit only *half* his wealth, that they pieced it all together. One family—wife, kids, dog—in Cleveland. Another of the same in Shaker Heights. By all accounts he was a loving husband, devoted father, a real stand-up guy. Provided for everyone. Always cheerful. Never missed a birthday or a graduation. Ever faithful to the end.

6

THE NEXT FRIDAY DEBRA AND I TOOK THE TRAIN INTO THE city for her performance with Carlos. I tried reading the *Times* while she wrote down notes in her composition book, preparing for her show, but I was too anxious to focus. I had to get up. I went to the café car and bought a Perrier and a bag of chips and paced up and down the cars for a while. I went back to my seat and tried closing my eyes, laying my head against the cold windowpane. My leg was tapping. I couldn't sit still. "You okay?" Debra said. I told her I was fine, but really I was all wound up, and she could tell. She said, "You'd think it was *you* who was about to perform in front of a hundred people." I closed my eyes again and feigned sleep.

We took a cab to the hotel from Penn Station. Debra had booked us a room at the Carlyle. La Quinta would have sufficed, but she had acquired certain tastes in the years since her books started being published, and who was I to argue. Stepping into the lobby and crossing the marble floor, I had to admit there was a part of me that enjoyed the perks of her success. I had grown attached to a measure of wealth, being with her. It helped separate me from the place I was from, a place I thought of as seedy and bankrupt, and which I'd failed to profit from even for creative material. The days of mildewed carpeting and Clorox-stained bath towels were behind me. Because of Debra I'd be sleeping tonight on Egyptian cotton sheets and drying my face on brand-name antimicrobial wash-cloths.

We checked into our room. Debra went into the bathroom and shut the door and started the shower. I sat down on the bed and watched cable news for a few minutes, but I soon got restless. I went downstairs to Bemelmans Bar to wait while Debra finished getting ready. I drank a martini and listened to the piano player. Normally I would have relished the time alone, tapping my foot to "Misty" or "Autumn Leaves," sipping from a gilt-rimmed cocktail glass, taking in the goofy cartoon wallpaper and the Third Republic furniture. But now it all seemed fusty and embarrassing, and I felt self-conscious and jittery, like a counterfeiter passing off a phony bill. In an hour I'd be seeing Sophie again, and everything else seemed trivial by comparison.

Debra found me in the bar a little later. Her hair was in two buns. She wore a white silk blouse and a black skirt. On her feet she wore red leather heels. Did she really want to wear those heels? I had visions of steam grates and sidewalk cracks, open manholes and escalator treads.

"You sure you don't want to wear flats?" I said.

"Since when do you know the word *flats*?"

"I pay attention."

"What's the matter? You don't like them?" She looked down at her feet.

"It's not that," I said. "We're gonna be walking a lot. Don't you want to wear something more comfortable?" In grad school, she'd worn Keds and cutoff T-shirts. She didn't seem to care how people saw her. She wrote stories as if no one would ever read them. I knew she'd gone to Miss Porter's, but I'd assumed that had been her parents' choice, that the cutoffs and Keds were a tiny rebellion. Now she was dressed exactly like her mother.

"We'll take a cab," she said. "I'll be fine."

*   *   *

We met John and Sophie before the reading at a bar in the basement of an Italian restaurant in the West Village. They were seated next to each other when we arrived, their backs to us. John was hunched over himself, elbows splayed, a glass of whiskey in his hands. Sophie's hair was up; loose strands swirled at the base of her neck. Her skin looked prickly and pale and I wanted to run my fingers over it the way a kid reaches out to touch a painting.

Debra took a wobbly step toward the bar, already scratching at her ankles where the straps of her shoes were rubbing into her skin. She took another nervous step. "I told you so," I couldn't help saying, and she turned and shot me a sinister glare. "Don't say another word," she said.

John turned around when we approached, stood up, and threw his arms around Debra. "Lovely as ever," he said.

Sophie and I juked left and right, unsure whether we should go in for an embrace, shake hands, or do nothing. What did we usually do? I couldn't remember. A kiss on the cheek? A hug? Nothing seemed adequate. I leaned in and put my arms loosely around her waist. I could feel her forearms against my hips, her fingers on my lower back. At once we both pulled away.

"Hi," I said.

"Hi," she said.

We all went and sat down in a booth in the corner. John started telling us about how he was involved in suing Google on behalf of a publishing company, he couldn't say which. Sophie sat next to me, close enough to touch. I lowered my hand beneath the table and let the back of it rest against her denim-covered thigh. She inched away.

"Anyone want a refill?" I said, hoping she might contrive to join me alone at the bar, even if just for a minute. But it was

John who said, "I won't say no," and followed me across the room.

"Why the sourpuss?" he said as we sidled up to the bar, ordering a couple of whiskies.

"What do you mean?" I was looking back at the table. Sophie wouldn't so much as glance in my direction. Had I completely misunderstood our texts those last few days? I'd thought she was flirting. Maybe she was rebuffing me instead.

"I know unpleasantness when I see it," said John. "Now tell your old pal what's the matter."

I took a belt of my whiskey and made myself turn back toward the bar. "It's nothing," I said. "Bad night's sleep."

John raised his glass and we toasted to bad nights. We both drank. Then John leaned in to me and spoke sotto voce.

"Listen, pal, I need you to tell me straight. Do we really have to go to this reading? I mean, do we really *have* to? Will anyone care if we bail? You just said you're tired."

"You have something better in mind?"

"How about we head to Koreatown instead." His eyes were bright and dreamy.

"Tempting," I said, "but I don't think that'd be the ethical thing to do. It's my wife who's reading, after all."

"Ethical? Pshaw! Ethics was a course I took in law school."

I sipped my drink. John shook his head disappointedly. Sophie sat across the room talking with Debra, ignoring me still. John went on about a place he knew where you could get a massage upstairs and then sing karaoke downstairs afterward. I watched Sophie and Debra anxiously, waiting for a signal, looking for a secret message in their gestures and movements.

By the time we got to Joe's Pub there was already a smattering of people clustered in various conversations. Debra's editor and agent were talking to each other at the foot of the stage. In the corner, Carlos Cross was doing a card trick for a group of fans gathered around him. The assignment that night was to tell an embarrassing story you'd never told in public before. I figured the card trick was part of his act. Last week a debut author had revealed to the world her considerable talent for juggling bowling pins. I'd had enough to drink that all these clustered little societies seemed to shimmer like film projections. I stood for a minute at the threshold, looking around in a daze. When my eyes focused, I realized Debra was staring at me. John had gone outside. And Sophie was already across the room at the bar.

"You doing all right?" Debra asked.

In the distance I saw Sophie resting her forearm on the bar as she waited for the bartender.

"I think I'll just go grab a drink," I told Debra.

"Maybe chase it with a water." Then she crossed the room to join her agent and editor in the footlights of the stage.

I raced through the crowd toward Sophie.

"I'm not in the mood," she said as I came up next to her. I could smell cigarettes on her hair, and the chalky aroma of her lipstick mixed with perfume and fabric softener.

"A drink then, that's all. We won't even talk. It would look weird if we avoided each other."

I ordered two martinis for us and we took them to the far end of the bar, away from the crowd. Across the room Debra could be seen laughing, her shoulders back, chin up. She knew every angle, every cast of light. She had poses, postures, an arsenal of writerly anecdotes and anodyne jokes to entertain with. I could almost see her mouth making the shapes of a story she liked to tell about Hemingway and Fitzgerald in the bathroom of the Rotonde café. Now she was shaking hands with people, smiling through her perfect white teeth. She was tall, with a sharp, androgynous face that I'd always admired but which she felt wasn't feminine enough. She compensated for it with fancy clothes, skinniness, and makeup. It occurred to me that she now looked vaguely like the anchor on Halbrook's local news. Outside, through the window, I saw John smoking a cigarette, shuffling his feet on the sidewalk, counting down the minutes till this thing was over.

"We could get away together," I said finally. "Just for a couple of days. I have a conference next week in Saratoga. All I have to do is one stupid panel, the rest of the time could be ours."

"Either that or we forget this ever happened," said Sophie, looking past me at Debra, who was now mounting the stage.

Debra stepped into the spotlight. The night's MC appeared beside her and delivered an introduction. *Author of* The Widower's Wife, *winner of the Rome Prize, recipient of an NEA grant, professor of English and creative writing at Eastern College*, and so on.

Debra stepped forward and approached the microphone, her voice suddenly booming through the PA speakers. "Can everyone hear me all right?" Moderate applause. "Okay, here goes nothing," she said. "So, um, this is a story about the first time I had sex," she announced.

"Uh-oh," I said.

Sophie looked at me. "Did you know she was doing this?"

I shook my head no.

Everyone around us laughed and cheered.

"And I've never told this story to anyone before," she said. "Least of all to two hundred strangers."

She went on to recount each awkward moment, even doing a pantomime of her nervous college lover slinking back to his dorm room after the deed was done, shoulders hunched as he tiptoed down the hall. I could barely watch. And it wasn't just because of the subject. There was Sophie, right next to me, with John all the way outside and Debra totally preoccupied by entertaining her fans with the sordid details of her first carnal embrace. Now might be the only time.

I leaned into Sophie and whispered in her ear. "What do I have to do to convince you?"

"Shh," she said. "My friend is onstage." Everyone was laughing loudly. Debra was really milking it, squeezing her mouth into a nervous expression of adolescent priggishness. Then after a while she delivered her coup de grâce. "Goes to show you what happens when you pick a Mormon for your first time!"

The crowd clapped and cheered and Debra hung the mike on the stand and started across the stage, waving and bowing like an opera diva. I turned back toward Sophie.

"Come on," I said. "It's one weekend. If it's a disaster, we'll never speak of it again. And then at least we'll know we gave it a shot."

"To what end?"

"That's what we'll find out."

Her eyes looked slightly askance. She was actually thinking about it. Maybe a weekend away together wasn't the worst idea.

"You know I want it, too," she said. "But—"

The room let out a loud collective gasp. Everyone turned at once. I swiveled to follow their gaze, and there at the foot of the stage steps was Debra, lying in a rumpled pile.

"Oh my God, Debra!" Sophie got up and ran toward the stage. I chased after her. As I got closer, I realized what I'd just missed: Debra tumbling down the stairs like a faltering race-horse as her ankle buckled beneath her high heels.

Sophie bent down and brought her friend into her arms. Some others from the front rows assisted in raising her to her feet. A couple of bartenders came around and scooped her up and carried her to a greenroom or someplace in the back. Sophie and I were left at the foot of the stage as Debra was carted off and a few others hovered in hushed astonishment. I looked to Sophie, still waiting for an answer.

"Maybe you should go after your wife," Sophie suggested.

I saw the door around back where they'd taken her. I nodded but I didn't move.

John came inside then. "What'd I miss?"

"Nothing," said Sophie. "Debra biffed."

John nodded, as if to say, *That sounds about right.*

I gave her a look. *Please, just promise me you'll think about it.* She screwed her mouth up like she'd tasted something rancid. *Now isn't the time,* she meant to say. "Go check on your wife," she said. I stood there dumbly until she gritted her teeth and pointed in frustration toward the back. *What are you waiting for, you philandering schmuck?* I shrugged, then headed past the stage in search of wherever they'd taken Debra.

Later that night at the Carlyle Debra went to bed early. She said she was tired from the night. She insisted her ankle was fine, she wasn't hurt, but I could tell she was embarrassed. "You want some ice or something?" She said she just needed rest. So I went downstairs for a drink. It was about midnight when Sophie finally texted, and when she did, it took everything in me not to leave the hotel, grab the first cab I saw, and cross the river into Brooklyn to see her right then.

Fine, she wrote. *Next weekend. I'm in.*

7

THE DRIVE TO SARATOGA WAS LESS THAN TWO HOURS, BUT by the time I hit I-87, I already felt like I'd been gone for days. It was a clear autumn afternoon, a week since Debra's reading. A canopy of blue and white was visible through the moonroof. When I rolled the window down I could smell the pine trees along the highway, and I filled my chest with several rich, deep breaths. Sophie was coming up from the city on the train. We were planning to meet at the Amtrak station and then drive together to the Hampton Inn downtown, where we would spend two nights alone, uninterrupted except by the one-hour panel I was expected to participate in to fulfill the ruse that justified my journey. The only hitch was that Sophie and John and Debra and I had been on so many vacations together, stayed in so many adjoining rooms, shared so many taxis, dinners, and hotel shuttles, that a part of me felt oddly guilty about leaving John and Debra out of this weekend. Whence Debra's weather consultations and hour-by-hour itinerary? Whence John's mental map of area watering holes? The four of us had always managed a delicate equilibrium, which depended on the counterbalances we each offered the others. To Sophie's sullen turns, John's puckish japes; to Debra's self-regard, my willing self-effacement. Like ballast, we kept each other upright. I didn't know how Sophie and I would do on our own. But as I crested a hill somewhere past Albany, and the distant peaks of the Green Mountains jutted up from the horizon like shark's teeth, the worry drained away. Halbrook was, minute by minute, more and more distant, and the weekend's prospects ever nearer.

I pulled into Saratoga around three. The train was scheduled to arrive any minute. I walked around the station house to the platform and looked down the tracks, hoping to see the train come rumbling ahead at any moment. I thought I saw the silver flash of a passenger car in the distance, but it was just a trick of the light, the glint of a tin-roofed barn spied through a gap in the foliage. The tracks remained empty. I waited, glancing down the rails every few minutes, pacing. It occurred to me that Tolstoy's tragic heroes first met on a train platform, and that it was perhaps a bad omen to be thinking of how it turned out for them. Of course, Vronsky had his mother in tow, or was meeting her at the station anyway. And Anna, she was all worked up because she'd left her baby at home with her boring husband. So their encounter was fraught to begin with. And besides, it wasn't as if Sophie and I were only meeting for the first time. Still, I couldn't help thinking we were perhaps a little doomed, because I knew the moment the train rattled into the station, and Sophie stepped down off the running board and I saw her coming toward me, a certain fate would be sealed. But where was the goddamn train? I kept tiptoeing to the edge of the platform, looking down the checkered tracks, waiting to see the railway switch flip and the blue snub nose of an Amtrak engine come roaring forth. But the platform stayed quiet. There was no preparatory rumble, no heavy undulation, no hiss and whine of steel on steel, just empty tracks and the almost imperceptible tweet of chickadees in the trees going *hey, sweetie, hey, sweetie, hey, sweetie.*

After a while, I went inside the station house, where the desk clerk informed me the train from Penn Station had been delayed half an hour. I sat down on a bench along the wall and watched the arrivals board tick off the minutes. If the train had derailed or broken down, then surely the station agent would have been notified. It probably would have been on the TV news, as well, which was showing only stock quotes on the screen above the restroom entrances. So probably it was nothing, just the usual boarding delays, your typically stubborn withdrawal from the city. I took out my phone, thinking Sophie was most likely as frustrated about the delay as I was, and shot her a text. *Everything okay?* But I heard nothing back. Eventually I went out to the car and got a stack of student stories—applications for my advanced fiction workshop next semester—to help pass the time.

Back inside the station house, I sat down with my reams of stories and watched the arrivals board until a new number appeared beside the 11:10 a.m. out of Penn Station. DELAYED 3:55, it said. Another twenty-five minutes.

I sat back and started flipping through the applications, but I was bored, and distracted, and growing anxious.

Soon it was well past four o'clock.

Anything to report? I wrote.

But again, no response.

Finally, about forty minutes later, the train announced its arrival with the usual ruckus of cabs pulling up at the curb, and family and friends of travelers stepping out of their cars and moving en masse across the parking lot. A crowd gathered on the platform and I went to join them. The train came trundling into the station, expelling smoke and whinnying to a halt. The doors slid open and the passengers descended the metal stairs, carting their rolling bags behind them over the concrete. Hugs and handshakes were exchanged, greetings called out, luggage hauled. I stood on the platform, waiting like a limousine driver with a cardboard sign. Passengers streamed by me on their way to the parking lot, where cabbies were lined up, smoking cigarettes outside their cars, ready to load suitcases into their trunks and backseats. I was still standing there when the last of the passengers had disembarked and the porters had begun boarding the next round of customers. Even the geriatrics, with the assistance of baggage handlers and wheelchairs, had cleared the station. I went up and down the platform, peering into cabin windows, thinking Sophie might have fallen asleep and missed the station announcement, but eventually the doors shut and the train plunged forward, picking up speed and rolling away down the tracks, and still Sophie was nowhere to be seen.

Maybe she'd gotten cold feet, I thought. Or John had found out about us. Or maybe she'd had to wait so long at a station stop at Albany or Schenectady that she finally wised up about what we were doing and fled the train before anything worse happened. Unless she'd missed her train to begin with and would be coming in on the Greyhound bus that was scheduled in an hour. But then why wouldn't she have called? Or returned my texts?

I sat waiting until the sun was low, and then I checked my phone one last time. It was past five. My panel was in an hour. I couldn't wait any longer.

I checked into the hotel alone and rode the elevator up to the fourth floor, standing dismayed before the parting compartment doors, staring blankly at the mosaic carpeting and vinyl wallpaper, before finally dragging myself down the hall to my room.

Inside, I stood for a few minutes at the window, looking down at the kidney-shaped swimming pool, which was already closed for the season, at the folding chairs corralled by the shed at the corner of the patio, at the custodian walking around inside the fenced-in area, picking up trash with a poker. I thought of the Last Resort, whose pool was always green with algae, half-empty, full of cracks, remembering an associate of my father's who used to come by in a blue lab coat and Bermuda shorts to administer chemical treatments that never panned out. Whenever any of the guests complained about the brown water and mold, my father would say, "You want a pool? There's one about a hundred yards that way"—pointing to the Atlantic Ocean—"it's open all year."

I lay down on the bed, remembering my childhood bedroom. It was room 2A, on the second floor of the Last Resort, cleaned and serviced every Monday by Jasmine, the housekeeper, and decorated—except for the books I kept on the nightstand—exactly like every other room at the Last Resort, with a watercolor painting of sailboats above the bed and a color television on the bureau along the wall. There was worn gray carpeting, a fiberboard desk, and, on the bathroom counter, a polyethylene ice bucket with a sheer plastic liner folded cleanly on the lip.

At night I would cup my ear to the walls and listen to the goings-on of my parents' guests. When I read *The Sun Also Rises* I thought I knew exactly what Jake Barnes was talking about when he said he had a bad habit of imagining the bedroom lives of his friends. When I'd see the guests in the morning—packing their cars in the parking lot, strolling down to the beach with their colorful terry cloth towels over their shoulders, cooking burgers on kettle grills in the sand—I was always surprised how much their faces didn't match their voices, how bad a portrait I'd painted of them in my mind the night before. Reality never lived up to my imagination. Young people would turn out to be old. People I'd thought were women would turn out to be men. You could never guess right at the Last Resort because uncertainty and doubt presided over the place like spirits. As Keats advised, the best you could do was to accept uncertainties and mysteries without any irritable reaching after fact and reason. When my parents extended dinner tabs and room credits to destitute guests on the empty promise that they'd send a check once they were home, there was never any real assurance they'd get their money back. When they traded beers and dinners with repairmen in exchange for services, there was no guarantee they would ever be reimbursed. When they waited out each hurricane, barricaded behind sandbags and makeshift plywood window coverings, they could never be certain their only home and livelihood wouldn't be deluged beyond saving. But like stoics, they never got their hopes up, and were therefore never disappointed.

I, meanwhile, had spent the last three hours in a daze of anticipation, dreaming about Sophie's arrival, only to wind up alone again in another drab hotel room. I thought of texting her once more, but there was nothing to say at that point. I'd chased after the wrong plot. Now there was nothing to do but put the whole affair behind me.

I went to the closet, grabbed a shirt from my suitcase, ironed it, buttoned it, pulled on a blazer, and headed out toward the Skidmore campus, where my panel was taking place.

8

WHEN I ARRIVED AT THE LECTURE HALL, THERE WERE ONLY about ten seats filled. I stood in the doorway at the top of the auditorium, looking down the sloping aisle toward the stage, where three empty seats had been arranged behind a long metal table, a pitcher of water and a stack of plastic cups sitting on top. I looked down at the brown carpet, combed into narrow, vacuum-brushed rows. Would anyone notice—or care—if I left? But when I glanced up at the front of the room, I saw a woman dressed in gray, with thick black-rimmed cat-eye glasses, waving me forward—tonight's moderator, I guessed. I put one foot out, and then the other, and doddered toward the stage.

The moderator—a Dr. Theresa Gault—handed me a name badge and a program. The title of the panel was *Truth in Fiction*. These words were arranged at the top of the sheet in squiggly *Twilight Zone* lettering. Underneath were the names and affiliations of the three panelists, myself and two others I knew vaguely from within the abbey walls of academic creative writing.

"Don't worry," said Dr. Gault, "the whole thing will be very casual. Just some friends having a conversation. I'm sure everyone will be excited to hear what you have to say."

I did not know this person, and as far as I was aware, she knew almost nothing about me. My chief credential was that Chet Bland, Chair of English, had gone to graduate school with her husband. I had watched as he paced my office last spring, relaying my bona fides to her over the phone, convincing her to let me join the conference. After a while he finally said the thing that clinched the deal. "Oh, perhaps I've buried the lede: his wife directs our creative writing program."

We assembled onstage a few minutes later. By way of an introduction, each panelist was to say "in their own words" what exactly "truth in fiction" meant to them. First up was a writer named Maggie Van Nystrom. We'd met at AWP two years earlier. She wore a leather jacket and tan cowboy boots and had fiery red hair. She was a fiction writer, but she was best known for having published a briefly infamous essay in which she disclosed the sordid details of her affair with a distinguished older writer who also happened to be her graduate school mentor. The man was fired in disgrace. The scandal and its aftermath were covered in a long piece in *Vanity Fair*. There were those who thought Maggie had exploited a more famous writer's privacy for personal profit. Others argued it was her story to tell, since it happened to her. Others, still, believed it was not only her right to tell the story but her duty; there were other young women out there like Maggie who needed to see their experiences reflected in literature, so the argument went.

"Fiction," she began, "is always about discovering the truth, even if takes a bit of lying to get to it." A couple of students in the audience clamored to copy down this assertion. Others pursed their lips and stared in wonder at the ceiling as if they were contemplating a Buddhist koan. "Because the truth," she continued, "is always relative. It shifts and morphs depending on who's telling it. What's true from my perspective might not be true from someone else's. Isn't that why we get ourselves into so much trouble? We can barely agree that two plus two equals four, let alone who's right or who's wrong, what's good or what's evil. So really, all we have to go on is our own point of view."

Next up was James Martin, a poet and novelist whose claim to fame was that he could write you a poem in sixty seconds or less. I remembered him earlier in his career, setting up his portable Smith Corona on street corners, university quads, and in hotel lobbies, taking five-dollar "tips" for every doggerel he clacked out. He had somehow parlayed this three-card monte into a robust online following and subsequently a full-time position at a college in Oregon. Now he was writing a novel on Twitter.

"The truth," he said, giving the kids in the audience an Uncle Sam jab of the pointer finger, "is entirely up to you. And no one can tell you any different. The way *you* see the world is the only way that matters." The students nodded soberly. "I often think of Oscar Wilde, who said that truth in art is one's latest mood. Think about that a minute. There's real freedom in knowing you can change your mind whenever you feel like it. That's why Twitter's such a wonderful medium," he said. "Your latest truth is only two hundred and eighty characters away."

The moderator turned to me now. "And how would *you* define truth in fiction?"

I must have appeared stupefied, because she tapped the microphone loudly, thinking it had malfunctioned and I hadn't heard her. Actually, I'd been feeling for my phone in my pants pocket, thinking it might have buzzed, that Sophie might have called to explain why she'd missed the train. I fished it out as the rest of the panel stared impatiently in my direction. There was no missed call, and no message, and yet I couldn't extinguish that last phantom smolder of hope that the doors in the back of the auditorium might open, and I'd look up and see Sophie burst in, frantic to make our date, taking a seat in the back, waiting out the panel just so I'd know she was there, it wasn't too late. Instead, two more students slinked in and slumped into the back row with their overstuffed backpacks.

The moderator leaned forward and spoke slowly into the mike. "Do you think the truth is always subjective? As your colleagues seem to believe?"

I looked over. "The truth?" I said. "I suppose one's own perspective is all any of us really has to work with."

"Some critics have argued that auto-fiction is the only honest mode left. Would you agree?"

"*Auto-fiction?* There's a word that needs the rescue of scare quotes."

"What makes you say that?"

"It all just strikes me as a lot of navel-gazing," I said. "There's something so unseemly about writing about oneself. The sheer number of times you'd have to write *I* and *me*—it's exhausting to think about."

"Then what *is* the role of fiction, if not to convey your own experience?"

"Every novel has only one job, in the end," I said. "To help you get to know the person on the next bar stool. That's what the truth is about."

"So where does it come from, then? Subjectivity? Lived experience?"

"The truth might be subjective," I said. "But I don't think subjectivity alone makes something truthful."

"And besides," Maggie chimed in, "you're never only writing about yourself. No person lives in a vacuum. We're all responsible for other people's stories, as well as our own."

"So how do you decide when it's fair to write about someone else's story?" the moderator said. "Or to include it in your own. I mean, *you* live with another writer." All heads swiveled in my direction. "It must be hard not to borrow things from each other sometimes."

"The solution would be not to read each other's writing, then," I said.

"That's one answer."

"Or don't live with a writer," I offered.

"And what about other people? Friends, family, coworkers, the guy on the bus, all the various private lives that might find a way into your fiction. Innocent bystanders?"

"All's fair in love and war," I said.

"But where does ethics come in for you? Where do you draw the line?"

"Me," said Maggie, "I want to be a good steward for my characters. Especially if they have some basis in reality. I feel like you take on a great responsibility when you decide to write about someone. Even if it's fictionalized. So I guess the answer has something to do with how sincerely those other lives are a part of your personal experience. What?" She was looking at me, her nose screwed up. "You don't agree?"

"I think we're all on our own," I said.

"That's a little pessimistic."

"That's the way it is. Which, Chekhov reminds us, is the only subject that matters in the end."

"Don't you see any redemptive possibilities at all in literature?" the moderator asked. I turned and saw James Martin wrinkling his forehead in strained concentration, perhaps contemplating the question. Then I realized he had his phone out underneath the table and was tweeting.

"Here's a little tip for you," I said. "Most people in life don't overcome obstacles, or gain insight, or make discoveries. And they almost never improve themselves. At best, they might learn to live with their faults. Which is why real art shows us the ugliness of life, the cruelty, the reality—the *way it is*."

"And how exactly is it?"

"It isn't pretty, I'll tell you that. People lie, they deceive themselves, they say they'll show up and they don't. The truth, as Schopenhauer said of life, is a qualified unhappiness."

"Isn't there a chance for people to understand each other just a little better through an author's search to understand herself?"

"I think we're all deluding ourselves," I said. "Most of all if we think we know what's going on inside our own minds. Our only consolation is that we're all guilty of the same things. Selfishness, narcissism, call it what you will. It's the mode of the day."

"That's pretty cynical."

I turned to Maggie. "You said it yourself; all we have is our own subjectivity. So what's the point of anyone trying to communicate with anyone else, as long as we're all trapped within our own blinkered viewpoints?"

"Why write anything at all," said Maggie, "if that's what you think?"

I didn't have an answer. Except the one that Debra had stumbled on long ago: *a paycheck*. And what was so wrong about that? At least it had a kind of proletarian dignity to it, a purpose. And after all, why should money, fame, or attention be any less honorable than the equally greasy motives we usually ascribe to quote-unquote "art," things like self-expression, social consciousness, political engagement, self-discovery. They all had the same basic telos, which is to justify your own existence. Cardinal Newman even had a name for it. *Apologia pro Vita Sua*. A Defense of One's Life. Norman Mailer had called it an advertisement for himself.

"Perhaps the only true integrity in art," I concluded, "is to say nothing at all."

I looked around at the bemused stares of the undergraduates in the audience. Everyone was glaring at me with crooked brows, as if I'd just stood up and started disrobing. I wiped my forehead. I had somehow worked myself up into a sweat. I pressed my pant legs, trying to gather my composure. I took a deep breath. James Martin was still over there tweeting the next chapter of his novel. Across the room, some caterers were setting out crudités, wine, and tabbouleh on a folding table by the wall. The moderator shuffled through her note cards.

"Perhaps everyone could offer a few parting words?"

Maggie said, "Be true to yourself. That's the most—and the best—you can do."

James said, "Follow me on Twitter."

I said, "Beware of happy endings."

"If anyone else has questions," the moderator said, "I'm sure the panelists will be glad to speak with you as we convene for snacks. We have three cheeses, if I'm not mistaken—and hummus."

We all repaired to the buffet. The students formed a phalanx around us as we began assembling paper plates of cheese and crackers.

"Do you know any agents?" someone wanted to know.

"Should I do National Novel Writing Month?" another one asked.

"What about screenplays?"

I pictured the Archaic Torso of Apollo telling them *You must change your life*, but instead what they wanted to know was whether or not they should take an online writing course. I poured myself a glass of white wine nearly to the lip of the disposable cup and gulped it down, then headed back across town toward the hotel.

I walked down Broadway, a tree-lined street with wide sidewalks dotted with black streetlamps. There were stores selling European foods, bespoke jewelry, and tailored suits. I didn't think I could feel much worse, but then I passed a bookstore. In the window I saw one of Debra's novels on display. *The Widower's Wife*. There was a note card affixed to the cover. In thick cursive, one of the booksellers had written a glowing appraisal. *One of my favorite books of last year!* Sex and the City *meets* Gone Girl. *What's not to love?*

I stepped off Broadway onto a sloping street called Caroline where there were half a dozen neon-lit dive bars. Inside one of them, I found a seat at the bar and ordered a whiskey and a beer and sat brooding over the bookstore clerk's note, remembering that when Debra had first conceived of that novel, she had asked me whether I thought she'd have better luck with a thriller or a romance. "You know, if you had to choose," she said. I told her, "Why not try both at once?" I'd meant it as a joke, but who was laughing now.

I drank the whiskey, sipped the beer, and shrank into my despondency. I felt my shoulders slump. My chin fell to my chest. There had been a moment of hopefulness earlier when I still thought Sophie might show up on that train, but it had all drained away. I felt like an embalmed cadaver, coursing with fraudulent juices, synthetic and ersatz. My plan, I guess, was to drink enough to pass out in the hotel room and forget the whole sorry episode, the debacle that was the fiction panel, too. Maybe a kind of retrograde amnesia would ensue, and I'd forget about the last four months altogether, go back home to Halbrook, and go on living insensibly as before.

But then I heard the bell above the door chime, and someone was calling my name, and my mind flashed to Sophie having taken a later train, wanting to surprise me, having tracked me down to this, my obvious refuge, a local public house.

I turned around with a restrained hope. Was it possible? Could something of the weekend still be salvaged? But of course it wasn't her.

Standing in the doorway were my fellow panelists from the conference.

Maggie said, "Fancy meeting you here."

"I could say the same," I said.

"So join us, then," said James. "I'll buy the first pitcher."

We moved to a corner booth beneath a green neon sign. Maggie slid in and tossed her leather jacket over the table. James returned a few minutes later with pint glasses and beer.

"Now that we're alone," he said, pouring beers, "tell us all about this famous love affair of yours. I know you were holding punches back there."

I wondered whether, in some kind of epileptic blackout at the panel, I'd unwittingly divulged my affair with Sophie, spewing God knows what nonsense like some kind of Holy Roller. But then I realized he was talking to Maggie.

She took a chug of beer and sat back. "If you want to know the truth," she said, "I felt bad about what happened with [Famous Writer]. But what was I supposed to do? You write what you know. You write from experience. And that *was* my experience. Oh, sure, I know what people said. That I only slept with him to get some kind of story from it, like I went into the whole affair with the express purpose of exploiting him for profit. I didn't. I loved him. But I didn't know why. I couldn't understand it. And that's why I wrote about it, to make sense of it. And besides, even if I *had* done it on purpose, so what? People do things all the time for art, and it isn't always nice. Get used to it, folks."

"No judgment here," said James Martin. "You do you, and that's all right by me."

He and Maggie clinked beer mugs. I signaled to the bartender for another whiskey to go with my beer. Maggie sat up in the booth and propped her elbow on the table and tightened her eyes. Suddenly she was looking at me intensely.

"What?" I said.

"I know you," she said.

"Hello in there!" said James. "You did a panel together like an hour ago."

"From before," she said.

"We met at AWP," I reminded her. "In Portland."

"No, it's not that. It's somewhere else. Where do you teach again?"

I told her.

"Yes," she said, "that's it. You're Debra Crawford's—"

I nodded reluctantly.

"I knew her at MacDowell," she said. "We were in residence together a few years back."

"Fuckers," said James Martin out of nowhere. "I've applied six times and I never even got on the waitlist."

Someone came up then and said, "Aren't you the guy who writes one-minute poems?"

"For you," he said, "I'll do one in thirty seconds. Follow me this way." And they found another table across the room, where James produced a notepad from his pocket and began hurriedly dashing off verses.

"So what's it like being married to a writer?" Maggie said after James had left. "It's one thing having an affair with one, I can tell you. But it's gotta be a whole other thing actually sharing a home."

"I wouldn't know the difference," I said. "I've never been married to anyone who wasn't a writer." Come to think of it, I wasn't even friends with anyone who wasn't a writer. Maybe that was my problem.

"It's gotta be hard. What with her being so—"

"Successful? Ambitious?"

"Prodigious," she said.

"I'm working hard to catch up," I said.

"Aren't we all. I've been working on an essay collection for six years, and no one will touch it. The *Vanity Fair* piece will stalk me to my grave. All anybody wants is another scandal. It's the classic story of the *it* girl who's lost her glitz. Only *it* is sex with a septuagenarian, and the *girl* is forty-three"—she raised her pint glass—"and *glitz* is Pabst Blue Ribbon. But what about you?" she said. "You're Mr. Perfect, or what? With your sharp haircut and your designer glasses and your oxford shirt? You're just the perfect portrait of a college professor, aren't you."

"I grew up in a motel by a marina," I said. "In a shitty town in Florida."

"So what is it then, this is all a costume?" She gave my collar a playful tug. "Who's the real Debra Crawford's Husband?"

I shrugged.

"Thing is," she said, "there's something you're not telling me." She reached into her leather jacket and pulled out a deck of cards and laid them on the table. "I'm a tarot reader," she said. "Whaddaya say."

She began shuffling the cards, then laid them out on the table, brushing them around beneath her palms until they were spread out like puzzle pieces. "Turn one over," she said.

I turned over the first card. It was a picture of a Greek orgy, or so it appeared to me. Naked seraphs dancing in the clouds, bare-breasted and suckling grapes. In the middle was a torture device.

"The Wheel of Fortune," she explained. "You're at a turning point, a crossroads. An important decision stands before you. You want to know what you should do, don't you?" Her voice was deeper now. I felt a little spooked. For the first time I saw Maggie Van Nystrom as a sympathetic figure. She had written something that mattered to her, but nobody cared what she had to say anymore. The #MeToo moment that made her briefly in-famous had abandoned her, and now she was a relic. It seemed unfair. Yet here she was, getting by, doing her best.

"Turn over another one," she said, and I did as I was told.

The next card showed a man and a woman with goblets spread out before them—the Ten of Cups, she informed me. The next one after that was a knight with seven swords balanced on his shoulders. "This card is about love," she said, "and this one's about betrayal and burden. You're confused," she said. "You love someone, but you don't know what to do. And you're carrying this burden around by yourself." I turned over another card. It was a bunch of people bathing. Maggie said, "Your creative life will be good with this other person, I can tell." I turned over a card that looked like Soviet propaganda. A worker was bent over a water pail, perhaps repairing a bench. I thought I saw a hammer and sickle in the corner. Maggie said, "This tells me everyone will be fine, whatever happens. This person here is a worker, someone who endures, no matter what. Debra?" she guessed. I looked more closely and the person in the image appeared eerily like my wife—long, thin neck, skinny arms like a high school boy. The only thing missing was a pair of running shoes hanging by the laces over their shoulder.

After I didn't say anything for a while, Maggie began cleaning up the cards. Once they were away in her jacket, she climbed out of her booth and came to join me on my side. She put her hand on my shoulder.

"Do you want to know what I think?" she said.

"I didn't ask."

"I'll tell you anyway. I think you're leaving your wife," she said. "You just haven't admitted it yet."

"Where do you get that from?"

"Listen," she said, "I'll let you in on a secret. They're just dumb plastic cards. All I do is pay attention to people's reactions. And I think I know what you want the cards to say." She patted my forearm. I took a sip of beer. "Thought so," she said.

James came back to the booth. "You two are suddenly very cozy. I'll write a poem about you." He produced a reporter's notebook from his back pocket and began scribbling, then turned the page around and revealed the poem he'd suddenly composed.

Late summer sweat,
Salty cheeks, thoughts in common,
So long, farewell, find me
@the-real-james-martin.

He ripped out the page, folded it in two, and slipped it across the table and was gone. I downed the rest of my beer. I stood up. "Thanks," I said to Maggie.

"Good luck out there," she said.

"I'll need it."

Soon I was on the Taconic Parkway with the windows down and the radio blasting and a flask of Jim Beam uncapped in the cup holder next to me.

Two hours later I was parked in a loading zone outside of PS 319. It was about 1:15 a.m. Sophie had to be around there somewhere. I set out on foot in search of her at one of the twenty or so bars I knew she and John always went to.

It was a Friday night. Bedford, Manhattan, and Driggs were packed with people, cars honking and backed up at crosswalks. I headed up Third Street toward Havemeyer, ducking into Banter, where European soccer was playing loudly on the TV. I tried Clem's, a few blocks up, where several groups sat on the patio smoking cigarettes. Inside, I checked the tables, checked the bathrooms, frightened a woman who was coming out just as I began to knock, almost hitting her in the face with my knuckles. I tried Lucky Dog, on Bedford, and Soft Spot, and the Gibson. I texted Sophie again but she didn't answer. I thought about trying John with the pretense of the two of us getting drinks. I gave him a try, but after three rings he didn't answer and I hung up.

I started back toward the car, dejected and sobering up. It had been three hours since I'd left Maggie and James in Saratoga, and I'd finished the Jim Beam somewhere around White

Plains. The sour taste of a hangover was starting to set in. I couldn't go home to Debra now. It would be too suspicious. What would be my excuse? Probably I'd end up sleeping in the car. It wouldn't be the first time.

Then I stopped at the three-way intersection of Union, Richardson, and Eleventh. There was Richlane, a dark triangular bar at the foot of an apartment building with vinyl siding. I had an inkling, or else I just remember it that way now. At any rate, if I didn't find Sophie there, then at least I could get a drink and begin rehearsing my homecoming.

I found a seat and ordered a Manhattan and drank it with my elbows on the bar. There was techno music playing and some people were watching *RuPaul's Drag Race* on mute on the TV. A guy from an HBO show sat alone in the window drinking a Shiner Bock. I had made a mistake, I thought. It was foolish to come down here. I should not have trusted my instincts. I had driven down to Brooklyn in search of my best friend's wife—my wife's best friend—and for what? Because a has-been writer read my fortune in a deck of plastic tarot cards?

But then I looked up, and I saw her coming from the restrooms around the other side of the horseshoe bar.

She stopped. Her face changed. Her eyes brightened. Her teeth showed as her lips parted, her cheeks spreading into a tentative smile. Her chest rose and fell as she took in a deep breath. Then she came around the bar—she had a whiskey in her hand—and sat down next to me as if she'd been waiting for me all along, as if she'd known I'd eventually join her there.

"Took you long enough," she said.

"I texted. I waited for you. What happened?"

"I lost my phone," she said.

"What about the train? You couldn't get another ticket? You're telling me you lost your wallet, too?"

"My phone *is* my wallet," she said.

"You could have emailed."

"My computer's at home."

"And where's John?" I asked.

She pointed to the entrance. I turned. John was coming in on a puff of smoke, tossing his cigarette behind him on the sidewalk as the door swung closed.

He stopped short when he caught sight of me. Then he rushed forward.

"Pinch me, I must be dreaming! Yet here you are in the flesh! Traveling solo?"

"I was up at a conference in Saratoga," I explained.

"And what brings you down here?"

"There were too many writers up there."

"So you came to Brooklyn instead? What about home?"

"There's too many there, too," I said.

"Then you'll stay the night with us. Nobody writes in our house anymore."

John leaned forward to order another drink, Sophie reached behind his back and felt for my hand. For a brief moment, in the time it took John to get the bartender's attention, our fingers rested in each other's warm palms.

Then John sat back down with his drink, and we let go of each other.

"So tell me all about it," John said. "Did you find the happiness you seek? Or is the answer still somewhere out of reach?"

part two

AMERICAN LIT

1

AND SO IT BEGAN. TUESDAYS AND THURSDAYS I'D GO INTO
the city between my 10:20 a.m. American Lit survey and my
5:00 p.m. fiction workshop for an afternoon *cinq à sept* with
Sophie. I let Debra believe I was at the library working on my
book those afternoons. We'd rent a room at the Washington
Square Hotel, meet for one drink in the lobby bar to calm our
nerves before heading up, then draw the curtains and grab
at each other, blind, searching, and desperate. Afterward, Sophie would go to the window, looking down on MacDougal
Street, and I would marvel at the most mundane artifacts of
her presence: a blazer coiled like a cat on the carpet, her yellow sandals overturned beside the bed, a wineglass with her lip
print smeared on the rim. I thought of Schopenhauer, who said
we should regard the world as a place of penance, a locus of
longing and perpetual discontent. But inside that hotel room,
in those flaxen postcoital hours, a kind of communion seemed
possible, redemption even. There were only the two of us in
that room, and it often seemed as if that was the way it had
always been—that we had only ever had each other to fall back
on, only ourselves to reckon with and rely upon. Debra had
her sister, her mother, her agent, editor, and publicist—even her
father was in her life these days—and John, he had his brother
in Connecticut, his legal clients, his barroom drinking pals, and
probably a paramour or two, to boot. Sophie, she had her in-

sane mother, which hardly qualified. And me, I had two beach bums for parents and a tattletale for a shrink.

Those afternoons, we talked about each of us leaving our jobs, leaving John and Debra, starting a new life together. And when we were apart, we sent each other texts with links to apartments and Airbnbs in remote places where we could afford to live without working—a bungalow in Oaxaca, a beach house in Tulum, a small flat in Cartagena. Both of us could write, we said. Sophie could start again—or keep going, because it turned out she'd never really quit. She'd simply given up on the idea of publishing. Over the years, whenever she found the spare time, and the quiet, she had returned to her old pages, revising the stories she'd written in graduate school, fleshing them out, filling in gaps, digging through the notebooks in which she recorded her daily impressions, because there was still so much more to say—about her mother's dementia, about her and John's seamy marriage, about her father's death. She didn't know what she wanted to do with it all, but she was starting to think she ought to do *something*. "There must be a thousand pages," she said, "more than a book's worth, at least." If she gave them the proper attention, and if she had the time—and if I could take her someplace where she could focus, and think—then maybe she could fit the work into a shape that made her reflections and recollections worth writing down in the first place. And me, away from the college, outside the shadow of Debra's success, and the constant pressure from Chet Bland and the dean's office to produce, produce, produce, I could finally find some creative peace and turn out something honest of my own.

But beyond the walls of the Washington Square Hotel, reality bore down like a vise, and it was all I could do to manage the time between trips into the city. My students' stories were getting worse, for one thing, and they probably thought the same of my teaching. To say nothing of the essays being churned out in American Lit, most of which I suspected were being written by AI software or a paid plagiarist with a bad thesaurus. I delivered lectures on the differing usages of *I* and *me*, *its* and *it's*, while surreptitiously checking my phone for messages from Sophie. I taught lessons on how to *lie* down in bed and *lay* down the law, to brush one's teeth *every day* and make oral hygiene an *everyday* habit, but none of it stuck. By the end of class, half the room would be slumped with their chins to their chest, resting mercifully, the other half listening to something else entirely on wireless earbuds.

Around this time, Debra also thought to immerse me in the deep end of department life—something like throwing a Labrador off a pier to see if he'll start swimming.

It seemed that during my summer abroad she had grown chummy with Chet Bland and his wife, Bonnie. Chet and Debra's work on the department bylaws had apparently given rise to certain extracurricular obligations. When she proposed we join Chet and Bonnie for a weekly wine night, I balked.

"Do you need to be sick?" Debra asked. "You look a little green around the gills."

It was true that Chet Bland had that effect on me. I suspected I wasn't the only one in the department who felt that way.

"Is this his idea?" I asked. "Or yours."

"It's something we've discussed."

"You and Chet discuss things?"

"Of course."

"Do I have a choice?"

"Not really," she said. "I already said yes."

So, once a week Debra and I walked the six blocks to Chet and Bonnie's house to dine on canapés and cheese. Chet would emerge from the basement cradling an armful of bottles like bowling pins, set them out on the table, and deliver earnest disquisitions on fermentation, clarification, and aging, while I supped the wine and waited for the ordeal to be over. Chet would bury his nose in the bell of his glass, inhaling loudly like someone breathing through a deviated septum, then produce a suckling sound, followed by a gurgling that seemed to be coming from deep inside the cavern of his mouth, finishing up with a noisy gulp as he flushed the gargled liquid down. Eventually, after we'd each gone through several glasses, the topic turned to department gossip.

"Melanie Presley's pregnant again, did you hear?" someone would say.

"She's, like, fifty."

"How many is that now?"

"Seven."

"Are they Catholics?"

"Mormons."

"You wouldn't know it from those low-cut blouses."

"Perhaps that's why she keeps getting pregnant."

By the end of the evening, Chet would lose himself in drink and begin gazing wistfully across the room at Debra. He'd get this peaceful look on his face, like little Marcel Proust waiting in bed for his mother's good night kiss. Oddly, this upset me less than the gargling. In fact, I found some comfort in seeing my department chair ogling my wife, his mouth open and his eyes staring in abstracted wonder while his own wife glared angrily at him from the other sofa. It took a lot of trust to let people see you that way. And in the end, I thought maybe wine night at the Blands wasn't really the torture I'd made it out to be.

But when I was alone again at the end of the night, I would fall back into a soul-queasy gloom, thinking only of when I could see Sophie again, counting—sometimes literally on my fingers—the hours until we reunited. Debra would go to bed, shutting herself down like a factory assembly line the moment her head hit the pillow, and I'd take Ernie for a walk around the block, ruminating on impossible hopes. Scooping his warm turds into my plastic-baggie-lined palm, I thought, *There's got to be something more than this.*

Debra didn't have those worries. Whether it was the minor celebrity she enjoyed as Halbrook's most famous author, or the distinction of tenure, or even the pleasure of setting a new PR on her morning run, she had endless reasons to be satisfied with her life. Of course, it wasn't by accident. She had had a plan from the start, and she'd executed it flawlessly. She had climbed the academic ranks just as she'd hoped; she had produced a new novel every twenty-four months for six years running; and she was entering her forties with the same firm, athletic figure she'd had in her twenties.

Her ambition was understandable. Her childhood had been a lonely one. Her parents had divorced early and dispatched her to boarding schools so no one would have to fight over custody. It made sense that she was motivated by a certain degree of attention seeking. She hadn't found any validation at home, so she went looking for it elsewhere, first in school literary awards and the Phi Beta Kappa Society, then in graduate school fellowships and publications in literary journals, and now in book sales and academic promotions.

At first, her ambition was something I'd admired. My family way was to reside in the margins, offstage, out of the scene. My parents reveled in a touch of failure. Laxity was their natural state. They were uncomfortable with too much success. Listening to guests through the walls at the Last Resort, I assumed the periphery was the place for me, too—a natural domain for a writer, after all. But I met Debra, and she seemed to know another way. She was determined to succeed, no matter what, even if it involved a little grift or unseemliness, the occasional flattery or extortion in exchange for a blurb, a friendship or two of convenience. I used to envy her self-assurance. I hoped some of it might rub off on me. For a while, it felt like it did. But eventually I realized it wasn't my own confidence, but hers, that we were both bolstering. Even when she introduced me to editors and agents and other writers as "the real writer in the family," she remained the actual focus. I became referential. As her stock rose, I came to see myself as a footnote in her life. My charms and witticisms—whatever cynical élan I had once brought to dinners and cocktail parties—eventually outlived their usefulness. Debra Crawford had arrived, and now I was just tagging along. Afternoons in the city were my only wrinkle of escape. But after several weeks of this back-and-forth, my mood began swaying like the bubble in a level.

One night I woke in fright, sweat-drenched and dizzy. Debra was lying next to me, mummy-shaped in a sleep as peaceful as the dead. I sat up against the headboard, breathing heavily, lapping at the air. I rubbed my eyes. I had had a terrible dream. Chet Bland was in his kitchen, cutting a wheel of cheese with a samurai sword. Debra and Chet's wife, Bonnie, were standing nearby, watching. Sophie was there, too. The three of them were wearing nothing but bra and panties, a glass of wine in each of their hands, as they watched Chet wield his horrible weapon. And me, I was strapped naked to a Catherine wheel like I'd seen on Maggie Van Nystrom's tarot card, spinning round and round like a roulette table. I sat up just before Chet's blade came hurtling toward me through the air.

The next day I called Dr. Judith Stern. It was only a matter of time before my terrors and hopes broke the seams and comingled in some untenable danse macabre.

I lay down on the davenport and told her about the dream, about the terrible size of Chet's saber, about the shiny pink top of his head. These kinds of details were exegetical catnip for Dr. Stern.

"That's a very specific image," she said. "Where do you think it comes from?"

"For one thing," I told her, "he really has such a weapon. I've seen him use it to open a champagne bottle." I didn't tell her about Sophie, or Debra—or Bonnie, for that matter—standing around in their underpants. That would have sent her over the top.

"And what do you think it means?" she asked. "This dream of yours."

"Isn't that your territory?" I said.

"I have a dictionary of Jungian symbols around here somewhere," she said, "but I don't think it would help. I'd rather hear what *you* think this means." I was lying like a Viennese housewife on the little sofa, staring up at the foam tiles in the drop ceiling. Dr. Stern's voice was hovering eerily out of view, for she always sat behind me at her desk and I never saw her during our sessions except when she opened the door to let me in and showed me out at the end. I heard the sleeves of her kaftan brushing the arms of her chair, her pen scratching the pages of her legal pad. In my mind she was a faceless specter, like a radio personality. This made her a difficult person to talk to, since only the truly insane talk back to the radio. Plus, you could never be sure she wasn't taking notes as fodder for gossip, the way a shock jock might twist a caller's comments into a punch line. I proceeded with caution.

"I'm not sure what the dream means," I told her. "But I suspect it has to do with monotony, torture, a sense of guilt, perhaps." Privately, I was calculating how long it would take me to drive to Manhattan and back tomorrow afternoon, trying to remember whether I had enough on my AmEx to book the Washington Square Hotel an extra afternoon this week, wondering whether there was any chance of me and Sophie spending a whole night together soon.

"What do you suppose you have to feel guilty about?" she

asked. I heard the pages of her legal pad turning over. "Spare me no details. I want all you've got."

"Nothing specific," I said. "The usual, I guess."

"Is it about your writing?" she asked. "Last spring you told me nothing in fiction matters anymore. Do you still think that's true?"

"Don't you agree?"

"Is my opinion important to you?"

"I'm paying you for it."

"That's rich!" She laughed. "Mind if I borrow that?"

"Why not," I said.

"Now tell me, how do you think Debra would feel to hear you sound so hopeless?"

"I'm not talking to her. I'm talking to you."

"Are there things you tell me that you don't tell your wife?"

"Isn't that how therapy works?" I said. "I come in here and unload all sorts of dirty secrets I wouldn't share with anyone else?"

"Do you think your secrets are particularly dirty?"

I thought of the dimples on Sophie's lower back. I saw her standing at the hotel window with a T-shirt barely covering her, thighs bare and glistening in the afternoon light. We were getting nowhere, Dr. Stern and I.

I stood up, wrote a check for the copay, dropped it on her desk, and left.

That night, Debra wanted to know what was up with me. What was the matter?

"Why should anything be the matter?" I said. We were sitting on the sofa, watching a late-night talk show. There was a scant bit of wine left in the bottle on the coffee table and I poured it into my glass.

Debra screwed up her nose. Something, she could tell, had the whiff of mendacity.

"Is it the book?" she said. "We can talk about it if you want."

Had Dr. Stern gotten hold of her? It was my impression that Dr. Stern's favorite pastime was to gab in barely anonymized detail about her clients and coworkers. It would only have taken a few minutes for her to plant in Debra the seed of suspicion.

"Everything's fine," I said.

"You don't have to lie."

"Who said I'm lying?" I drank the rest of the wine in my glass.

"I know you," she said. "Maybe even better than you know yourself. You get this way when the writing's going poorly. Come on, let me help. Give me some ideas, let's hash this out together." She turned her body toward me on the sofa, tucking her calves up underneath her butt, and reached for a notepad that was lying on the console behind us. It was a pantomime of the way we used to be, drinking wine on the sofa and watching TV, when one of us would suddenly turn to face the other, an idea percolating, and the other would hop up to grab a cardboard coaster or an envelope or a magazine subscription card—anything to write on—and start taking dictation as the other spitballed ideas. Soon both of us would be riffing. Hours would pass this way, another bottle of wine would be opened, and eventually we'd have five or six pages of notes jotted down, no recollection of whose ideas had been whose, or what belonged to whom, and no care to sort it out. We were in it together then. But that was a long time ago. I could barely make out the people we were, like the faded, dewy impression of a handprint on glass. Debra touched my arm.

"Okay," she said, "I see you're not in the mood." She put the notepad down. "But be patient. You'll get through it, I promise." I picked up the wine bottle to pour another glass, but it was completely empty. "And maybe you should scale it back a little on the booze," she said. "It makes you anxious and depressed." Across the room Ernie whimpered in his sleep. "Tell me you'll think about it, at least?"

"First thing tomorrow," I said. She rolled her eyes.

My phone buzzed on the entryway table and I darted to retrieve it. A message from Sophie. A link to a rental house in Colombia. *$800 a month*, she wrote. *Can you just imagine?*

"Urgent call?" said Debra. I looked up, clicking the screen off.

"My father," I said. "Something about repaving the parking lot at the hotel. It's nothing. Don't worry about it."

2

It was the second week of October, and an early cold snap blew through Halbrook, sending everyone in town scrambling. Hats and scarves and hooded sweatshirts were hauled out of storage. Students who hadn't brought winter clothes from home were forced to improvise with whatever accessories they had lying around. All over campus you could see people in mismatched outfits like snowmen dressed up by little children. They wore cutoff jean shorts with big puffy vests on top, T-shirts wrapped around their necks like scarves, athletic socks on their hands for mittens. Girls in summer skirts could be seen crossing the quad with their thighs blistered and splotchy from the cold, plush-lined boots barely covering their calves. Cars were parked off-kilter all over town (there was a rumor of snow), and grocery store shelves grew disorganized and empty almost overnight. And inside the Humanities Bloc, a very specific kind of climate crisis was taking place. The radiators had come rumbling to life after their long summer hibernation, and now all the classrooms and offices were unbearably hot. Everyone had to open their windows to fight the heat, but with the sudden cold outside, you also had arctic blasts cutting through the hot air inside. Turning a corner, you'd hit a low-pressure front that would stop you in your tracks. Then you'd open your office door and feel a steam furnace heat that would suddenly fog your glasses like you'd just stepped inside from a blizzard.

I told Debra she ought to take a break from running until the weather passed. It was too cold out, and dangerous, and there was frost and there might also be ice. But she kept up with her morning runs as if nothing had changed. She was laced up and out the door by six thirty every morning—frost, fog, and freezing rain be damned. And that's where trouble set in.

I got up to walk Ernie one Saturday morning and noticed Debra still wasn't home from her run. Usually she was back in the kitchen drinking a protein shake by the time I was out of bed. But not today. This wasn't entirely uncharacteristic. She *had* been acting a little strange lately. Last week I had come in through the back door at just the moment Debra was coming in through the front, looking unusually disheveled, her sweat-band down at her neck, hair a mess, cheeks flush and weather pocked. We found ourselves squaring off at opposite ends of the hall, the front and rear doors barely shut behind each of us. Then, after a period of mutual, unspoken suspicion, we reached a détente, silently passing each other in the hall like the changing of the guards. I told myself afterward it was nothing, I was just projecting. But where had she been? And where was she now?

I looked out the window, rubbing a smudge clear in the frosted glass. The sky was white; snow had started coming down. I couldn't fathom why she'd gone out in this weather.

I pulled a wool hat over my ears and attached Ernie's leash to his collar and opened the door. Ernie put a tentative paw over the threshold, but even he had the good sense to rear back as soon as he felt the cold concrete underfoot.

"It's okay, buddy," I told him, "fortune favors the bold," and together we stepped into the fray.

We set out on our usual route, first up Poplar, then left on Myrtle, then up and around Berkmar Park, where Chet Bland lived. The dog and I passed his house, stopping for a moment to observe the venue of our wine dinners and the setting for my recent *cauchemar*. The place appeared empty, or at least Bonnie was gone. There was only one car in the driveway, a silver Lexus, the roof and hood thick with a layer of fresh powder, the letters on the license plate—C-H-A-I-R—visible beneath a dusting of snow.

Now it was really coming down. I looked up the road. No one with any sense was out and about in this, and it was time Ernie and I got back, too. But when I looked down at the freshly covered sidewalk, I detected the almost imperceptible tracks of two size-seven Asics Metaspeed running shoes stamping a path toward the park. I knew this was part of Debra's circuit. She usually stopped a few blocks up, at the swing sets, to pause and stretch. Maybe we could catch up to her there.

It was three blocks later that I noticed a strange figure across the street. Ernie's tail perked up. Then I realized, from across the intersection of Myrtle and Adams, that the distant lump on the sidewalk was my wife. There she was, lying on the ground with her foot in her hand, her shoe unlaced beside her like a child's overturned Tonka truck. She was rocking back and forth and wincing on the icy salted sidewalk.

I let go of Ernie's leash and he darted across the road and ran up to Debra and started sniffing her face, licking her cheeks, aware, with his dog's intuition, that something was seriously wrong.

I came up a minute later and put words to his worry.

"Jesus, what the fuck happened?"

"What does it look like?" she said. "I fell." Her mouth was twisted up in pain. She clutched her foot, quivering.

"Is it broken?"

"I don't know, I can't tell. It's just throbbing, and it hurts."

I crouched down and lightly squeezed her ankle. She gritted her teeth—"Aaahh."

"Can you stand?"

"I don't know." She pushed herself up off the sidewalk. I gave her my hand for support, but as soon as there was pressure on her foot she crumbled back down to the ground.

"It's too cold," I said. "You shouldn't have gone out when it was this icy."

"So it's *my* fault now?"

"It's the weather's fault," I said. "Plus, your ankle was already weak from when you fell down the stairs at Joe's Pub. Remember?"

She set her jaw, teeth clenched. "Get the car. Please."

I grabbed Ernie's leash. "Come on, Lassie, let's go get help."

The doctor's prognosis was that Debra would be out of commission for at least six weeks. The ankle was fractured. She needed to keep her leg elevated. She would be mostly bedridden. But with luck and physical therapy, she could be running again in a few months.

Debra shimmied herself up in the hospital bed. She was wearing one of those blue cotton gowns and it was falling off her shoulder. I pushed it up for her. Her foot was in a cast. Her leg was suspended in a sling. I sat down in a chair at her bedside and held her hand.

"What about my classes?" she asked the doctor when he came back in.

"Is there anyone who can substitute for you? At least for the next several weeks?"

All eyes were on me. It took me a moment before I realized what was being asked.

"Yes, of course," I said. "I'll ride swift to the rescue!" But how would I find the time? And what did this mean for my trips to the city?

"Better if you just take attendance and deliver a few lectures," Debra said. "I'm sure I'll be back in no time."

"Eventually we'll get you a knee scooter," the doctor said. "It'll give you enough mobility to get around the house, but I wouldn't try to stray too far from home for the time being. You're lucky you've got a husband who can cover for you."

"I serve at your pleasure," I said. But then it occurred to me I didn't know exactly what I was signing up for here. "What are you teaching right now, anyway?" I asked.

"Studies in Women's Fiction," she said.

"No sweat," I told her. "When it comes to fiction and the fairer sex, I'm practically an expert." Even through the haze of prescription painkillers her look said *do not fuck with me right now*. I put my hands up in surrender. "I'll just follow the syllabus."

"Good," she said.

"Good, then," the doctor said. "Someone will call in a prescription. In the meantime, go get some rest."

"Will she be okay?" Sophie wanted to know when we talked on the phone that night.

"Eventually," I said. "She's in a lot of pain right now, but she seems to be all right. Mostly I think she feels embarrassed."

There was silence on the line. We both remembered Debra's fall at Joe's Pub.

"She shouldn't have worn those high heels," said Sophie.

"That's exactly what I told her."

"Where is she now?"

"On the sofa in the living room," I said. "She can't go up or down the stairs."

"You have stairs?"

"It's a house," I said.

"Sometimes I forget you don't live here in the city. Like a rat, like the rest of us. You have this whole other life. A house, a dog. You have stairs." In the background I could hear John's voice. He was intoning something in Latin.

"Is that the *Metamorphoses* I hear?"

"He's on an Ovid kick," she said. "I have no privacy here. I can barely get away from him for ten seconds. I'm wasting myself. And now this? Come down soon, will you?"

"As soon as I can."

"I guess I should be in touch with her, huh? Wish her well or whatever?"

"It's what a friend would do."

"I'm quickly growing tired of this arrangement, you know."

"It gets worse," I said. "My course load just doubled."

3

I LEFT AMERICAN LIT THE FOLLOWING TUESDAY AND headed down the hall to Studies in Women's Fiction. I peered through the window panel in the door before entering. There were young women everywhere. A blotch of fog appeared on the glass, spreading with my breath, and I looked through it as if into a mystical other world. But I was confident about my prospects. I had done my homework, studying Debra's syllabus the night before, scanning the notes and underlines in my old copies of *Cranford*, *Villette*, and *Mrs. Dalloway*, refreshing my memory on the goings-on of the Jenkyns clan, Lucy Snowe, Clarissa Dalloway, and the rest of them. Plus, when I looked past the congregation in the middle of the room, I spied an assured ally in the back. In the last row, sitting at a distance from his fellow students, with a curly black mane half covering his eyes, attending quietly to a heavily creased paperback copy of *Emma*, was Winston Armstrong, my most stalwart disciple. I took his presence as a welcome surprise and ventured forth.

Pushing through the door, I was met with a waft of pleasant smells—lilac, lavender, orange blossom, jasmine, vanilla, lemon peel, bergamot, coconut, quince—a panoply as rich and varied as the Macy's perfume counter. I inhaled the heady aroma. Maybe this class would turn out all right. I tossed my satchel on the desk by the whiteboard and pulled out the lecture notes

Debra had given me as a cheat sheet. Today we were discussing Jane Austen.

"As some of you may know," I began, "I'll be subbing for Professor Crawford until she recovers from her recent mishap. This is not usually my subject, as you may have guessed, but together I think we'll have a lot of fun rooting around in this thorny territory. So, how 'bout we check in with ol' Emma Woodhouse." The students opened their notebooks and laptop computers.

"Some critics have argued that Emma Woodhouse's greatest sin is that she plays God by trying to rule over other people's affairs. Would you agree with that claim?"

A young woman in the front row raised her hand.

"Yes?"

"You say she's playing God," she said. "But I think she's playing *man*."

"Interesting assertion," I said. "Can you explain what you mean?"

"Her sin is that she defies the sexual hierarchy. That's why nobody likes her."

"Do others agree? Is Emma generally unlikable on this count?"

"I mean, she's kind of selfish," someone said. "And she's always trying to force Harriet into this fantasy of how she thinks she's supposed to be."

The palm of the student in the front row appeared again, elevated like a crossing guard's white glove, about two feet from my face.

"Yes?"

"The thing is, it's fine for a man to control the affairs of a woman, but not for a woman to do the exact same thing? Is that the lesson?"

"Well said," I replied. "But what would you say about the fact that Emma finally *does* marry in the end? Wouldn't that imply that the novel is less critical of the sexual hierarchy than you suggest?"

"It tells me the novel is flawed."

"Not a fan, huh?"

"I don't think Austen was brave enough to show us what a truly independent woman would look like."

"In other ways, don't you think Ms. Austen does just that?" I was attempting to play devil's advocate.

"Why is it *Ms.* Austen, and not just Austen to you? You wouldn't say *Mr.* Dickens, would you?"

A teaching moment!

"As a matter of fact," I said, "it was once the norm to refer to all authors by such distinctions as *mister* and *missus*. I suppose I was attempting an amusing anachronism. But if it upsets you, then by all means—"

"Upsets?" she said.

"If you find it irksome."

"*I* find it offensive," another student chimed in.

"Those terms are rooted in the patriarchy," someone said.

I forged ahead.

"But the story ends with Knightley moving into Emma's house, the man attaching himself to the woman's wealth." Not dissimilar to my own arrangement, I had to admit.

"Maybe she should have gotten a job and not married anybody at all," one student suggested.

"It wasn't the norm during the time," I said.

"But Austen herself never married," another student offered.

"Fair enough," I said. "But in Jane Austen's time, the financial opportunities available to women were almost entirely bound up in matrimony. Austen's particular situation was an anomaly."

Now the conversation was really taking off. I dispensed another argument to spur the debate.

"Is Jane Austen, in her own cunning way, challenging the

established system by inventing a character as authoritative as Emma?" I asked.

"Cunning?"

I looked out at the group. All eyes were fixed on me, their collective gaze as tense as a drawn bow.

"What I meant," I said, "was *sly*. I meant Austen is sly as a narrator. As in clever, or tricky."

"Tricky?" someone said.

"Yeah," another volunteered. "These words feel gendered to me. You'd never say a man was tricky, would you?"

"Actually, our thirty-seventh president was frequently called Tricky—"

"Um, Richard Nixon was a criminal," someone said.

"All I meant," I tried again, "was that Austen's a capable narrator; she's able to trick us into feeling two ways at once about her heroine."

"Of course she is capable. But when you say it like that you sound surprised she would be."

Some of the students in the middle scooted in closer behind their leader in front, marshalling themselves like a female tribunal in a Fellini fever dream. The end of *City of Women* flashed to mind. I looked all the way to the back for support, but only found Winston Armstrong drawing curlicues with a Bic pen on his left forearm.

I put up my hands. I had lost them. The ship was taking on water. The cockpit was flooded. Nothing left to do but evacuate.

"Why don't we all turn to chapter thirty-seven," I proposed, "and just go around the room reading aloud from the text for a while. I'm sure everyone would enjoy a break from hearing what I have to say. I know I would."

* * *

The debacle in Women's Fiction soon carried over into my other classes. One morning I heard myself delivering to my students' weary gazes a long extemporaneous lecture on the myth of "Syphilis." Then I told them to go outside and gather rosebuds. "It's a metaphor for sex," I heard myself telling them, as if someone else were speaking through me, as if I were my muse's ventriloquist dummy. My mind traveled places, I couldn't focus, and I felt like I was being shadowed by some other, less clever self.

Finally one afternoon I had a full-on out-of-body experience. I had asked my students to read a Melville story aloud. They were going around the room, taking turns. I felt my eyelids grow heavy. My chin fell to my chest. And then, in slumber, I saw myself rising above myself, until I was looking down upon the specimen that was me—almost forty, skinny in the arm and leg, a paunch developing, hair graying slightly at the temples, engaged in an affair with his best friend's wife, who was also his wife's best friend—and I saw this figure start to age, slowly at first, then rapidly, like in a time-lapse video of a decaying flower, until his jowls were loose, his hair was white, his chin was a formless bag beneath his lips, while all around him teenagers recited tonelessly from a hundred-and-fifty-year-old short story about a disgruntled office clerk.

I came to, sweating and breathless. Waking, I heard the colorless incantations of Chase Morrison—lacrosse player and luckless creative writing student—murmuring the ending of "Bartleby, the Scrivener" aloud. "Um, Bartleby?" he said, as if it were a question. "Um, humanity?"

I sat up in my chair, taking a deep breath. The students were staring at me, nonplussed, from around the seminar table. No one spoke. I looked around the room at them. Their red-eyed, half-stoned faces awaited some kind of commentary.

"'Who looks outside, dreams,'" I said. "'Who looks inside,

awakes.'" Several of them took out their notebooks to copy down my remarks. "But don't take my word for it."

I left the room in a daze while the rest of them stayed behind packing up their things.

Dissociative fugue was the clinical term for what had happened, Dr. Stern informed me. "Formerly psychogenic fugue," she said. I had caught her just before she left the office for the day. "Sometimes brought on by depression, post-traumatic stress, extreme fatigue," she said. "And alcohol abuse," she added. "It's the mind's attempt to escape psychological distress. People often wake up in strange places," she explained, "with no idea how they got there. I knew a guy in the Economics Department who suddenly and mysteriously wound up on a beach with no clue what he was doing there. Just looking around in amazement, like he was in a dream. An assistant professor in History—you may know her—experienced something similar last year. Funny story, really. It happened a month before she went up for tenure. As soon as she made associate, it never happened again. She even quit seeing me. Apparently she was totally cured. Anyhow, others wind up on a mountaintop, or an airplane, all sorts of places."

"But I didn't go anywhere," I said. "When I woke up, I was still right there in class. It was horrible. I would have preferred an airplane."

4

THE GOOD NEWS WAS THAT IT COULD ONLY GET BETTER. And knowing Debra, she'd probably recover in record time and come charging back in to reclaim her mantle in a matter of weeks.

The recovery, however, was off to a shaky start.

The first week home, Debra spent the whole time on the sofa with her leg elevated on a stack of pillows and a teapot within reach on the coffee table, watching a lot of daytime television, and apparently doing very little to rehabilitate herself. The sounds of cheering studio audiences and shampoo commercials filled the house. In between episodes of *Ellen* and *The View* she scrolled through social media. She put up photos of her broken leg and sat swiping at her phone, waiting for people to "like" her posts. She spent hours browsing the Internet for new boots and purses, running shoes she couldn't use, and leather jackets she had no occasion to wear. She kept tabs on her Amazon page to see whether her ranking had gone up or down.

I thought she was simply wallowing in her suffering—which would have been extremely out of character for her—but of course there was something else brewing within this solution of daytime television and Internet shopping. A creative flame was lit, and before long all this sitting around had served to conjure up a new project. I had no idea where this inspiration was coming from, hearing Hollywood celebrities boast about their winter vacations in the background, but for Debra Craw-ford it was creative fire. A stack of manuscript pages eventually grew on the coffee table as she printed out each day's writing and spent the evenings reading over what she'd written earlier. Within a couple of weeks she must have had fifty pages.

"Where the hell is this coming from?" I asked her.

"I got a spark," she said. "What can I say?"

"From where? You haven't left the house in three weeks."

"It's like it was sitting right in front of me the whole time," she said. "All I had to do was open my eyes."

There was nothing in front of her but me and the dog, yet somewhere in that fifteen-by-nineteen room she'd found inspi-ration. Go figure. The muse was a tricky priestess.

Meanwhile, I was running to CVS to fetch Debra's prescrip-tions, heat pads, and mentholated ointments, cooking dinners, preparing lunches, vacuuming the house, sanitizing the toilet bowls, spraying the countertops, folding the laundry. I was also having to make extra time to read all the books on Debra's women's lit syllabus before class. Plus, the last time I'd made a getaway to the city, I'd nearly gotten caught. Coming in the door in the blue of night, thinking Debra was already in bed, I saw her through the length of the hall, hobbling around the living room on her orthopedic boot, reading over that day's work. When she turned, hearing the kitchen door open, I had to quickly grab a leash from the counter and thank my good luck that Ernie rushed to my side in time for us to make a tableau of Man and Dog returning home from a late-night walk.

All this was taking a toll in the social realm, as well. Because of Debra's injury, wine nights had to take place at our house instead of Chet and Bonnie's. They would come over with a cardboard box full of Chablis or whatever, and the four of us would swig as much as we could, while Chet would offer Debra his sincerest encouragement that she'd be back on her feet in no time. Once, when Bonnie and I were clearing glasses to the kitchen, and Chet had forgotten we were still in earshot, I overheard him telling Debra, "I'd do anything for you, you know. Anything."

After Chet and Bonnie left one night, I tidied up the space around the sofa where Debra had stationed herself, while she mutely opened the laptop and returned to writing the Great American Novel, as if the intervening hours of drink and talk had done nothing to interrupt her flow. I tried to engage her. "You want to watch a movie or something?" She shook her head no, still typing. I picked up a few empty bottles and rested them under my arm, cleared the cheese plate, wiped some crumbs from the table, asked again whether she needed anything—"I could make some popcorn? Ice cream? Nothing?"—and she barely responded, just shook her head once more and continued typing. It was strange. Suspicious, I'd say, if I were that way inclined.

Finally I said, "Is this just you in the throes of another book, or should I take it personally that you've gone radio silent these last few weeks?"

"This is me"—she held her arms out like the Buddha, the laptop resting where the Buddha's crossed legs would otherwise be—"doing my best."

"You seem a little detached is all," I said. "Are you sure you're not taking too much of this stuff?" I picked up the amber pill bottle on the coffee table and rattled it to see how much was left of her painkillers.

"I'm fully attached," she said.

I balled up Chet's soiled napkin in my fist, the last of the night's detritus.

"Well, you'll let me know when you've got some pages you want me to read," I offered.

"Noted," she said. "But I don't think you'd like it."

"Why not?"

"Cuts a little close to home," she said. "At least you might think so."

She was being weird, I thought, and I wondered whether Sophie had talked to her, whether Debra had told her anything that might explain her weirdness. I repaired to the kitchen and called Sophie to get some answers, but it was John who picked up Sophie's phone.

"Hello, old friend," he said.

"John," I said, surprised.

"You were expecting my wife, perhaps?"

"Just seeing how you two were doing," I lied.

He put on his poet's voice and began to deliver a slurred reading of Philip Larkin.

"'Someone else,'" he said, "'feeling her breasts and cunt, / Someone else drowned in that lash-wide stare . . .'"

"Drinking alone?" I surmised, but really I was worried. Had he been waiting for me to make this call? Waiting to ensnare me? How long had he known?

But he went on with another recitation, meaningless, harmless.

"'One should always be drunk,'" he declared. "'So as not to feel time's terrible burden.'"

There was a commotion in the background. I heard Sophie's voice telling John it was late, time to hang up. I looked for hidden signs in the sounds on the other end of the phone, in the static, in the murmured dispute she and John were having as the two of them tugged the phone back and forth.

Finally the line went silent. John—or Sophie—had hung up. Ten minutes later I got a text message.

Don't call after six. Are you trying to fuck this up?

It was late by now, but Debra was still at it in the living room.

I heard her faintly reading aloud. I was at the sink, cleaning Chet and Bonnie's lip marks from the wineglasses. I cut the faucet and went to the kitchen doorway and listened from the end of the hall, the wheels of Debra's knee scooter scraping the floor as she hobble-paced back and forth, reading to herself.

"'He thought he was the smartest guy in the room, and sometimes he was. But mostly he was delusional and self-obsessed. And like most men, he was in love with his own emotions. His depression, his addictions, his lust, his self-deprecation—he carried them all around like a little girl with her dolls, petting them from time to time, probably talking to them, too.'"

I crept halfway down the hall, keeping my back to the wall, listening.

"'He wasn't always that way,'" she continued. "'He used to be ambitious, hardworking, industrious even. But he became too resentful of other people's success. He prided himself on being a realist—he thought he always knew the right answer—but actually he was a fantasist. He was delusional and sentimental and nostalgic.'"

Boy, I thought, this was one sad sack she was writing about, and Debra Crawford was really giving him hell. Whose life and times had she pillaged now? One of her sister's boyfriend's? The poor fucker.

"'Nurse, maid, muse, Madonna,'" she went on. "'What did he want in a marriage? Or a love affair, for that matter? All of them, probably. What man didn't?'"

She was really going for the jugular.

I crept a little farther down the hall to hear more, but Debra caught sight of me standing dumbly in the half-lit hallway with a drying cloth dangling like a cornerman's towel from my waistband.

"Just checking if you needed anything," I said.

Full-voiced, she said, "No, thank you, I've got everything I need."

I went back to washing the dishes. Soon I heard the familiar rustle of pages—she was closing down shop for the night—and the thud of her walking boot mounting the stairs to bed.

5

THE NEXT MORNING THERE WAS A KNOCK AT THE FRONT door. I was jittery and empty-stomached, drinking the morning's first cup of coffee. I hadn't slept well. John's voice on the phone last night had haunted my dreams. Like an earworm I kept replaying in my head the lines of Philip Larkin he'd recited. The words *lash-wide stare* kept waking me up, his voice ringing in my ears. I lay there watching the moonlight track the ceiling, saying those words over and over in my head till dawn. In my unease the next day, I felt the knock at the front door like an electric jolt and shuddered. I dashed clumsily to answer, banging my shin on the corner of the coffee table along the way. Debra's pages had been neatly stacked on top, with one white cover page concealing the writing underneath, and the stack went flying. She was on the sofa with her laptop open. With a huff she rose to her feet, scooted around the coffee table, and started picking up the pages I'd spilled. I turned the knob, wincing from the throbbing pain as I opened the door.

Outside, Carlos Cross was standing on the stoop with a bouquet of carnations pressed to his chest. He seemed surprised to see me. "Oh, it's *you*," he said. "These are for Debra."

I stepped back out of the doorway, kneading my leg with my thumb, feeling a bruise puff up.

Carlos stepped inside. "Here," he said, peering around me to gain access to Debra's bent-over form. "I didn't know what you liked, but these seemed bright, so . . ." He lay them on the entryway table. Then he made sense of what was happening: Debra picking up manuscript pages from all over the floor. He made a beeline for the coffee table and proceeded to help her, weighing the pages in his open palm as he scooped them up.

"Something new?" he said, and started thumbing through the manuscript.

Debra stood up and snatched them away before Carlos could read them. Maybe *he* was the sucker who'd inspired her, I thought.

"Couple weeks old," she said, tucking the stack into her side with her elbow.

"Damn, at that pace you could have a new book in two months."

"Yeah, I should break my ankle more often," she said.

"Damn right," said Carlos.

They both had a good laugh. But when I said, "Maybe I should try it myself," Debra just gave me a cold stare.

"Why don't I get a vase for these," she said.

She grabbed the flowers from the entryway table and wheeled away to the kitchen. Carlos looked around, like a social worker surveying a foster home, his forehead wrinkled with doubt. After a minute he turned to me and placed his hand on my shoulder and ushered me to the corner of the room, away from where Debra could hear us. In a voice barely above a whisper, he said, "If you don't mind my saying, things aren't looking very good from where I'm standing. Is everything all right?"

I glanced down the hall. Debra's cast was peeking out from behind the kitchen wall. I could hear the tap running, scissors snipping the flower stems. Back in the living room, the remains of Debra's writing frenzy were spread out like so much trash. There were mugs, coasters, teabags, magazines, candles, match-books, pens. The TV was still on, though muted. It was not a good scene, and I could understand why Carlos might be concerned. But that was Debra's process. Buttoned up on the outside, a frenzied mess behind closed doors. I was used to it.

"She always writes in bursts like this," I explained. "Plus, she's on painkillers, so she's acting a little wacky."

Carlos squeezed my bicep and looked me in the eye. "I wasn't talking about her," he said. "I was talking about you."

I stepped back and gave myself a once-over. I hadn't slept well, it was true. I was still wearing yesterday's clothes, as well. And I hadn't showered today, or shaved. My eyes were probably bloodshot. John's voice rang in my ear, and Sophie's rebuke. *Are you trying to fuck this up?*

"I'm just overworked," I said to Carlos. "Between my own classes, plus Debra's—"

He was distracted by something. His eyes were downcast. He seemed fixated, like someone tracking the tiny movements of an insect.

"What is it?" I said.

He just kept staring at my leg.

"What?"

"I think you're bleeding."

I looked down. There was a gash in my pants, and a spot of blood was spreading in the fabric like tie-dye. I walked over to the coffee table and found a smear of red on the edge of it. On the sofa arm, which I must have brushed against on my way to the door, was a streak the color of iodine ointment.

"Just a stupid accident," I said. "I wasn't paying attention."

"You need to settle down. You're burning the candle at both ends, I can tell. Is it the book? Is that what it is?"

Et tu, Carlos?

"I'd be happy to look at it if you like," he went on. "Give you some notes."

I didn't tell him there was nothing to read.

"I don't mind passing it on to my agent either," he offered. "I'm at your disposal. Seriously. Use me."

My own agent had not officially dropped me, but she was no longer accepting my calls. Now when I phoned, I had to spell my name out and give my number and email to the intern at the front desk as if I were querying for the very first time.

"It's tempting," I said. "But no, I'm fine for now."

"Well, anyway," he said, "go easier on yourself. None of this is worth getting so worked up about."

"Probably not," I said. "You've got me there."

Debra came back in, the flowers in a tulip-shaped vase resting on the handlebars of her scooter. She set them down in the middle of the coffee table, then lowered herself onto the sofa and reached for her laptop. "Now if you two will excuse me," she said, "some of us have work to get back to."

6

Sophie and I met under the awning of the hotel. We hadn't seen each other in three weeks. The last time I heard her voice was when I'd called and John had answered. She was unusually quiet today. Taciturn, really. It was a cool afternoon. The sky was clear, the air was brittle with autumn. My train had arrived on time. I'd caught all the walk signs coming down Broadway. These alone were reasons to be optimistic. But when Sophie showed up, she had a look of disdain on her face. Maybe it was indifference, or dislike. I could see it the moment she came around Waverly and Sixth Avenue, where she stopped, perhaps fifty yards away, as if she was thinking of turning back. I could see her sigh. She looked down for a minute, as if to gather herself. Then, like someone gearing up to mount a steep hill, she made herself come toward me. I put my hand out as she approached, but she didn't take it. "Not today," she said, and kept walking past the hotel, past me, up into Washington Square Park. I followed after her, saying nothing.

We ambled in mutual silence for an hour or more, zigzagging languidly up and down the streets, letting the quiet grow between us like fog. Eventually we headed up Broadway and into the Strand for lack of anything else to do. We had browsed the stacks so many times together as friends, I hoped this might ease the tension, our falling back into a familiar pattern.

We walked up and down the crowded fiction aisles, tipping

spines back from the shelves, reading the back covers. But when I looked up at one point she was gone. I saw her heading for the stairs to the second floor. I figured I'd let her be alone for a while, if that was what she wanted. I couldn't push her. So I went downstairs and skimmed the philosophy and psychology in the basement. I opened a copy of *Either/Or*. *Being a perfect human being is after all the highest goal. Now I have corns . . .* So much for the Danish perspective. I shelved the book and continued ambling around the basement. The affair had only been going on six weeks and yet she was already tired of me, I thought. For all its sordid nondisclosures and tacitly understood betrayals and reconciliations, at least there was a pattern to the life she had with John. It had a plot she could follow. What did she have with me?

I found her on the mezzanine, flipping through a collection of Egon Schiele paintings. I looked over her shoulder at the spread legs and twisted mouths, the red lips and vulvas and nests of hair splotched like Rorschach tests on the pages. In the one called *Friendship* two people held each other, nude, kneeling. Others swarmed around us up and down the stairs, and I felt a twinge of guilt looking down at the pubic blots in full view of other people.

I closed the book in her hands and, reaching around her, slipped it back up on the shelf. I could smell her, a tantalizing aroma of fabric softener and cigarette smoke, lip balm and coffee. I breathed in. I put my hand on her lower back. She turned and, in full voice, in front of everyone moving up and down the stairs, said:

"Your wife thinks you're depressed."

"Can we take this outside?"

Sophie started down the stairs, snaked through the throng at the registers, and pushed through the doors. I went after her, knocking into someone's overstuffed tote bag.

Outside, I said, "You talk to Debra?"

"She's my friend." She lit a cigarette and took a drag.

"And what exactly did she tell you?" I asked.

"That you're rudderless. Her word, not mine. She sounded weird. Worried."

"Suspicious?" I asked.

"Is that what you're afraid of? Being caught?"

I wouldn't have put it past Sophie to tell Debra herself, if the mood struck, if she felt cause for retribution, if she was really through with me and wanted to dispatch me in a hurry. She could be erratic, unpredictable.

"What else did she tell you?" I asked.

"She said you mope around. And when you're not moping, you're manic. She says you act frantic, like you think someone's chasing you, like a paranoiac, and then other times you're co-matose. She said you're like a caged lion doing figure eights in the sand. Again, her words." Caged lion? Debra was never great with metaphors. "And you drink too much, she said. And you complain all the time. She says she's in the middle of a new book. The best thing she's done, she said. Are you even writing at all?"

"Now you're on my case about it, too?"

"It's just like I thought," she said. "You don't really want anything to change. All that stuff we talked about. It's just entertainment for you. That's all it is. That's all I am. A way to avoid reality."

The cold glare from the end of the block, the reluctant trudge down the sidewalk toward the hotel. She'd been angry at me from the start.

"What do you want me to say?" I lowered my head, tried to lock sight with her downcast eyes, seeking a truce, a connection. She blew a puff of smoke sideways out of her mouth and looked up.

"I'm smoking three packs a day," she said. "I don't sleep. I'm shaky and queasy in the mornings. It's making me sick. And you—what do you want from me? Do you want to run away to Mexico? Or do you want to stay and get tenure. Do you want to write a novel?" she said, stomping her cigarette out on the sidewalk. "Or do you just want everyone to tell you how smart you are."

I looked at my phone. It was almost five o'clock. "My train," I said.

"*My train, my train,*" she repeated. "You really don't get it, do you? Everything waiting for you up there—Debra, the school, the goddamn dog—it's a detour, my friend. A mistake along the path."

"It's my life," I said. "How can you be sure it's a mistake?"

"Because I knew you before all that," she said. "And you knew me."

"And what about us? What if *we're* a mistake?"

"Oh, dear," she said flatly. "We're all we've got left."

"I need time," I said.

"And in the meanwhile, I wait for you to figure out what you want out of this? No thanks."

I checked my phone again. "I only have ten minutes."

"I'm supposed to meet John for drinks in twenty anyway. We've all got things to do."

I reached for her hand. She made a show of stuffing her fists in her coat pockets.

"And one last thing," she said before turning away. "I don't want to lie to your wife on the phone anymore. Or lend an ear while she complains to me about your precious ennui. That's too perverted, even for me."

She strode quickly up Broadway, toward Union Square and the L train back to Brooklyn. I followed her down the block, hoping she might turn back, but she disappeared into the mouth of the subway.

An hour later, as I sat in the café car drinking a rum and Coke, I pictured Sophie hunched over some Greenpoint bar with John, and a curdling nausea came over me.

What do I want? I wrote her, somewhere near Poughkeepsie. *I want you. That's all.*

Several minutes later the little dots started squiggling on the screen as she was writing me back. I wondered how she had the privacy. John must have left the bar to have a cigarette or gone to the bathroom, I thought. Then I felt a tremor of excitement thinking maybe he hadn't left at all, that she was texting me with her phone in her lap, hidden from view, while John sat right next to her. I waited, short of breath, the café car trembling underneath me as the train reeled upstate.

See, that's all I was asking, she wrote. *Now prove it.*

7

I WAS IN MY OFFICE THE NEXT MORNING, CRAMMING TO FIN-
ish the day's stories before workshop, when suddenly there
came a tapping as of someone gently rapping at my office door.

I looked up, and there, darkening the doorway and swaying silently over the threshold in a gray overcoat, was Winston
Armstrong, tall and lanky, wearing a wool hat with greasy hair
sticking out of it. He had a habit of appearing in alleys and
doorways without anyone's notice.

"Come in before you scare somebody," I told him.

He stepped inside. He was nervous, shaking a little.

"And take a seat," I said.

He pulled the chair out and sat, resting on the edge as if he
were afraid his hundred and thirty pounds might break it.

"Yes?" I said.

He sighed. "I saw that your door was open." Outside in the
hall I could hear old Fletcher Mills shuffling ever so slowly toward the bathroom like the ghost of Jacob Marley hauling his
chains.

"I really should keep it closed," I said. "Now, what was it
you wanted?"

"Well, sir, it's my senior year, as you know. And I've been
thinking about what to do next. And you know how much I
like to write. And so I was wondering . . . if maybe it isn't too
much trouble . . . if you'd be willing to help me out . . ."

"Don't tell me," I said. "You want to go to graduate school for this stuff."

"Yes," he said. "I do. Very much, sir. With your recommendation, that is."

"What is it you want to do with a graduate degree, Winston? Where do you see yourself when you're my age?"

"I want to write, like you," he said. I sat back. The chair croaked. "I want to be a man of letters."

"Is this a phrase you use regularly, Winston?"

"I learned it from you," he said.

A vague recollection of last year's intermediate workshop came to mind. For some reason I had quoted from Proust. *A man of letters, merely by reading a phrase, can estimate the literary merit of its author.* I didn't tell him it had been a long time since I'd written anything decent myself, or that my first and only novel sat unpublished in a 658KB file on my desktop.

"Listen," I told him, "it's hard to make a living as a writer. Scratch that, it's hard to *live.* What makes you so sure you want to take the risk?"

"It's all I care about in the world," he said.

I remembered a story he'd written last semester for class. It was about a Civil War photographer. There were long, descriptive passages detailing the materials and procedures involved in the photographer's work. There was an important scene in which the photographer has the mother of two dead sons sit for a portrait. Afterward they eat the last of the family's pickled vegetables together. The students were unanimous in their praise. "I felt like I was there." "Really cool details." "So good it was like watching a movie." Their only suggestion was that Winston reconsider his hero's name. "Something like Malcolm," one of them said. "Or Harold." "Or Benedict." "Something more old-timey," they agreed. For reasons no one could understand, Winston had named his hero Chad.

"And what if you don't succeed?" I asked him.

"It doesn't matter."

"So you're decided."

"I am."

It was only two hours later, before class, that it occurred to me I might use Winston Armstrong to my immediate benefit—that his arrival at my doorstep had in fact been providential after all.

The other students were already seated in their circle when the two of us ran into each other outside the classroom. Everyone had their laptops out, ready for the arrival of their instructor, backpacks at their feet. I looked through the window. Some of them were looking toward the hall to see whether I was ever coming in to instruct them. I looked at the time on my phone. I could be in the city by seven o'clock if I left right now.

"You want to be a teacher? A man of letters?" I said to Winston. "*Comme moi?*"

He nodded soberly. Suddenly he had the serious, unhappy look of a scholar.

"Okay then," I said. "Why not get started right now?"

"I don't understand."

"You've taken my classes the last four semesters. You know how they go. I trust you'll figure out what to do."

"You want *me* to teach your class? *Our* class? Right now?"

"Just sit there and let the others talk. If inspiration strikes, tell them something funny."

"What if they don't say anything?" Winston wanted to know. "What if I can't think of anything funny?"

"Then read them a story," I said. I fished through my bag. *What We Talk About When We Talk About Love* was peeking out. It was the eighties Vintage copy with the yellow lettering and the watercolor of a woman smoking a cigarette in bed on the cover. I thought of Sophie's bare shoulders, the little patch of fleece on the small of her back, the way she shivered when I ran my fingers over her skin. "Here, read them this," I said, handing him the book.

He looked curiously at the cover, thumbed through some pages.

"It's a little, um, white, and male, don't you think?"

"It's all I've got."

"And what about the other students?" he said. "You don't think they'll think it's weird you're not there?"

I placed my hands on his shoulders and looked him gravely in the eye. "I believe in you, Winston. Besides, this gives me something to write about in my recommendation." I turned him around by the shoulder and patted him on the back, ushering him slowly forward.

He opened the door and entered the classroom. I watched through the glass as the students began popping their earbuds out of their ears and stowing their cell phones in their backpacks. Winston went to the whiteboard and wrote out his name in schoolboy print. As an afterthought he added a little *Mr.* before it. Then he took a seat in the circle and said something I couldn't hear. But soon I saw Madison Parker's lips start moving, and I knew things were working out all right. She was reading her story aloud, looking up and down at the pages as the others followed along with their own copies. I hurried off down the hall, confident that I'd left my pupils in trusted, if shaky, hands.

8

SOPHIE AND I HAD OYSTERS AND MARTINIS ON BERRY STREET that night. Usually I didn't go all the way into Brooklyn (there wasn't time), but with Winston Armstrong's help, I had a few extra hours tonight. We sat in a small round booth facing the bar. The bartender was pouring drinks in fancy etched glasses. The lights flickered on the zinc countertop. Now that we were away from the hotel together—alone in Williamsburg, not hiding, not hurrying, listening to the clamor of other nearby voices—it seemed possible we might actually make a real couple one of these days. Maybe we really should move to a little town in Maine, I said as we sipped our drinks. We could rent a house near the water, I mused. Or maybe we should go to Mexico, like we'd talked about before.

I went on like that for a while until eventually a look of sadness came over Sophie's face. I realized she hadn't spoken in some time. Meanwhile my lips were still flapping like sheets in the breeze. I could hear my voice babbling something about the weather in Buenos Aires. She looked past me, settling her gaze somewhere over my shoulder. Her eyes appeared tired, like they were about to close.

"What's wrong?"

She shrugged.

"Is it something I said?"

She shook her head. "It's nothing. I know you like to daydream, it's fine."

"Who's daydreaming? I thought we were making plans."

"Argentina?" she said.

"Why not?"

"I don't believe you anymore."

The next round was set down a few minutes later, and we sat in silence, sipping our drinks. When we'd started this at that bar on Lorimer three months earlier, after I'd just come back from France, Sophie had said I never should have gone home. She'd said I should have gone to Mexico, or anyplace else. She might even join me, she'd said. At the time I'd thought we were joking, flirting, having fun. But I remembered her stiff lips, her stony stare. She hadn't been teasing. And she hadn't been daydreaming either. Once an idea took root in Sophie's mind it was already a foregone reality, with only the logistics of seeing the plan through remaining. What did I want? she'd asked. How would it work between us? If I really wanted to make a new life with her—if either of us actually thought we stood a chance of becoming a real couple, like the twinkling amber bar light convinced me we might—then how exactly did I plan on doing that? These were the things she wanted to know. Forget whatever I had to say about empanadas and Eva Perón. Sophie wanted facts. *Prove it*, she'd said. And she was right. How long could we keep sleeping around behind Debra's and John's backs, carrying on the way we had been? The current arrangement couldn't last much longer. I'd wrangled Winston Armstrong into my scheme for tonight, but how many more times would that trick work? The moment called for action, decisiveness, fortitude.

"It doesn't have to be Argentina," I said after a while. "Or

Mexico. Or anywhere else. It could be right here, in the city. Just you and me. All I want is us."

Sophie set her glass down. Our forearms touched. She looked me in the eyes, her eyes lustrous and eager. "You'll leave her?" she said.

"Yes," I said, feeling a chill at actually saying it out loud. "Eventually."

"And what'll you do for work?"

"I'll figure something out," I said. Then I thought about it for a second. "Better yet, I'll keep my job at Eastern, just until I get approved to apply for tenure. Then I'll negotiate a sabbatical leave next year. It happens all the time. Then we'll go wherever you want."

"That's a whole year from now," she said.

"It'll pass like that," I said, snapping my fingers.

"What'll we do in the meantime? I'm sick of hotel rooms. They're not natural. It always feels like night. It's too easy to dream inside them. Everything feels false." I didn't remind her that my childhood had been spent in a hotel room.

"Just trust me," I said. "It'll all work out."

She nodded. Her lips were tight. She wasn't exactly brimming with confidence, but she believed we had reached a tenuous understanding.

A few minutes later, in the soft tone of a wish, she said, "Come home with me tonight?"

John was out of town, she said, visiting his brother in Westchester. It was probably the only night we'd get like this, she said.

"Please?"

"I don't know," I said. "I want to. But how?"

"You mean Debra?"

I nodded.

"Make something up. Isn't that what writers do?"

126

"That's one way of putting it," I said.

"Besides, didn't you tell me Debra's going crazy with her book right now? She's so self-absorbed she probably won't even notice you're gone."

She had a point.

The apartment was dark when we entered. It smelled faintly of cigarette smoke. Sophie flipped the light on. It was the first time I'd been there since we slept together over the summer. The futon where we'd made love was folded into a sofa now. An afghan hung over the back of it. On the coffee table there were half a dozen books with bookmarks sticking out from between the pages. A couple of back issues of the *New Yorker* lay in a pile beside an empty coffee mug and a couple of drink coasters. Sophie asked if I wanted anything. "We have some wine, I think. And a bottle of Sobieski." She was going through the cupboards, looking for the bottle.

"I'll take the vodka," I said.

She came back into the room with two rocks glasses and the Sobieski. I was at the bookshelves, looking at John's poetry collections. She unscrewed the cap on the vodka and poured two glasses as I kept looking through her and John's possessions. There was a glass jar full of sports memorabilia, tickets from Mets games and the US Open. Next to it was a saucer full of opera tickets, Film Forum passes, tickets to the Whitney Biennial. In another jar there were matchbooks from bars and restaurants they'd been to together. There was a plane ticket from a trip the four of us had all taken to New Orleans. On the wall, above a tiny secretary desk, were John's diplomas—his BA, his MFA, his JD. I felt like a historian or a biographer looking over the artifacts of someone else's life, sorting through the evidence of their existence, spying, making interpretations. On the credenza there was a letter tray containing Christmas cards addressed to John and Sophie. In the pile I found one from me and Debra. I remembered buying it at the stationery shop on Merchant Street, in Halbrook, one chilly December day last winter. We'd stopped afterward at the Irish pub downtown in order to warm up before heading back home. We sat before the fire with two glasses of Powers Irish whiskey, writing out our holiday cards. It had been a nice afternoon, I remembered, but by now the day had taken on the worn glow of a distant recollection. Snooping around Sophie and John's apartment, I realized we weren't on the cusp of change. Everything had already changed. We were already dealing with the aftermath. Even if I never left Debra, our marriage would never be the same again. Events of six months earlier now seemed like decades-old memories. I thumbed through some theater tickets that were lying in a mug on the table. The date on them was from last fall, a year ago. The paper was already yellowing. The person who came up next to me and handed me a glass of vodka was not the same person who had gone to see *Hedda Gabler* with her husband a year earlier.

I took the drink and went to the futon and sat down. Sophie sat down next to me with her thigh pressed against mine. The window was cracked. A cool breeze blew in. Outside on the street a laundry cart could be heard rattling over the sidewalk. A truck beeped, backing into a loading dock down the block.

Sophie took another sip of vodka and then put her glass down and lowered herself, resting her head on my lap. The street noise quieted and there was only the sound of the wind and the bare autumn branches. I ran my fingers through her hair as she closed her eyes.

"Now tell me what we'll do again?" she said softly, her voice trailing off into sleep. "This sabbatical thing," she said, barely above a whisper. "It's in a year from now? I can wait a year, if that's what you're asking me. What's a year?" she said, drifting off to sleep. I covered her in the afghan hanging over the back of the sofa and slipped down into the cushion and closed my eyes. "It's nothing," I heard her murmuring. "Nothing, nothing . . ."

9

THE ENGLISH DEPARTMENT HAD A FACULTY MEETING TO vote on the department's new "learning outcomes" the next day. This was a document two years in the making, a wish list of what we hoped our students would take away from our classes, as well as official evidence to the college's accreditation association that we were taking our duties seriously. Chet read from a photocopy.

"Learning Outcome Number One: Students completing our courses will be able to assimilate disparate sources in the annotation and interpolation of bibliographic materials." He looked up for comments and reactions.

Debra had patched into the meeting from home, via Skype. Chet had pulled down the projection screen on the wall at the end of the conference table, and Debra's visage shone down on us all like the face of the Sphinx. I sat with trembling bowels as her voice boomed through the speakers like the voice of Zion. Chet watched her as if she were a silver-screen starlet.

"I don't like the word *assimilation*," she said. "It strikes the wrong note, I think."

"*Diverse* sources would make me feel better, too," Chet said.

"*Assimilation* has an icky connotation," someone else agreed. "*Diversity* sounds much better."

"What constitutes *bibliographic* materials anyway?" someone else wanted to know. "*Huffington Post? Bleacher Report?*"

"And who's to say what's *material*?" This from the resident poststructuralist. "The meaning of existence, Foucault suggested, is to never accept anything as definite."

Soon it was old Fletcher Mills's time to weigh in.

"Could someone pass me another sheet?" The window behind him was open and his photocopy, along with his hair, had been blown forward in a flurry. His head looked like the plume of a legionnaire's helmet as he reached across the table for another sheet. I pushed a copy toward him. He nodded in thanks and placed a trembling hand over the paper so it wouldn't blow away again.

"Maybe we should take ten and revisit this after a break," said Chet, appraising the situation. "Do I hear a second?"

"Second!" came Debra through the PA.

"All in favor?"

Hands raised.

"Okay, then. Meet back here at two thirty."

Everyone pushed their chairs out and repaired to the hallway. Fletcher gripped me by the elbow on my way out the door. "Save yourself," he said in a timorous baritone. I remember his breath smelled of bananas.

I decided to heed his advice. I felt weary and disjointed. That morning I had told Debra a well-rehearsed lie about getting drunk at Cafferty's last night and sleeping it off in the car, so as to cover my tracks. She'd responded by saying, "I didn't ask." Even for her, this was a suspiciously cool answer.

When I got inside the house it was quiet and the air was stale. It had been a brisk morning, but it had warmed up by the afternoon and no one had bothered opening the windows, so the place was musty. "Hello? Anyone home?" I called out. Maybe she'd climbed the stairs to take a shower. "You up there?" But then I noticed Ernie's leash missing from the hook. Not to mention the dog himself. They must have gone out for a walk after the meeting—or a scoot on Debra's knee scooter, as the case may be. I threw open the sash and a rush of cool air blew in. That's when I noticed the pages of Debra's manuscript fluttering on the coffee table. I crossed the room and saw a Post-it note stuck to the cover page, demanding no husband's favorite words: "We need to talk."

I picked up the manuscript and started reading. It wasn't long before I got the gist of the plot. A self-obsessed professor struggles with his writing, marriage, and the difference between what he tells himself and what's unfolding around him. The wife, of course, is *tall, patrician, and poised.* And the hero *deluded and arrogant, and not as handsome or clever as he thinks.* I felt a chilly recognition.

I took the pages to the sofa, put my feet up, and dove into the record of our hero's dissipation, depression, and latent alcoholism. I read about the way he mocks people whenever they pronounce a word wrong or forget the title of a play, how he loses his temper driving the car and slams the steering wheel like a petulant toddler, the way he sublimates turpitude and degeneracy with self-deprecation and humor, how he casts judgment on others as a substitute for self-improvement. Everywhere, he's crippled by intimations of greatness and resentment toward the successes of others. It only gets worse when he starts an affair with his wife's best friend, who promises only *false, fleeting fantasies of the type he deludes himself with already.*

I flipped back to the cover page. *Summary Judgment,* the thing was called. *A novel by Debra Crawford.* Our home address was typed in the lower corner.

A novel? I thought. It was more like a transcript. Every line, every word of dialogue, every gesture and detail came straight from my life. Debra had somehow copied down my every phrase and deed like a court stenographer. I remembered how she'd written *The Widower's Wife* while talking on the phone to her sister, transcribing her sister's complaints verbatim, spreading the quotes throughout the novel to give the impression of a story developing. One critic had said the novel rang true with "the unvarnished pap of real life." This time it was me she'd plucked for material. I should have known.

Where she wasn't quoting from my emails and text messages, or from things I had said, she was freely making up passages in my voice, launching into internal dialogues and daydreams and flashbacks—about me and Sophie running away to South America together, about my childhood at the Last Resort, about the burden of my parents' financial ruin and their constant begging for money—things that only a person who'd spent the last decade living with me, or the last two months spying on me, could have known.

I flipped ahead, feeling suddenly embarrassed, like I was staring at myself nude in the mirror.

"You know what the cost of living in Ecuador is?" the character asks his paramour. *"We could last for almost two years on my savings alone. I could write. You could start writing again, too!"*

These were the kinds of delusions he'd concocted, she'd written. *He'd lost touch with reality. He was completely unhinged.*

Reading, I felt the queasy sensation of having heard myself on a tape recording. Where had she gotten this stuff? The only answer was that she'd read my emails. I must have left my laptop open at some point. And my text messages, too. But how long had she known? How long had she been compiling evidence against me? Building a case. And what was this thing anyway? A memoir? Biography? She called it a "novel." But it was clearly not *that*. Some passages were more in the category of recipes and movie listings than fiction. One section was merely a litany of psychological diagnoses. An uncited contribution from Dr. Stern? *Major depressive disorder, dysthymia, dysphoric disorder, adjustment disorder, erotomania, delirium . . .*

The kitchen door creaked open.

I rushed to put the papers back in order, tapping them frantically into a tidy stack on the table.

I stepped away in a hurry, just in time for Debra to come into the room.

"How was the rest of the meeting?" she wanted to know, rolling in on her knee scooter, Ernie trotting behind her. She seemed almost bubbly.

"You're mobile now," I noticed.

"I had to move on at some point," she said, a pleasant smile on her face, her cheeks rosy from the sun. I thought I might puke and raised my arms above my head and took in three deep breaths. Finally I managed to say, "What's with the good cheer?"

"I talked to Beth" (her agent). "She loves the new book. Thinks it's hilarious. A terrific spoof of white male angst, she called it. Just a few rounds of edits and she wants to send it out." She crossed the room on her scooter, scooped the pages up that I'd been reading, and put them under her arm. Then she smiled knowingly at me and carted herself, and her book, up the stairs. Ernie trotted after her. I swallowed, coughing to avoid choking on my own sputum.

I went to Cafferty's in search of ministration. I drank two martinis, working through my thoughts. So I'd been having an affair. Like plenty of men before me, and nearly all the great fictional characters. And maybe Debra was right, in a general sense. The course of recent months had constituted a sort of dissipation. Had I been depressed, irritable, self-indulgent, as she'd said? Sure. But what was in the realm of appropriate responses? Resentment, the cold shoulder, an affair of your own. All fair game. But skewering your own spouse in a novel? That was treason! Probably the French had a word for it. And besides, it was one thing for my friend Maggie Van Nystrom to write a book about her old lover. He was famous. He had earned the scrutiny. I was nobody! I looked up from the bar and noticed one of those placards staring down at me from the shelf. TAKE MY WIFE. PLEASE, TAKE HER. Someone's idea of a joke.

I remembered, at the symposium on truth in fiction, saying all was fair in love and war. But that was when we were talking in the abstract, about *other* people's love and war. This was about me! What's more, Debra wasn't even writing to find out what she thought, to understand herself—or even to understand me. She had already made up her mind. This was an exposé. A hatchet job. A takedown.

I finished my drink and drove straight home.

Debra was in the kitchen with her orthopedic boot propped up on her knee scooter when I came in. She had a glass of wine in her hand, as if she'd been waiting for me. Seeing me, she rolled across the tiles, grabbed another glass, and poured it full and handed it to me. Then she sat down at the kitchen island. I sat down across from her.

"How long have you known?" I said.

"A month," she said, as coldly as if we were going over the utility bill. "Maybe a little longer. Since just after the injury," she said.

"Why didn't you say something sooner?"

"The book wasn't finished."

"How did you find out?"

"You've been acting weird for months," she said. "Ever since you got back from France. At first I thought it was someone abroad. I wouldn't have minded so much if it was some French girl with hairy legs. Who would care? But you kept getting weirder, leaving at strange hours. So I used Find My Friends on my phone. Can you imagine the irony?"

"And the book?"

"While you were pretending to be a character in a novel,"

she said, "I was writing one. I mean, what were you thinking? We'll live in Mexico together! We'll run away to Colombia! A beach house in Maine?" She put her hand on my thigh. "Sweetie, you're such a fool." She laughed. "But it's good for material."

I couldn't believe how nonchalant she was being. Did she not care at all? Or had all her interest and passion for the subject of our marriage gone into making her book?

"What happens now?" I asked her. "What do you expect me to do with this?"

"You can do whatever you want. Isn't that what you've been asking for? Ever since the day we arrived here, all you've talked about is moving to the city, or going back to Chicago, anything so long as you don't have to stay in Halbrook. Now there's nothing keeping you." She made a flourish. "Be free," she said. "I'll survive without you."

Despite the boot, she still had a regal air about her. She was wearing a white blousy shirt and black dress pants. Her hair was up, her neck was long and stately. She was wearing earrings we'd bought together on a trip to Rome several years earlier. Another man might have wanted to say the right thing to convince her he'd made a mistake. He might have wanted to tell her he'd gone temporarily insane, he just wanted to work things out, he knew how stupid he'd been, how bad he'd fucked up, but he was fighting for her now, he'd do anything to keep her. He might have explained the drain that all his failures had taken on him—as a writer, as a husband, as a teacher, as a man. He might have admitted he'd been envious of her success since the moment she sold her first novel, that it was something he'd been trying to come to terms with, but it was hard, she had to understand. He might have told her how he always felt like a second-class citizen at Eastern, how he couldn't get over the indignity of having gotten his job on *her* merit, not his own. He might have tried to explain how sleeping with Sophie was really just his way of *feeling* something again, anything. Maybe all he wanted was to feel young. He was turning forty in two months. That did something to a person. He might have reminded her of the conversation they'd had before he left for his fellowship last summer. How they'd been at Cafferty's, sharing a cheese plate, when he asked whether she'd be all right with him leaving for three months. It was a warm April night, two weeks before the end of the spring semester. He might have reminded her about how he'd suggested she visit him in France sometime in June, just to break up the separation, so they wouldn't have to be alone that long, and how she'd said, yeah, maybe, but did they really want to go to all that expense? How she'd said it wasn't worth it to her. She'd be fine by herself for a few months. She was even looking forward to it. And how he'd started to think, at that very moment, that she might have left their marriage a long time ago. He might have reminded her that, before he departed for France, he wrote down all the recipes he used to make for her so she could cook them for herself while he was gone, and that while doing so he felt like he was orchestrating his own disappearance, making himself dispensable. He might have tried to make her see that when he got to Brooklyn that night last summer, after three months alone, he felt so relieved to be back in the company of people who knew him when he was younger, and who still wanted to spend time with him now, that his feelings bordered on the ecstatic. What was he supposed to do, after a dozen drinks, or maybe more, when he felt the warm hand of his old friend, and a kind of possibility of renewal presented itself? People make mistakes, he might have told her. I'm only human, he might have said. Things happen, he might have argued. But I didn't tell her any of that stuff.

"What'll people say when you publish it?" were the words that came out of my mouth. "They'll know it's about me. They'll know it's about you."

"Good," she said. "People like to believe there are facts behind the fiction."

"You've worked it all out for yourself, haven't you."

"Maybe I'll put your name in the dedication," she said. "You know, as thanks for the inspiration."

I felt a cold queasiness come on. I needed another drink before the numbness wore off and I accidentally felt compelled to do something stupid like argue with her or tell her I was sorry. I crossed to the cupboards and pulled down the Dewar's and drank a slug from the bottle.

"Oh yes, one last thing before I forget." She rolled herself over to the drawers and pulled out an envelope and tossed it to me. There was a lawyer's name stamped on the outside. "Everything's taken care of. I've even paid the legal fees. Consider it a parting gift."

Ernie had his chin on the tile floor. His maw was slack, his jowls hanging over his teeth onto the ground.

So this was how it happened, I thought. One day you were married to a person, the next you were signing divorce papers. But what about Ernie? And the house. The books. The furniture. Dishes. Pots and pans.

"Is that really what you're worried about right now?" said Debra.

I shrugged, took the lawyer's papers, and said, "Thanks for taking care of this. I guess I'll find a hotel for tonight?"

"That would be wise."

I put the envelope under my arm. "So I guess that's it."

"Guess that's it."

"Okay, then," I said.

"Okay."

As soon as I got in the car, I called Sophie.

"Why wait till the end of the year?" I said when she answered. "Let's move in together now. We'll get a place in the city. Maybe Harlem or Washington Heights. That way I can commute up to Halbrook easier. It's what we should have done months ago."

"You sound a little manic."

"I'll still come up to teach my classes," I explained. "I'll commute till spring semester's over."

"And then you'll get your year off?" she said.

"Yes, yes, exactly, like I promised."

The line was quiet. Then there was a hissing sound. Sophie was lighting a cigarette. I could hear her exhale.

"What is it?" I said. "What's the matter? Isn't this what you wanted?"

"What changed?" she said. "Why now?"

I was pacing the street. The neighbors' bedroom lights were clicking off up and down the block. Up in Debra's room I could see the tremulous ocher glow of her bedside lamp against the curtains, her shadow sliding across the room. Then the window went dark. My cheeks felt flushed, my legs, my arms, the ends of my fingers tingled.

"It's like you said, why wait any longer. I told her everything. The time is now."

part three

PUBLISH

1

IN THE FIRST WEEK OF DECEMBER SOPHIE SCHILLER AND I moved into a second-floor apartment at the corner of 204th Street and Sherman Avenue, above a deli mart and a nail salon. Street parking was easy to find and there was a Hudson Line train station eight blocks away with twice-daily service to Halbrook. The apartment was a one-bedroom with a kitchen that had a pass-through to the living room. There was a working fireplace with a brick mantel and the windows opened onto a fire escape where Sophie and I sat the first night in knit hats and gloves, drinking gin on ice from foam coffee cups, as stacks of cardboard boxes lay waiting inside to be opened. An air mattress was blown up on the living room floor. We were hopeful.

I had spent the last two weeks staying by myself at the Washington Square Hotel, waiting for the apartment to be vacant and for Sophie and John to complete their disentanglement. John took the news of our moving in together in stride, I was told. He said he'd had his suspicions about me and Sophie for a while, but he appreciated her finally coming clean. "In a lot of ways," he said, "this makes perfect sense. The two of you, I mean." He added an envoi in Latin. "*Pax vobiscum.*" She couldn't tell whether he was being sincere or not.

They conducted their separation while I stayed alone at the hotel, reading my students' end-of-year portfolios on my laptop around the corner at the Village Tavern, then stumbling, blind drunk, back beneath the familiar gilt awning of the Washington Square Hotel at the end of each night, falling asleep on top of the duvet before the charismatic tremble of television light, waiting for the next phase of my life to begin.

I wondered those nights whether Sophie and John were still sleeping together in the same bed. Did they make love? Eat dinner together? Reminisce over lost times, weeping and laughing? I never asked. Once during that period I picked up the phone, meaning to call Sophie, but instead I found myself dialing Debra's number. She answered, and like the idiot lover in a movie I hung up without speaking.

One afternoon, after Sophie was almost all moved in to the new apartment and all of her things were out of the old one, John and I met for beers in an effort to remain friends. For almost a decade—no matter what else was going on in our lives—we had managed to catch up over drinks at least four times a year, what John called the Quarterly Concern. "Why should this most recent dustup get in the way of tradition?" he said.

It was a sunny December day. The bar we went to was an Irish pub somewhere in the Financial District where the cobblestone streets went crooked and there seemed to be water glittering at the end of every street and alleyway. It was near John's office.

"So you're really going through with it," he said, stroking his chin between his thumb and forefinger like some kind of oracle. When I said of course I was going through with it—it was too late not to—he said, "You're a goddamn fool, but so be it." Then he sat back smiling, pleased by the apparent truth of his assessment.

I shrugged. "And what about you? Where will you go now?" Would he stay at the apartment in Greenpoint? Maybe move somewhere else in Brooklyn? Find a studio in Manhattan that was closer to work? Or leave the city altogether? For a moment I envied his freedom to choose.

"Maybe I'll enter the seminary," he said. He sipped his beer and gazed wistfully into an imagined future in the spartan attic room of some parish house in the Bronx.

"You can't be serious," I said. "A priest? Not really."

He looked back from his reverie. "No, not really," he admitted. "But it's time for something meaningful. The moment calls for change, don't you think?"

"You could start writing again," I suggested.

He laughed. "A monastery would be preferable."

A few minutes later, as we neared the end of our drinks, he said, "A couple of pointers, while I've still got your attention. She gets hungry every couple of hours. Keep snacks around. And she's got this thing about the temperature. Crack a window when the radiator's on. She gets hot if it goes above seventy degrees." He went on for several minutes, as if he were giving weekend instructions to a dog sitter, before I realized he was talking about Sophie.

"Oh, and one more thing," he said, raising his glass. "To love. The one true subject of farce."

We clinked glasses. John slugged his beer and slammed the mug loudly on the countertop. Down the bar, a beautiful young woman in a navy pantsuit looked up from her drink and said, in our general direction, "Is that a quote or something? Who said that?"

John turned to her. "I said it. Just now. Do you like it?"

She said, "I thought it was someone else."

"May I recite you a poem?" he said, and suddenly he was off of his stool and down at the end of the bar.

Sophie and I spent most of the next few weeks setting up the apartment. We ordered a mattress from the Internet. It showed up in a cardboard box, and when we cut the box open, the foam expanded like a sea monkey in a pot of water, filling the bedroom nearly wall to wall. We'd each brought a few things from our lives before—clothes, toiletries, a few pots and pans, dinner plates and glassware, books and records—but most of what we'd brought remained in boxes for weeks. Maybe I felt like we were still getting away with something, like we might run into an old acquaintance on the street who'd rat us out to Debra or John, and, having been caught, we'd have to pack up again and each go back home. But eventually, day by day, we unpacked and organized and the apartment came together like a finely sutured wound.

We trekked over snowdrifts to Key Food and CTown and Ace Hardware, buying bleach, detergent, coat hangers, laundry baskets, disinfectant, toilet brushes, dustpans, and sponges. In the aisles of Target, on 225th Street, we stood before the shelves of hand soaps, examining the brands, choosing from among the endless scents and formulas. I picked up the lemon verbena. Sophie shook her head. "I used to buy that one with John," she said. I put it back on the shelf and picked up the rosemary lime. "What about this?" She shook her head again, reaching for the lavender mint. "What about this one?" she asked. "No, not that one," I said. "That was in our guest bathroom."

"You had a guest bathroom?"

Eventually we settled on cucumber lemon. Then we humped our wares up the tiny staircase to our new home, unspooled the contact paper from the roll and lined the cabinets, sprayed the counters and bathroom tiles, and began building something like a life.

I admired the work Sophie put into scrubbing the insides of the cupboards, the care she took in pulling the refrigerator away from the wall to mop the hidden tiles, how she got down on her stomach, in the bathroom, to clean behind the toilet and underneath the sink. I'd had no idea she was so industrious. I went out one afternoon to buy pantry items—flour, rice, oats—and when I got back, the rickety bookshelves we'd found on the curb around the block two days earlier were suddenly standing upright and sturdy against the wall, filled with books organized in perfect alphabetical order as if they'd always been that way. The houseplants that she'd brought from her apartment in Greenpoint, which two hours earlier had been sitting on the kitchen counter, roots and soil spilling all over the place, were now perched elegantly on stands around the apartment. In a matter of days, we had cobbled together a living space. That it all had the makeshift quality of a stage set—that only three weeks earlier I'd been living with Debra, and Sophie with John, and that we were both dangerously aware that at any moment this new life could be thrown overboard, too—didn't matter. I tried to embrace the impermanence. When I was growing up at the Last Resort, the fleeting and the ephemeral were all you could count on. People came and went. Friendships were flimsy. And Sophie knew that feeling, too. She'd lost her father when she was just a girl. Anything could happen, at any moment. Nothing could be counted on but doubt and uncertainty. Yet here she was, bothering to alphabetize the books, organize the cupboards, arrange the spices, executing a stay against the chaos. Despite the odds, we were both marching forward.

On Christmas Eve we bought a log in a chemically coated paper bag and lit it in the fireplace. It filled the hearth with a blue-green flame, sending a burst of smoke up the chimney, then settled down to a pleasant orange flicker that reminded me of beach bonfires at the Last Resort. We bought a tree from a lot on Dyckman Street and carried it home on our shoulders and set it up in the corner of the living room, in front of the window. We hadn't brought any ornaments from our lives before, so we made do with things we could make ourselves. With construction paper and Scotch tape we sat on the love seat we'd found at a used furniture store in the Bronx and cut out stars and snowflakes and snowmen and angels. As our only gift to each other we bought ourselves the most expensive bottle of bourbon we could find at Uptown Wine and Liquors and drank it in Styrofoam cups over bagged ice. At midnight we heard the bells from Our Lady Queen of Martyrs and stepped out onto the fire escape to listen to the chimes and watch the empty snowy roads glimmer in the quiet glow of the street-lights. A mother and father in dark overcoats, each holding the hand of a little girl in a red parka, were headed in the direction of the bells.

"*In splendoribus sanctorum*," said Sophie. "How many times did I hear those words every Christmas, when I was just about that girl's age."

"Somehow I always forget you're a Catholic," I said.

"Once upon a time I was," she said. "A long, long time ago." She was nine when her father died. She couldn't really remember what Christmases were like before that. But afterward, everything was about her mother, and for her mother the Catholic church was both a salvation and a curse.

"She woke us all up at eleven thirty one Christmas because she'd suddenly decided she wanted to go to midnight mass," she said. "*Needed* to. So, I got all my siblings into their coats while she was running around the house trying to find her car keys, the TV blasting, the radio on, the oven door open, and the kitchen smoky because she forgot she put a roast in. We all packed into the Volvo station wagon. She swerved through the icy streets. Then, twenty minutes after mass started, she lost her mind. Stood up and started screaming, 'You're a fake!' at the priest, who'd barely begun the homily. It was the first year they didn't do the liturgy in Latin, and she was pissed," she said. "Betrayed, forsaken, I don't know—but my mother went crazy about it. The curate and some others had to carry her out, kicking. I never knew what to do about her rants and tirades, how to look after my little brothers when she locked herself in the bedroom for days, or what to feed them when the cupboards started getting empty."

I asked why she didn't write about that stuff anymore. I thought of her short stories, their urgency, how they seemed to emanate from necessity. "Don't you think people other than me would want to hear about that stuff?"

"Oh, shush now," she said. "That's enough about me already. Tell me something you've never told me."

I told her about the Christmas season in Florida, as a kid. Down there the holidays always seemed like a facsimile of the real thing, I said. "I used to imagine that somewhere far away," I told her, "here in New York perhaps, or maybe even in a backwater like Halbrook, other people were living the real thing. But at the Last Resort," I said, "everything was a simulacrum." The hippy sailors would festoon their mainstays with string lights and decorate their bowsprits with inflatable Santa Clauses and blow-up dolls. My parents would set up a tin tree in the small first-floor lobby of the motel. The regulars at the bar would hang stockings made of fishnet on the hooks beneath their stools and fill them with airplane bottles of liquor, bonbons, tubes of sunscreen. The weather never changed. It was still eighty degrees and sunny, with one four o'clock burst of rain every afternoon, which dried thirty minutes later. But the melancholy songs would come on the radio—"I'll Be Home for Christmas," "Blue Christmas," "White Christmas"—and I would listen to their sentiments of loneliness and longing, sensing I was missing something. I also remembered it as a season for immoderation and forgiveness, which the drunks at the Last Resort took as license to perform lewd and mawkish displays of affection, smacking kisses on each other's lips underneath the mistletoe my father hung in almost every doorway, playing grab-ass till all hours. "Giving me little nips of brandy and Thunderbird wine," I said.

"Explains a lot," she said, sipping the bourbon from her Styrofoam cup, giving me a wry smile.

"A product of my environment," I said.

"Aren't we all."

I thought about Debra, who had probably gone to her brother's in Wisconsin. That's where we'd spent the last five Christmases together. He lived in a giant colonial house twenty miles outside of La Crosse, with horses and stables and woods with walking trails. Early on, Christmases at his house had seemed like the quintessence of what all those holiday songs were talking about. There were literally sleigh bells hanging from Nathan Crawford's front door. When Debra and I arrived and tugged the end of the leather strap it jingled like a band of carolers coming over the hill. But eventually the novelty wore off. Other than wood chopping and casual hiking, there was nothing much to do around there. "The nearest bar was five miles by county road," I told Sophie.

"Far cry from a stocking full of mini bottles," she said.

Every once in a while Debra and I used to sneak out and make the trek down the highway, shoot a game of pool at the local tavern, drink rail whiskey and beer. Of course, that was a long time ago, too. More recently, I just spent the days reading and doing crossword puzzles while the others petted the horses, fed them carrots and sugar cubes, and took long walks where they reminisced about their quote-unquote "fucked-up" childhood—mom's neuroticism, dad's chicanery, et cetera, et cetera. I remembered them coming in from the cold with a ruddy air of self-satisfaction. I imagined Debra now, alone in the tall four-poster bed we used to sleep in at Nathan's house. Perhaps her sister was sleeping in bed with her in my stead. She was newly single, too.

"You won't miss it?" said Sophie. "The money, the board games, the fine trimmings, all those nice family traditions . . ." She cracked a toothy, sardonic smile.

"I wouldn't trade this for anything."

We clinked the lips of our foam cups and drank. Inside on the radio I could hear John Tesh delivering his baritone supplication to kindness and brotherly love, followed by a report about the salubrious effects of gingko biloba. Then Nat King Cole came on. *Chestnuts roasting on an open fire* . . .

Sophie laid her head on my shoulder. The sky was platinum, promising snow through the night. In the distance you could see the skyline of midtown Manhattan. The Empire State Building, the Chrysler Building, MetLife, and the new skyscrapers on Park Avenue and the strange glass obelisks jutting up around the old residences of Central Park West, their lights flickering like air traffic control towers through the mist.

We drank the rest of the whiskey and lay back against the window frame and watched the snow coming down for a while longer. We had nothing planned for tomorrow, and no one expected anything of us, and, looking out upon the city, I realized with solemn acceptance that there was no going back—we were finally alone together—and it occurred to me that if anyone other than Debra ever wrote a novel of our lives, it might somehow involve this moment, the fireplace roaring inside, the snow coming down in plush white flakes, and the two of us with our boots dangling off the fire escape, and Sophie's head on my shoulder, and a companionable hope on both our faces.

2

CLASSES RESUMED TWO WEEKS LATER, AND I BEGAN MY thrice-weekly commute up to Halbrook. Despite the cold and the icy roads, and the typical dross of faculty committees and student papers, I embarked on the semester with optimism. I even looked forward to going up to Halbrook, knowing I'd be returning to Manhattan at the end of the day.

In the mornings, before work, Sophie sat on the sofa with a mug of coffee, writing in a little yellow notebook, while I finished marking up student short stories before heading out. The room was silent but for the busses and cabs rattling the windowpane. There was no radio playing, no TV in the background, no dog barking or whining. And seeing Sophie trace her pen across the pages every morning in peaceful quiet helped me believe I might actually be able to sit down and write something, too, one of these days. Looking back, I realize those mornings were some of the happiest times we had together.

Afterward, we'd get bundled up in our wool coats and hats and mittens and head down the steps and out onto the street, walking to the 204th Street stop, where Sophie took the A train downtown to work. Sometimes we stopped for coffee or a Danish at the bodega on the corner. Underneath the elevated train we kissed goodbye for the day, and then I turned and headed toward the car, or the Hudson Line, depending on the time and the weather, and departed for Halbrook.

My classes were composed of the usual combination of disaffected artsy types in dark clothes and weary C students looking for an easy A. I was glad to give them what they wanted. For the disaffected, a healthy dose of Russian tales full of existential dread and spiritual longing, and for the C students three opportunities to revise their work for a better grade. I was surprised that Winston Armstrong was not among them, though. In his regular seat in Advanced Fiction was a young woman who sat knitting through every class period. By the third week of the semester she had a complete pair of socks.

On days I wasn't teaching I'd find a coffee shop in the neighborhood at which to grade papers and prepare the following day's lesson plans, happily taking lunch at one of the local delis or Chinese food storefronts. Then at night Sophie and I would meet for martinis at L&M, a tavern down the block, or go for dinner at one of the neighborhood Dominican restaurants, and return to the apartment, listen to records, play gin rummy, drink cognac or bourbon until we were tired, and then fall asleep in a tangle of each other's naked limbs.

I had accomplished something significant, I often told myself in those early weeks of January. I had taken the bull by the horns. I was swinging the world by the tail. When Fletcher Mills stopped me in the hallway one morning soon after the start of the semester to ask how I was doing with everything, I said, "Tell you the truth, old man, I've got the world . . ." *By the short hairs? Balls? Curlies?* What was the saying?

"On a string," he concluded.

"Yes," I said. "That's it exactly."

But then one morning in February—the day of my fortieth birthday—I woke with a queasy sense of foreboding. Sophie was already up. I could faintly hear her rustling in the other room. When I found her, she was sitting in the windowsill, smoking a cigarette, sipping coffee, and writing in her notebook. She already had her work clothes on—black slacks, a gray cashmere sweater with the sleeves pulled up, revealing her forearms tense with activity. Her hand moved quickly across the page. I liked to see her face fast with thought, her lips moving almost imperceptibly as the words came to her, her jaw twitching. I came up and kissed the back of her neck. She shut the notebook.

"Don't stop on my account," I said.

"Oh, it's nothing." She stood up and stubbed her cigarette out in the ashtray on the windowsill and tucked the notebook in a canvas tote bag slung over the back of the sofa.

"You've been writing so much lately," I said. (I seemed to have that effect on women.) "What's it about?"

"Nothing really. Just putting down some thoughts."

"I knew it would come back to you," I said.

"Who said it ever left." She sipped her coffee. "And besides, that was the point of all this, wasn't it?" She had moved to the other side of the kitchen counter and disappeared behind the refrigerator door. When she stood up again with the milk carton she said, "And anyway, it only looks like I'm writing a lot because that's the only time you see me during the day. The other eight hours I'm writing white papers about electrolyte water."

"We'll see if I can do something about that," I said. "Soon," I promised her. "Soon."

"You've said that before."

"And I meant it," I said.

She was quiet the rest of the morning. Neither of us spoke as we walked to the train station. At the turnstiles, she turned back. "I'm sorry, I almost forgot. Happy birthday."

I entered the Humanities Bloc a few hours later with a sour stomach and an anxious mind. I thought I heard hushed voices around darkened corners. Everything had seemed okay the last few weeks, but I wondered what rumors had circulated since the break. Did Debra paint me the craven philanderer? The volatile nutcase? The dissipated drunkard? I walked down the hall on the first day of my forty-first year and I thought I saw people averting their gaze when I approached. There seemed to be bowed heads everywhere. Probably I was overreacting, I told myself. Maybe there was a surprise party in the works. At least that's what I thought when, checking my campus mailbox, I found what I took to be a gift. A first edition of *Portnoy's Complaint* underneath missives from used textbook buyers and a note from Chet Bland demanding a meeting. A thoughtful gesture from some kind soul, I thought, until I read the inscription on the title page and remembered why I recognized the faded, slightly torn yellow cover. *To our favorite Philip Roth fan on his thirtieth birthday*, it said. *Your friends, John and Sophie.* One of the books I must have accidentally left in Debra's library when I moved out.

I went down the hall to thank her for returning it, but through the parted door I could see she was deep at work. The overhead lights were off, the Tiffany lamp was glowing. The dim gray sky outside her window coupled with the blue of her computer monitor made the room look like the East German office of a Cold War spy, and I thought better of knocking. She was probably putting the finishing touches on her novel, so deep was she in the contemplation of our marriage and its decline that she failed to register me—the hero of her story—standing life-size in the doorway. I slapped a Post-it Note to the door that said *Thanks* and went off to teach another session of Advanced Fiction.

But when I arrived, the room was empty. I checked the time, thinking I was early and everyone would start filing in soon, but in fact I was a few minutes late. The wooden chairs stared back at me like naked mannequins. Where was the corps of naive, hopeful, earnest young writers who hung on my truisms and shibboleths like they were religious edicts, the ones who stopped me after class to ask if it was really true that literature is the axe for the frozen sea inside of us and whatnot? Why did everyone seem to be avoiding me today?

I went back outside and checked the room number, thinking I'd made a mistake. Maybe I was on the third floor instead of the second, or else I'd absentmindedly gone counterclockwise around the building instead of the other way and entered the odd-side room instead of the even. But no. I was in the right place. I checked the time again. Perhaps I'd gotten confused about the date. Had classes been canceled without my knowledge? Maybe there was a boycott or a protest going on. But I heard chatter starting up in classrooms down the hall, the peal of PowerPoint presentations beginning, the chuff of papers being passed around, the creak of chairs being settled into. I went to the window, and outside on the pale winter quad there was no one. Everyone was in class. Except for my students.

I left in search of an answer and spied Winston Armstrong across the quad a few minutes later. I made to approach him, but he launched into a lanky gallop past the Mental Health Center. Arms and coattails flapping like a skein of geese taking flight, he disappeared before I could reach him. I was certain he'd seen me. We had locked eyes before he opened his mouth in mute shock, gasped, and took off running. Now I was staring down the empty alleyway between the Mental Health Center and the Diversity and Inclusion Office, seeing if I could track him, but he hadn't left a trace. Something was most definitely up. That's when Dr. Stern came down the stairs of the Mental Health Center.

"Looking for something?" she said.

"Always," I said.

"Always," she said. "That's rich!"

"Have you heard anything weird today?" I asked her. "Is there something going on that I don't know about?"

"Weird?" she said, in her usual Socratic retort. "What do you mean by 'weird'?"

"Oh, I don't know. Any rumors you've heard. About me, perhaps."

"I haven't heard anything *too* bad," she said. "But I'll let you know when I do."

"*When?*" I said. "You mean *if.*"

"If," she said. "That's what I meant."

I headed back to the Humanities Bloc to see whether there was anyone who could shed light on whatever was going on. I felt vague and uncertain. The department secretary's office was locked. A note was on the door saying she'd be back in twenty minutes. Everyone else's doors were shut, too. It was midafternoon, and almost all the other faculty were in class. Even Debra's door was shut and locked now. I turned around, thinking it was time to throw in the towel and head back to Inwood for the day, when suddenly there appeared Chet Bland's glistening crown, shimmering like custard skin under the halogen lights.

"Did you get my note?" he asked.

"Shit, I forgot."

"Walk with me awhile."

We headed down the hall, outside, and started across the cold barren quad like Master and Man crossing the frozen steppe.

"Is it true, what I've heard?" he said. The air was thick with his breath.

"You'll have to tell me," I said. "It's been a very odd day so far. What's going on around here?"

"I was hoping you'd make this easy by telling me yourself. I didn't want to have to drag it out of you, but I guess that's the way it'll be."

"I'm at a loss," I said. "What are you talking about, Chet?"

"I've heard some very upsetting things."

"There's a lot of bad information out there in the world," I said. "Fake news, disinformation, conspiracy theories."

"You're suggesting your students are lying to me, then? For what purpose?"

"They're a mysterious lot," I told him. But I couldn't guess what they had to do with any of this. Unless he had an answer as to why they'd all disappeared on me.

We stopped outside the music library. Chet stuffed his hands in his pockets and pulled the hood of his parka over his head and became nothing but a pink nipple of a face. Then I saw Winston Armstrong again at the end of the walkway, hunched into a curlicue beneath a streetlamp, sucking on a cigarette and shivering. Again he flapped his coattails and scurried off.

"Is that what this is about?" I said. "Young Winston there?" Chet must have caught wind that I let Winston take over my class last semester, and now it was this week's department gossip. Probably one of the other students complained. Out of jealousy for Winston, probably, resentful that I'd designated him my replacement for the day.

"I thought it must be something worse," I said. "You had me worried for a second."

Chet sighed. "Come on," he said, putting his hand on my shoulder and turning us both in the direction of the employee parking complex. "We'll go talk someplace warm." He looked at his watch. "It's almost five. Buy you a drink?"

We went to Cafferty's and found two seats at the corner of the bar. Leaning casually on my elbow, I explained to Chet how I'd given Winston a chance at leading the class. But it was no big deal. Didn't Chet ever give his students teaching opportunities? Didn't he know that students learn best by demonstrating knowledge? That is, by doing the teaching themselves? "Haven't you read *Pedagogy of the Oppressed?*" I asked him. "This stuff is Engaged Learning 101."

I went on like that for some time, until Chet started seriously fretting. If he'd had hair, he would have been wringing it. As it was, he squeaked his finger against his brow like a marker on a whiteboard.

"I've been told it went dangerously bad. Someone could have gotten hurt."

"Hurt," I said. "Now you're mistaking language for violence, too? I thought we were above all that."

"Objects were thrown. Tears were shed."

"Objects?"

"At least one Nalgene bottle," he said. "And an iPad mini."

"Jesus."

"It was bedlam," he said. "The reports I've read—"

"It can't be that bad."

"It was worse. It was a Hobbesian free-for-all. Every man for himself. And what did you expect? You left your students in the hands of a twenty-year-old. Their own classmate, I might add."

"These are advanced undergraduates," I said. "Some of them may be in graduate school next year—next semester even— teaching their very own classes. So I gave one of them a head start. So what."

"There's a lawsuit pending," he said. "I had hoped the complaint would go away, but there are multiple parents involved. They want damages. Do you understand what that means?"

"Damages?" I said. "You've got to be kidding me."

I downed the rest of my martini and signaled to Charlie, the bartender, for another one. I sat back in my seat. Cafferty's had always been a sort of sanctuary for me, a place for calm contemplation and relief of pain—a port in the storm that was my life. But now I felt none of the usual solace. Looking into Chet's watery blue eyes, I realized he'd taken me here precisely because it was a place where I was known and felt comfortable, a place where I wouldn't make a scene.

"The department's in enough financial trouble as it is," said Chet. "Add the lost revenue if parents start asking for tuition reimbursements and we're doomed." He sipped his drink. My next martini arrived and I took a bite of the olive.

"What is it you're saying to me, Chet?"

"I'm saying there's one way they might be willing to drop the suit," he said, "and I'm sure I don't have to tell you what that is."

"I think I can guess."

"So you'll comply?"

"What's the alternative?"

"There isn't one. Not really. Either you go," he said, "or I make you."

"I think I'm getting the picture," I said.

"Who knows," he said after a while, "maybe this'll be good for you in the end. You could use the time off, maybe finish the book at last. Wouldn't that be something?"

"It sure would," I told him.

He dropped some cash on the bar. Then he turned back and, either because of my unaccountable charm or because he had his own secret and particular reasons for being nice to me, offered a concession. "I know some folks at the community college, by the way. The Composition Department. I could put in a call and see if they can make room for you over there."

"Freshman comp?" I said. "At the community college? I'd rather die."

"There's no need for hyperbole. They're very nice people."

"I'm being literal," I said. "I think I'd rather kill myself."

"I'm trying to help you here," Chet said.

"And why is that?" I asked. "Is there some reason you think you owe me something?"

"After the divorce . . ." he said. "Things with Debra . . . financially, I mean . . ."

"Say what you're saying, Chet."

He pulled his coat on. His cheeks looked flushed, roseola spreading across his neck and ears.

"Never mind," he said. "Forgive me for trying."

After he left, I sat back with my drink and saw, on a shelf behind the bar, one of those insipid inspirational placards that decorated the walls of Cafferty's restaurant:

LIFE IS SHORT, SMILE WHILE YOU STILL HAVE TEETH.

3

I EMPTIED MY OFFICE THAT FRIDAY. DEBRA CAME BY BRIEFLY while I was unloading the drawers and packing the books. There were boxes everywhere and there was no place to stand. She stood in the doorway, biting on her lip. After a while she said, "I guess you got your wish."

"I'm not sure I imagined it going like this," I said, laying the flaps down on another box and taping across the seam. I pulled down a few more paperbacks and continued filling the boxes. I noticed one of the spines. It was a Carol Shields novel, left over from Debra's women's literature class that I'd been teaching last fall. I took it out and handed it to her. "One of yours?" She grabbed it and slipped it into her big leather purse.

"Are you on the job market yet?"

"I've dabbled," I said. "There's nothing much out there right now."

"I suppose you didn't call the community college."

"Would you?"

She cocked her head.

"Exactly."

"And the writing?" she asked.

I said nothing.

"If you need a recommendation, I'd be happy to write one."

"Will it read like your novel?"

"I'll lie if you want me to."

"I don't doubt it," I said.

"Well, anyway," she said, "I'd better leave you to it." She smacked the flat of her palm against the doorframe. "See you around, I guess."

"See you around," I said, and continued boxing up the office as Debra's heels clacked away down the hall.

After she left, and I finally had almost everything boxed up and ready to go, I realized I had no place to put it all. I hadn't told Sophie I'd been fired, and I couldn't rightly cart all these boxes into our apartment without explaining myself. Over the last few days I'd tried to find the right moment to tell her but it never worked out. Over martinis the night before I'd thought up several approaches. *I'm finally out,* I thought of saying. *How 'bout a toast! To starting fresh!* But the time wasn't right. She went to the restroom, leaving me alone at the bar, and I rehearsed my lines, drumming up courage, but by the time she returned, I couldn't risk undoing everything we'd constructed those last eight weeks, the plans we'd made for the following year, the schemes we'd concocted for my imaginary sabbatical year and my nonexistent tenure appointment. I understood the fragility of our situation. Our tenuous happiness needed coddling like a sick child. It couldn't survive on its own. If I just told her I'd been fired, then we were doomed. All I knew was that I had to get my stuff out of there before the office was turned into a storage closet for the department's stockpile of old printers and desktop computers and office chairs. The rest I could figure out in time.

I borrowed the hand truck from the custodian's closet and started carrying the loads out to the car, stuffing everything inside. Once the cabin was finally full, I realized that was where it would all have to stay until I could sufficiently explain the situation to Sophie.

I shut the trunk and was about to climb in when Carlos came trotting out of the building and down the ramp in my direction.

"Say it ain't so!" he said, jogging toward me.

"Looks like it."

"I hate to see you go like this," he said.

"They left me no choice."

"There's some bad juju in the air, if you ask me," he said.

"What else?"

"Well, first you and Debra split up," he said. "Now I hear Chet and Bonnie are on the skids. And this thing with you getting the boot? It's just one bad thing after another."

"Chet and Bonnie?" I said. "I hadn't heard."

"Probably I shouldn't say anything. Not my news to tell."

"But it's true?"

"That's the way I heard it," he said. "But who knows. Anyway, how's the new digs? Maybe I'll come down to the city one of these days and we'll hit the town. I haven't been to the city the whole time I've been in Halbrook. Can you believe that?"

I told him I could. It was one of Halbrook's special curses. "The town has a heaviness to it. It weighs you down, won't let you leave. Until it kicks you out. You should be glad you're only visiting."

"It's not Portland, that's true," he admitted, which was where he was from and where he'd be returning at the end of the year. "But it's better than the alternative. You know what I was doing before *We're All Gonna Die!* was published? I was working at a Barnes & Noble. I shit you not. I was thirty-eight years old. I'd published one short story, and I'd written three manuscripts that no one would buy. I never thought I'd do anything else in my life. My big goal was to become assistant manager. That was the extent of my ambitions."

"Are you suggesting I get a job at a bookstore?"

"I'm saying you never know what might be coming your way."

"Thanks for the advice."

"Hey, listen," he said before I left. "I was serious what I said a while back. If you ever want me to share anything with my agent, just send it along. Anytime." He nodded sincerely. "That's an open offer."

4

I PARKED ABOUT TEN BLOCKS FROM THE APARTMENT SO SOPHIE wouldn't see the car packed to the gills with all my office material when she was walking around the neighborhood. But then I realized I had another challenge to deal with. I had to keep up the impression I was still commuting to Halbrook and teaching. Your typical working man would have had to keep up this charade five days a week, but of course I was no working man, I was a professor, so I only had to put on a show three days a week. On days when I was supposed to be in class and Sophie decided to work from home, I spent the working hours in the car, doing crosswords against the steering wheel, or playing chess on my phone at the park, or walking aimlessly around the neighborhood until six o'clock, when it was safe to return to the apartment. I'd come through the door sighing, spout some complaints about the sorry state of young people's grammar, drop my coat on the sofa arm in wearied relief, and silently tell myself that tomorrow I'd come clean to her about everything. But I never did.

One morning I walked her to the subway, letting her believe I was headed up to Halbrook for the day. I invented a meeting with Chet, lunch with Fletcher Mills, and a one-on-one with Winston Armstrong to give the lie more credibility. I'd be back by dinner, I told her.

But I knew it couldn't go on like this much longer. Eventually I'd run out of money. I'd already gotten my final pay-check. Now I really had no choice. I had to get a book done in order to get a job. It was March now. That left April-May-June-July-August-September—six months to get a contract before the academic hiring season started in earnest. But of course if I did get a decent advance, then I wouldn't need the job. The whole thing was a mess. My muddled thinking was only the half of it.

I walked up to 220th Street, where the car was parked, and unearthed an old hard drive from the trunk of the Saab with the idea of salvaging the various drafts and revisions I'd made over the years to *The Last Resort*. I thought I might refashion them into something salable. The disk also contained hundreds of other false starts, vignettes, and sketches, ideas for stories and essays, film treatments, and who knew what other rem-nants. Walking with it back to the apartment, I had a depress-ing thought: I'd been at this the better part of a decade, and the record of my achievements was as disjointed and inchoate as my actual self. It would not have taken a genius—even Dr. Stern was up to the task—to connect the desultory scraps on that hard drive to the lassitude that was my existence. I had a mind to throw the thing in a dumpster. But maybe there was a snippet worth saving, the germ of a new idea buried in an old chapter, a detail or a character sketch worth mining. So I took the hard drive back to the apartment, plugged it in, and started rummaging through the files, clicking and clicking. I was des-perate.

I found a story about a runaway who seeks refuge at a dilap-idated seaside resort.

I found scraps about a prostitute who becomes an inspira-tional speaker.

I found the first forty pages of a novel about a fisherman struggling with his finances—a thinly veiled version of my father, I realized, mustachioed and hobbling on a cane, but with a Greek fisherman's cap covering his bald spot instead of the green poker visor he actually wore.

It all had the ring of what John called "that stuff about boatyards and boardinghouses." It didn't matter that in real life I'd kept my distance from that place for the better part of two decades; somehow my parents and their people kept showing up on the doorstep of my fiction anyway.

The night before, Sophie and I had stayed in and ordered Chinese food from the restaurant underneath our building. Neither of us had the energy to cook and we didn't want to go out. She was tired. I was angry and frustrated and drinking a lot. We'd uncapped a bottle of Jameson and were almost halfway through it before the food arrived. I could hear the delivery guy shutting the jangling door of his restaurant downstairs at the same time that our buzzer started ringing. I ran downstairs, stumbling, and took the food from him, bleary-eyed. Outside it was cold and gray and starting to snow and the food was steaming through the paper bag. The guy sighed when I stumbled, trying to grab the bag. He shook his head ruefully. Even to strangers I had the look of a man in distress. While we ate, we tried to watch a movie on Netflix, but neither of us could remember our passwords, so we kept trying and failing to key them in, fumbling, growing frustrated, trying again and failing again. I thought Debra had canceled my account, or else changed my password just to thwart me. Eventually Sophie managed to log into the account she used to share with John. The screen flashed with three boxes. There was a name in each one. The boxes said *Sophie, John,* and *Sophie and John.* Above the names another box said *Who's Watching?* We ate our food. The screen kept flashing *Who's Watching? Who's Watching?*

I kept thinking about that as I opened and closed computer files one after another, searching for something, anything. *Who's*

Watching? I kept thinking. In the back of my mind I could hear Debra's old inducements. *Just sit down and write. Something will come.* That's the way it worked for her. She just put herself in a trance and let her fingers start typing. She had a real knack for cutting through the psychic barriers. I wondered whether her brain was even activated when she was writing. Perhaps the process for her was more like performing the triple lutz or driving a golf ball; the less you think about it the better. I was often surprised that what she came up with made any sense at all, since I'd never seen her write a plot outline or even a pre-liminary sketch. It all just came out more or less wholly formed after four to six weeks of moderate labor on a par with her medium-intensity jogs. But me, I couldn't work that way. In Debra's characterization of me I was too neurotic, too bound up with ideas of perfection, which was probably true. I liked to call it a Platonic idealism; in Debra's account I was just plain-tive and depressed. In her new book she had me going around the house in a bathrobe, muttering to myself, searching out little errors and mistakes everywhere I looked—cabinet doors left open, bathroom lights left on, run-on sentences discovered in my students' stories, typos spotted in the *New York Times.* These were the things she had her hero fretting about. The guy was a nuisance and a bore.

Later that afternoon I was talking to Dr. Stern on one of our Skype sessions. She'd offered to finish out a final month's worth of treatment pro bono after I told her I could no longer afford her services since losing my job. So there I was talking to the blank screen. (To better mimic our usual in-person experience in which I'm lying on a davenport while she sits behind me out of view, she had angled her computer camera toward the foam tile ceiling of her office so it seemed like I was lying on my back as I looked at the screen; her voice emanated invisibly through the speakers.)

"Does it scare you to think nobody's paying attention?" she wanted to know. "That you might be living in oblivion?" She had a way of taking my worries and recasting them as existential crises.

"Who said anything about oblivion?"

"How would you characterize the feeling then?"

"Are you asking if I believe in God or something?"

"Is that a subject you want to talk about?"

I thought of poor Vladimir and Estragon waiting with their trousers at their ankles for Godot to show up and save them from their gloom.

"Tell me again about the hotel where you grew up," she said after a while. "All those people coming and going. It must have been hard to make any lasting relationships outside of school, to know anyone intimately, to think that anyone could know you in return." I'd told her about pressing my ear to the wall of my room, about listening to the guests, about watching through the window as they drove out of the parking lot in the morning, about wondering where they were going, and writing stories about them, guessing, making up what I couldn't know firsthand, imagining the lives they were returning to. Their time at the Last Resort had been a retreat, an escape, a holiday. But to me, whenever they returned home, that was the real escape. An escape to normalcy, financial solvency, social standing, respectability.

"Tell me why you decided to leave," I heard Dr. Stern saying.

"Why did I leave?" I said. "Who wouldn't? And besides, I had to go to college."

"I meant your home in Halbrook," she said. "Your wife."

"Oh, that? Who knows. Pick a cliché."

"What's it like at home now?" she asked.

"Which one are we talking about?"

"Where you live at the moment."

"It's the same as anywhere," I said. "We watch Netflix, order Chinese food, buy toilet paper when the roll runs out."

"But you thought it would be different."

"Yes."

That night Sophie and I got drinks around the corner at L&M again. I looked at the curve of her lip in the carmine glow of the Narragansett beer sign, the peach tip of her snub nose, the black dots of her nostrils, the line of her collarbone. Most mornings she was up before me, writing in her journal at the kitchen counter, taking stock of yesterday's events, preparing for the day, heading out early to write blog posts on behalf of the senior executives at Creative Industries. I sensed her growing as I unraveled. Every day I didn't tell her I'd lost my job made it that much harder to admit it, so I didn't, and the secret knowledge of my mounting failures—which six months earlier I'd been so happy to disclose over dinner with her and John— was metastasizing. I felt us growing apart already. I looked at her eyes. I wondered what she was writing in her journal every morning.

Maybe we just needed to go out one of these nights and do something different. A change of pace, I thought.

"Let's go down to Harlem," I said. "Let's go hear some music." I was willing to try anything.

"I have a nine o'clock meeting in the morning," she said.

"It's early still. It's not even ten."

"If you can figure out a way I don't have to work for a living, then by all means tell me. But until then," she said, "I have to be up at seven."

5

Sophie was gone by the time I got out of bed the next morning. I went to the sofa and laid down for several hours in my underwear reading Schopenhauer, trying to glean some insight into my malaise. What Schopenhauer had to say was that my malaise was in fact the total of my existence. That was little consolation. I turned to Aristotle, who thought happiness was something you did, an act of virtue. William James came to the same conclusion two thousand years later. *Fake it till you make it*, they seemed to agree. I read from the Buddhist sutras, Camus, Augustine, and Epicurus. I flipped through the latter pages of *Anna Karenina*, trying to remember how Levin solved his weariness, but stopped reading when all Tolstoy wanted to talk about was farming techniques. I read desultorily for another hour from *The World as Will* and the *Nicomachean Ethics* and *Pragmatism* and *The Varieties of Religious Experience*, until finally I gave up and carted them all to the Salvation Army on Lenox Avenue and tossed them in the big red bin to the benefit of someone else's deliverance.

It was a sunny day and the snow had melted, leaving the sidewalks spackled and glistening with rock salt. I had nothing to do and nowhere to be, so I trudged over puddles and ice to the Dyckman Street stop and took the 1 downtown with no particular destination in mind, simply hoping for the city's noise and activity to take me away from my thoughts for a while. I was hungover and felt a need to move.

I got off at 116th Street and headed toward a bookstore I knew of on Broadway. If I'd had a wise older brother or a precocious little sister to call upon for advice, I might have done that, but I didn't know those sorts of people. I knew writers.

I browsed the new releases for a while. Maybe Chet was right, I thought, looking at all that literary content arrayed on the tables like Netflix series. All I needed to do was publish something—*anything*—it didn't matter what. Look how many books were being printed these days. They couldn't all be great—or even good. Many of them were downright bad, I suspected. Maybe I could write one of *those*, I thought. After all, it was time to stop thinking about *The Last Resort*. Nobody wanted to read about me. *I* didn't want to read about me. No, it was time to write something timely instead, something current, trendy, fashionable. I browsed the tables to see what was selling these days, thinking maybe I could trace the lines of someone else's bestseller as a tailor does a suit jacket and fashion something new from it. Who knows, with enough of my own panache I might even turn out something decent. How hard could it be? It seemed like hundreds—thousands!—of people half my age were doing it every day. But the browsing was difficult. The New Releases table was jammed with colorful covers that were almost indistinguishable from one another. The old telltale signifiers of culture and quality—hand-cut pages, French flaps, embossed card stock—had been replaced by a boilerplate style that made everything from young adult novels to Scandinavian murder mysteries look exactly the same. There were titles like *The Thousand Things, Five Hundred and a Hundred More*, and *Seven Days and Six Nights*. I thought a savvy editor might have seen fit to do a little trimming. *M, 600*, and *One Week* would have sufficed. But I hushed my inner critic and flipped through a few of them anyway, reading the blurbs and opening chapters, trying to figure out what appealed to readers these days. There were novels about infanticidal babysitters, zombies, and murderous PTA moms—but I knew I couldn't hack a genre novel, so I put those aside. Then there were tales of refugees, child soldiers, and exiles—but those were subjects you had to live to earn the right to talk about. Something else then. I flipped through a few more, searching for the perils of the petite bourgeoisie. The quiet indignities of married life. The laments of the middle class. It wasn't only that my name wasn't there among the book jackets, it was that there was *nothing* of me inside those pages. I felt like a tourist in a foreign land. There were words all over the place, but I could understand none of them. What were these people saying? Whom were they talking to?

Weary, I bought the zombie book and the PTA murder mystery and took them around the corner to a pub to start reading. I'd thought they were pulp, but in fact they each had blurbs from prize winners, and the zombie writer had even been short-listed for the National Book Award, so I decided to give them each a shot. Probably I had been uncharitable and envious in my earlier rejection. I ought to open up to the possibility that either one of these books might be very good. So what if these weren't the subjects I was usually drawn to. Who was I to say what should go on in another writer's mind? They must have had their reasons for telling these stories. And what was so wrong about zombies anyway? Mr. Kurtz was a kind of zombie. So was Frankenstein's monster. And the lady from that Ibsen play—she was a ghost anyway. But I couldn't do it. The thing read like the script for a cheap slasher. I looked at the jacket again. A notable critic had praised the author for having "learned as much from comics as from Conrad," as if that were a good thing.

I glanced down the bar. There were a few parties scattered about the booths and tables. Maybe someone else wanted these things.

"Anybody want a free book?" I said, holding it up for display. "I just bought it. Barely used. Never read."

A guy in a Mets sweatshirt came over and took it in his hands and turned it over a few times as if he were assessing a melon, then handed it back. "Thanks anyway, man." He returned to his table empty-handed.

"Anyone?" I offered, feeling a certain sympathy with the rose peddlers and squeegee wipers of the world. "It's a free book," I said. "There's no catch. I just don't want it."

"Me either," the guy said.

"Maybe the lady would like it?" I suggested.

She came up, scanned the back, then said, "Nah," and went back to her friends.

I tried the other tables. "Anyone? Free book? Really? Nobody?" I threw my arms up. "You're telling me I can't even *give* this thing away?"

They all shook their heads and went back to sipping their beers. Perhaps there was some strange principle of consumer psychology working against me. Maybe when I said *free*, everybody thought that meant my goods were *tainted*, *damaged*, *worthless*.

"Five bucks, then," I proposed. "Do I hear four? Four dollars. How 'bout two for six."

"You just said it was free, like, two minutes ago, dude."

"So you'll take it?"

The guy looked at it again and considered—crinkled nose, scratch of the chin. Then he waved it away again. "Nah, never mind."

"It's a book," I said. "You could learn something from it. It could change your life, expand your capacity for thinking and feeling. Who knows, it could transform you."

The guy raised his eyebrow. "Who thinks that's possible?"

"Emerson."

"I don't buy it."

I sighed. "Yeah, me either."

I ended up dumping the books on the sidewalk outside the bar and walking the eighty blocks home through sludgy streets. I felt tired and disheartened. When I got home I went straight to the cupboard and got down the vodka and pulled out a stool and sat with my drink. I couldn't understand what they were publishing these days. I sipped the vodka and opened my laptop, and that's when I got my answer. In my inbox was the latest edition of the Publishers Lunch newsletter. And there it was:

Fiction: Author of The Widower's Wife *and Professor of English at Eastern College Debra Crawford's* Summary Judgment, *a mordant satire about a middle-aged professor's crumbling personal life, sold to Knopf in a good deal by Marjorie Klein.*

6

"What do you think a *good deal* means?" I asked John. We were having lunch the next day at P.J. Clarke's, at my behest. I couldn't stop thinking about Debra's book. All night I'd rolled around in bed, waking up in a sweat, turning over and over, obsessing about how much she'd gotten for it, what would happen when the thing was published, what it would mean for me and my career. I had gotten it in my head that I deserved some compensation. If she was going to take me down, and turn a profit from it, then I ought to be indemnified in some way. She owed me that much. "Hundred thousand?" I said. "Two hundred? More?"

"Depends," he said. "But somewhere in that range, yes."

We'd both ordered hamburgers but neither of us was eating them. I was too upset.

"Too early for a martini?" I ventured.

John shook his head. "Never." I ordered a round from the waiter and we drank them while we talked.

"It's all about *me*, you know."

"I don't think I need to tell you how that sounds," said John.

"No, it really is. I read some of it. I'm everywhere. She basically transcribed things I said to her, emails I wrote to Sophie, things I said in . . ." I stopped. For a moment I'd almost forgotten that John and Sophie had been married, that in fact the ink was not yet dry on either of our divorces. "Anyway, things I said in confidence. Point is, the character is so obviously me it's ridiculous. And I guess I'm wondering . . ."

"What your legal options are."

"Exactly."

"Well, there are certain standards we'd have to meet before we can even begin to contemplate legal action. The characterization in Debra's book would have to share such a transparent likeness to you that any reader who knows you would link the two. We're talking biographical facts, quirks of character, identifying features." He began to appraise me. "The eyeglasses, for example. But not that alone. The guy would also have to be tall and thin. Graying at the temples." He looked toward my lap. "Perhaps gaining a little weight in middle age. And he'd also have to be a professor at an East Coast liberal arts college."

"Assistant professor," I reminded him. "And not even that anymore."

"He'd probably need to be raised in Florida, as well. The son of hoteliers."

"Let's not be generous."

"Flophouse operators?"

"Better."

"Does the character in her book look like you? Did he do the things you've done?"

"I don't know exactly," I admitted. "I think so. He *sounds* a lot like me, from what I've read."

"That's almost impossible to prove, though. He would have to say things that you've said on the record, things you've published in essays or short stories, anything like that?"

"I'm not sure."

"She'd also have to write something defamatory about you. It's not enough that she simply borrowed your likeness. Defamation suits claim some kind of injury. Does this guy come off as crude, violent, abusive, criminal? Something that would damage your reputation. Is he a pedophile? A thief? A rapist?"

"I hope not," I said.

"A philanderer?"

"Well . . ."

John took a moment to think. "That's not exactly defamation then, is it." He sipped his drink. "So what's your problem?"

"Don't you understand?" I said. "She stole my persona. It's all I've got left."

We ordered another round of martinis. I bit into my burger, thinking I ought to try eating something. It oozed all over my chin, and I wiped my mouth and put it back down. I had no appetite. The room was loud with midday business lunchers, and I was feeling alien and peevish.

John, however, was in his element. He rolled up his sleeves and bit into his burger. Still chewing, he said, "What do you want out of this anyway? Is it the money?"

"Yes," I told him. "But that's not all."

"Then what?"

"I don't know," I said. "Credit, maybe. Justice."

"Tall order."

"She made a story out of *my* life, John. I deserve a share of it."

"Of what?" he said, wiping his mouth. "Your life? Or the profits."

"What's the difference?" I said.

"I get your frustration," he said, "but is it Debra you're upset with, or the fact that the industry deems fit to continue publishing her, and not you?" He leaned forward on his elbows. "Listen," he said. "Unless you can demonstrate at least one specific way that you've been injured by Debra Crawford's success, then I'm afraid there's nothing I can do for you."

I drank the rest of my martini. "Show me one way in which I *haven't* been injured by Debra's success."

"Understood," he said. "But still."

He straightened his necktie. His phone dinged and he pulled it from his pocket, pressed a few buttons, then tucked it away again.

"I have a massage in an hour," he said. "I should get a move on soon. I'm sorry I can't be of more help." He pulled out a credit card and laid it on the table, waiting for the waiter to come back around.

"Word of advice?" he said as we waited for the check.

"Sure."

"Worry less about what other people are up to. All you can manage is yourself. The rest is stardust."

"You're a stoic now?"

He shook his head. "Just go and write something, for God's sake."

"Who says I'm not?"

"I've heard," he said. I looked at him quizzically. "Come on," he said, "you must know we talk from time to time. Sophie was my wife after all. She's still my friend."

My drink was empty, I couldn't eat, and I wanted to leave. "Thanks for meeting," I said, and stood up from the table. I fished in my pocket for cash to cover the check and dropped four twenties on the table. It was more than I could afford—my checking account was almost empty—but I didn't want to look cheap. John picked up the cash and tossed it back at me.

"Your money's no good here."

I picked it up and threw it back at him.

"Fine," he said, "I accept. But only for the sake of your dignity."

Outside on the sidewalk, we started in opposite directions up and down Third Avenue. I headed west at Fifty-Ninth Street and entered the park. I had always liked walking alone in the city. I found it meditative. Sometimes I'd look up and realize I'd been nearly catatonic for a dozen blocks or so, strolling in a pleasant daze, alert only in some primordial dreamlike way to the sounds of cab horns and horse buggies and bicycle cogwheels whirring, as if the world were emanating from my own imagination. But now everything was a terror. I remembered walking through the park after my agent told me she thought we had a deal for *The Last Resort*. Debra and I had come down from Halbrook so she could meet with her publicist—one of our rare excursions into the city after we'd moved. She went to lunch, so I went out walking. Over the phone my agent said Grove was interested, she just wanted to drum up a little competition before pressing them for an offer. Now she was calling to say she was *this* close to getting one. The editor was waiting for his publisher to get back from Germany. All he needed was the green light. "Keep your phone on," she said. "I'll call you soon." I remembered turning my ringer on and walking aimlessly around the park, waiting. I wound up in one of those bird-watching spots. I checked my phone again. No missed calls. An hour later I was by the boathouse, watching the stupid paddleboats twirling around the pond, compulsively checking my phone. But she never called. It was two days before I heard from her again. The editor at Grove had been fired. The truth was, she explained, he had been our last chance. Everyone else had passed, she just hadn't had the heart to tell me.

Now I started climbing toward the Ramble, stepping over outcroppings and tree roots, trudging miserably. I made it to Belvedere Castle, where I looked out from the parapet at the glass roof of the Met shimmering in cold late-winter sunlight. I pictured the Temple of Dendur underneath the glass carapace shining in the sun. The stone columns and the carvings, the iPhone-laden tourists ogling the tombs, posing for selfies before the icons of gods and heroes, later making their purchases at the museum gift shop. Usually I'd want to head over there. Now I had no interest in going inside. I could make no connection between my soul and the rest of the world. Also I resented that they'd started charging an entry fee.

I exited the park, spilling out onto Fifth Avenue with the tourists and carriages, marching along like an act of self-flagellation, pushing forward hatefully. On Seventy-Ninth Street I walked past the Rudolf Steiner School, sandwiched between doorman buildings with heated awnings. Inside I could see the children's heads bobbing silently in the windows as their instructor filled them with goodness, godliness, godlikeness, or whatever anthroposophy is all about.

At Madison Avenue I headed downtown, passing J.Crew, Starbucks, Capital One, and the Carlyle, where Debra and I had stayed last fall when she read at Joe's Pub. I went inside the bar and drank a Dewar's. The pianist was playing "Days of Wine and Roses." A few minutes later a woman from the bar joined him to sing a slow, somber version of "Summertime." There were only five other people in the bar at that hour, two of them obviously the teenage children of a guest, drinking underage. We clapped, out of sync, when the woman finished. The teenagers laughed at her viciously behind their hands as she beat an anxious retreat to her Bloody Mary, which was waiting for her on the bar. It was hard to remember what I'd ever liked about these gilded rooms.

Around six I tried to pay the bartender with my American Express card, but it was declined. I tried several others until eventually the Chase card—with perhaps three hundred dollars left on it—went through. Then I headed out, wandering downtown under gray skies, hoping I might catch Sophie at her office before she left. It would be a surprise. It would be just the thing we both needed.

It was dark by the time I reached Union Square. I texted Sophie but got nothing back. I was starting to think she was avoiding me for some reason. "Does it ever worry you," Dr. Stern had asked once, "knowing that relationships that begin in affairs nearly always fail?" I'd said it didn't. "Sheesh," she'd said, "it would worry me." I tried Sophie's phone again but still got no answer.

At Houston I headed west, in the general direction of Sophie's office. I stopped into Fanelli's, on Mercer, and drank a shot of whiskey. I remembered that on a long day of heroic drinking John and I had played craps there with the bartender. Now the place was full of shoppers and tourists. I looked at the logos and brands on their bags, the computer-generated names and vector graphics. With glum acceptance, I realized that Sophie was probably, at that very moment, concocting catchphrases for just such an array of products. I could not find a welcome or comely face in the whole bar. On the television everyone looked distorted and perverse, like a gallery of caricatures come to screeching life. I felt bellicose and numb. I tried, half-heartedly, to argue with the bartender when he put the bill down. "Fifteen dollars for a shot of rail bourbon? How do you sleep at night!" But he just looked at me blankly and, having delivered his line so many hundreds of times before, said plainly, "Welcome to New York."

I marched past the brightly lit boutiques—weaving, bobbing, listing in and out of shoppers' throngs. As I walked, I thought about the wretches and scamps out of Fred Exley and Denis Johnson, I thought of the luckless antiheroes out of Leonard Gardner and Harry Crews, the hustlers and scroungers out of Nelson Algren and Charles Jackson. I felt old before my time, out of touch, sympathetic only to the fictional losers who were my kin. Who the hell had even heard of Charles Jackson or Leonard Gardner anymore? I had enshrined myself in fallacies and fantasies, like a zealous follower of a fringe religion.

The walk sign came on at the corner of Spring Street and Crosby and I lunged forward with the crowd, carried across the intersection as if on a wave, lost in self-absorption. I got dropped on the opposite sidewalk as the crowd dispersed in all directions, and I came to a stop, awakening for a moment.

And that's when I looked up and saw the grand crimson awning of Balthazar. And inside the window, sitting at a table near the bar, amid a clamoring after-work crowd of lawyers, tourists, and minor celebrities, was Debra Crawford, drinking champagne and eating hard-boiled eggs with her agent.

I stepped forward, watching Debra's mouth move. I watched her agent nodding sagely at everything she said. I watched Debra dunk the empty champagne bottle upside down into the chiller beside the table, ordering another one when the black-vested waiter came back around. She had on her white silk blouse, the one she always wore to readings, salons, and sundry literary events. She was wearing it with tight, dark jeans and leather boots. She was a book jacket photo come to life. I wanted to be charitable—I was the one who'd fallen in love with someone else, after all; I was the one who'd spent autumn sneaking back and forth to the city—but watching her dine out on *my* emails and text messages and hopes and plans made me bilious and spiteful. I wanted to go inside and overturn the table. And to think that I'd colluded with her all those years. And for what? Steak dinners and martinis?

She looked toward the window, I turned in a hurry, and then suddenly the crowd on Spring Street pulsed forward, pushing in around me, and I got knocked off balance, stumbled into the crosswalk, and fell to one knee in the glare of oncoming head-lights. I heard brakes screech, tires squealing to a halt, and when I looked up, there was the grille of a yellow cab staring me down at about six inches' distance. The cabbie had his hairy fist out the window. He was screaming. I stood up as a crowd circled around me. "Sorry, sorry . . ." I said. Then I ran at a sprint to the A train and headed back up to Inwood in a state of weary dismay.

7

AT HOME, I FOUND A BOTTLE OF IRISH WHISKEY IN THE CUP-board and drank a few slugs. I was shaken from falling down, and from almost getting hit by the cab, and from having been yelled at in the street. But my failure had no recourse. John had more or less said so himself. Debra's book would come out next year, she would get richer, and apparently there was nothing to be done about it.

Except, possibly, for one thing. I knew I had a bad track record when it came to being jealous of other people's success, but I wasn't the only one. There was nothing that stoked Debra Crawford's ire more than the success of a close peer. For Debra, who *was* successful by most of the metrics that mattered to her, being beaten out by a close friend was too much to endure. Coming in second was, after all, worse than not placing at all.

I went to the bedroom closet and took down the banker's box filled with Sophie's notebooks. There were scores of them, yellow and spiral-bound. She'd been writing in them since she was a child, adding more to the tally year after year. And every day these last many weeks she'd been writing a little bit more. Whenever I asked what they were about, what she planned on doing with them, she said she didn't know yet, she was just getting ideas down. But I knew—as everyone had back in the day—what she was capable of. I had promised her I'd give her time to write again. I'd figure out a way, I told her.

I started reading greedily through the pages.

The date at the top of the first page I opened to said 1989. Sophie must have been about ten at the time. I read the various entries, her notes and observations, sketches and records of yesterday's activities like the crop reports of ancient annals. *Rained yesterday, dinner was meat loaf. Mom threw the salt-shaker at the wall and it shattered.*

It was nothing, just the static report of a kid's day. But as I read more, moving through the months and years, I saw a story starting to take shape. I saw Sophie's mother breaking into the funeral home where her dead husband's body lay waiting for interment. I saw her—as Sophie had—opening the casket and lying down with him, cleaving, until she was pulled out by two funeral directors who had to tie her wrists with decorating ribbon in order to restrain her. I read about her mother being taken to the Ridges, a mental asylum in Ohio, after Sophie's aunt hauled her and her siblings out of the funeral parlor, Muzak playing on the PA, and shoved them into her Cadillac to take them up to live in her house in Cleveland. I read about the feel of the leather seats on Sophie's thighs as her aunt kept driving and driving, never saying aloud until Sophie understood on her own that she would be living with this woman now. I read about how Sophie showed up at college and decided she hated every single person there, because they all got care packages in the mail from their fathers, who would show up in the flesh a week later and take them out to dinner. And I read about how she met a professor who encouraged her to enroll in a writing class, and how it seemed like a light flipped on, and she could see things clearly, and she could stand beside her sadness like it was something other than herself, like it was just a thing to carry around, not a thing that was inside of her, but an accessory. I kept reading.

The journals spanned years of Sophie's life, from her mother's incarceration at the mental asylum through high school and college and on into her marriage to John. There was humor. There was suspense. And unlike everything I'd seen at the bookstore the other day, there was authenticity. There was raw sincerity, and a total lack of pretense. This was the writing of someone who had no intention of anyone else ever reading it. It was exactly the opposite of Debra's style, and it occurred to me that if Sophie ever published a book, it would be like torture for Debra, because she would know that her friend had accomplished something she hadn't: she had gotten to the bottom of her story. She had said something necessary. I thought about Debra sipping champagne in the window of Balthazar, the fraudulence and gamesmanship that was her brand, and I felt consumed with vengeance. And I felt defensive of Sophie, and the girl she'd written about in her diaries—the girl she had been. Meanwhile Debra was dining out on another pilfered narrative. Maybe it was true the law couldn't do anything about it. But perhaps there was another way to expose her, I thought. And maybe that way was also the solution to my financial woes, and to Sophie's ennui, and to my own publishing failures, too. I looked down at all the notebooks spread out all over the floor, all those words, all that story, just waiting to be edited into a narrative. There were pearls on every page. They just needed a string. A sense of connection. It wouldn't take that much work. The characters, incidents, themes—they were all right there. The pall that Sophie's achievement would cast on Debra's work! To be outdone that way, it was Debra's worst nightmare. And if it also meant Sophie getting a payday of her own—well, that was what I'd promised her, wasn't it. A way out. And maybe this was it.

I took another sip of whiskey, got out my laptop, and started writing, filling in Sophie's older diary entries with dialogue and narrative, giving them a novelist's touch. With the more recent journals—everything covering her marriage with John, the last

few years of sordid drinking, her work at the marketing firm—
there was hardly an edit to be made. They already read like
finished chapters. It was only about getting things in the right
order. Overall, it took several hours, but soon I had about thirty
pages that felt like the logical beginning of a novel. I got Carlos
Cross on the phone.

"I might have something for you," I told him.

"You all right, buddy? You sound a little messed up."

"Now listen," I said, "this is in confidence. For now anyway."

"Is it your book?" he said. "I can't wait. Send it along."

"No, yes," I said, "well, not exactly. But it's something."

"I'll clear my desk."

"I'm emailing you now."

I sent him what I had. Beside me there were still dozens more
notebooks—a seemingly endless supply of material. *There's
more*, I wrote him. *Lots more. This is just the start. Send it to
your agent. Let me know what she says.*

Finally I shut the computer. Downstairs I heard the front
door to the building slam, and I thought Sophie might be home.
I wanted to hear back from Carlos before I let her in on what
I was doing—better to lead with good news—so I hurried and
gathered all the journals and stacked them back at the top of
the closet as quick as I could. I shut the closet door just as I
thought I heard the front door squeak open. But it must have
been a sound out on the street. When I opened the apartment
door there was no one there. And then I remembered that Sophie wouldn't be home till late tonight. She had gone to a work
event downtown. That was why she hadn't responded to my
texts or calls earlier.

I left the apartment and went around the block to L&M,
feeling a little like I was fleeing the scene of a crime or an unfor-
tunate one-night stand. But in the end, I was confident I'd done

the right thing. If Carlos and his agent thought Sophie's pages were even half as good as I thought, then we'd be hearing good news soon. I distractedly watched the second half of a Knicks game, checking my phone every few minutes to see whether Carlos had written back yet, waiting.

8

A WEEK LATER I GOT A MESSAGE FROM CARLOS CROSS. "HEY, listen," he said, "there's good news and there's bad news. I talked to my agent. She's super excited. She's gonna email you." This was the call I'd been waiting for. "But I'm afraid there's some not-so-great news," he went on. "It's old man Mills. He's had a stroke. He's at Presbyterian, up here in Halbrook. I went to see him earlier. It'd be good if you paid him a visit."

It was early afternoon. Sophie was still at work. I didn't particularly want to drive all the way up to Halbrook, but if I didn't go now and see Fletcher, I didn't know when else I could. Besides, I couldn't spend all afternoon waiting around like a debutante for an email from Carlos's agent, so I got in the car and headed upstate.

I arrived at the hospital around four and followed signs for the neuro-trauma ward. Fletcher was alone in a dark room. The shades were drawn. The only light was from the heart monitor screen next to his bed. Fletcher opened his eyes as I pulled up a chair and sat down. "They don't have a bar around here, do they?" I asked him. He smiled crookedly. His mouth was limp from the stroke. He had a gauze bandage on his head. He must have fallen. "What have they got you in for anyway?" I asked him.

He said something but I couldn't hear him. I leaned in to listen and he whispered hoarsely in my ear. "I'm innocent."

"That's what they all say."

The door opened then and a triangle of yellow light from the hallway widened across the floor and up the walls. Fletcher squeezed his eyes shut. A nurse in green scrubs came in with a clipboard. She marked down some observations. Fletcher made a hissing sound and she left, leaving us alone in the dark again. Out in the hall I could hear the nurse talking with her coworkers at the desk.

"No family at all?" they said.

"His wife died years ago."

"No kids either?"

"None that I know of . . ."

There were several books on Fletcher's nightstand. In the pale, dim glow of the heart monitor I could make out a copy of *Paradise Lost*. Beneath it lay six or seven recent studies. I glanced at the spines. *Genderqueer Christianity and the English Epic. Milton in the New Arab World. Gates of Heaven and Borders of Empire.* The scholarship had left poor old Fletcher Mills in the dust. But unlike others of us, at least he had tried to stay abreast of the trends, even if he couldn't make heads or tails of them. When he saw me looking at his books, he turned toward them with an infant's dismay. What were they doing there? What did those words mean? Who was he to them, or they to him? he seemed to wonder. It was slightly reassuring to think that Fletcher had given his life to the study of something that would endure long after he was gone, but it was depressing to think his sole contribution had already been out of print for twenty years, and that before long his name would not even appear in an MLA search.

"Is there anything I can do for you?" I asked him.

His lips trembled as he tried to speak. I put my ear to his mouth. He made a breathy, tongue-smacking sound.

"Take me with you," he said.

I looked at the crack of light underneath the door. Did he mean for me to help him escape?

Then I saw a cup of Jell-O beside his bed. "Make me a spoon" was what he was actually saying.

After he ate, he closed his eyes and fell asleep and promptly started snoring. I sat with him for another few minutes. There was nothing more to do but keep the old man company. He came to from time to time, peering out through slit eyes, and then laid his head back down, having found nothing interesting outside of his mind worth staying awake for. I put my hand on his wrist. It was thin. The skin was papery. I could smell his sour breath in the air as he snored. I thought of all the grading rubrics and learning outcomes the department had put him through over the years, the accreditations and budgets and trigger warnings and assessment contracts and research plans and grant proposals and performance reviews. I opened the book on the table next to him. *So farewell hope,* the Devil says, *and with hope farewell fear, / Farewell remorse! All good to me is lost. / Evil, be thou my good . . .*

Out in the hall I heard footsteps. I saw the light under the door darken with the shadow of someone's feet. Fletcher had more visitors. My old colleagues, no doubt. I had better leave, I thought.

I stood up and patted Fletcher's arm goodbye. He opened his eyes, squinting. "So soon?" he said. I was about to sit down again, stay a while longer, but he just kept talking, repeating himself, until I understood what he was actually saying. "Some soup," he said, "some soup, some soup . . ."

In the hall I told one of the nurses that Fletcher was hungry. Then I drove back to the city, hopeful for a message from Carlos's agent, and a little weary from the visit. I had a sick feeling in my stomach. The hospital had inspired some of it, with the smell of institutional food and antiseptic cleaners and sterilized tubes and hand lotions and sanitizers. But I also had a vaguer sense of apprehension—that maybe Carlos's agent was not as eager as he'd made it seem, or that Sophie would respond worse than I hoped to the news of my having sent her pages out. But of course that wasn't the half of it. She still didn't know I'd lost my job, that I was nearly busted, too. I owed her the truth, and I told myself that as soon as I got through the door, I'd give it to her. Seeing Fletcher breathing painfully, torpid and practically mute, had made me penitent.

But by the time I got home it was already too late. The apartment door was ajar. From all the way down the hall I could see a sliver of light coming from inside. I could hear the muffled commotion of papers being sorted, boxes being packed . . . It wasn't clear.

I pushed the door open and entered. Sophie was seated at the little island that separated the living room from the kitchen. She had a stack of envelopes ripped open before her. She had a glass of white wine and a half-empty bottle uncorked next to her. I came up beside her. She said nothing. Over her shoulder I recognized on the uppermost envelope the seal of Eastern College. *Nil Certum Est*. Nothing Is Certain. I reached for it, but before I could get hold of it she wrenched it back, stood up, crossed the room, and waved the papers in my general direction.

"When were you going to say something?"

In a flash she was over by the window. She had her elbow tight to her hip, her forearm out at an angle, her hand wagging the envelope in the air. I stepped toward her. "I was about to tell you. Just now in fact. As soon as I got home." She pulled back, making an invisible barrier between us.

"You quit your job?" she said. "You seriously quit your job?" She was incredulous. "Of all the stupid things you could have done." She shook her head and turned her eyes toward the ceiling, where she seemed to observe the litany of idiotic things I'd done lately. "All the bullshit about tenure, your sabbatical, taking me off for a year. And the stuff about me leaving *my* job. You were just gaslighting me, weren't you? You knew I couldn't leave. Because you were living off my salary. How long did you think that would last?"

"I wanted to tell you," I said. "I tried, but it was never the right moment. Besides, you're not understanding."

"So explain."

"I didn't quit my job," I said.

"Then what do you call this?" She flung the envelope at me. It twirled to the floor and I bent to pick it up. Contained inside of it was my contract termination, signed by me, Chet, and the dean.

"It's not how it looks," I said. Then I turned around and shuffled through the other envelopes. There was paperwork from the college about rolling over my retirement accounts, filing for COBRA benefits, archiving my campus email account. Underneath those there were credit card statements, past-due notices, debt consolidation offers. She must have seen I was broke now, too.

I tossed it all across the counter and turned around.

"You have to understand. It wasn't my choice. They made me resign. I was basically fired."

She backed away toward the window, pulled it open, and sat down on the sill. She drew a cigarette from her shirt pocket and lit it, blowing the smoke outside.

From across the room I kept trying to explain what had happened, that it hadn't been my fault, and that it had probably been Debra's plan to have me fired all along. Debra was a powerful figure in the department now, I explained. What she said went.

Sophie stared outside, blowing wreaths of smoke through

the window, refusing to look back at me. Finally she stubbed her cigarette out on the fire escape and shut the window. She came forward and stood at a few feet's distance with her arms crossed over her chest.

"You didn't fight for anything when you left," she said. "The house, equity, the dog, nothing. And don't get me started on Debra. Her new book."

"How do you know about that?"

"I read Publishers Lunch, too," she said. "First Debra writes a book about us, as if that's not embarrassing enough, and now you tell me you don't have a job anymore either. So why don't you go up there and talk to her, like the man you think you are, and figure this out. Maybe they can reinstate you. Or at least give you severance. Worst case, you try and get some money out of the house. She owes you that much, doesn't she? And in the meantime, leave me by myself."

She walked past me and closed the bedroom door behind her. I took a moment, then I followed after her and tried the handle, but it was locked. Inside I could hear the squeak of the bed frame as she lay down.

I looked at the time. It was early evening still. Not quite six o'clock. I could make it up to Halbrook to talk to Debra and still be back in the city before midnight.

"I'll go now," I said through the door. "I won't be long."

I heard the bedside light click off. Or that's what I thought it was. But then I realized it was Sophie tapping something on her phone. I pressed my ear to the door and heard muffled conversation, but I couldn't make it out, and I couldn't tell whom she was talking to. I finished the wine in the kitchen, grabbed my car keys, and headed out.

9

THE TACONIC WAS CLEAR. THE SUN WAS DOWN AND THE
headlights etched a narrow path toward Halbrook. I didn't
know what to say, how to start, but I imagined something
would come to mind once I got there. I would find the right language. I would come up with an argument. And Debra would
have to understand. She would have to see that, however icy
and distant she felt, she owed me something. If not for the years
I'd put in at Eastern, or the money I'd invested in the house,
then at least for the material she'd taken from me for her book.

I took the exit for Halbrook and headed past the car deal-
erships and fast-food restaurants leading into town. I passed
the sign that said HISTORIC DOWNTOWN. I passed the old nickelodeon theater, with its marquee of amber bulbs shining down
upon the asphalt. I passed the hardware store. The library.
Finally I turned down Myrtle Street, passing the park where
Debra fell, and I couldn't help thinking she might have done it
on purpose, to ensnare me, to keep me from going to the city to
see Sophie. How long had she really known about the two of
us before she started writing her book? Maybe the whole thing
had been a plot from the beginning. And driving toward the old
neighborhood, I thought of all the strange double meanings of
that word, like *scheme, scenario, conspiracy, plan . . . homesite.*

I turned left onto Poplar. The elm trees stood stately and
bald on the lawns up and down the street. Winter had left the

ground straw-colored and patchy. It was about eight o'clock by now, and in most driveways there was a car parked for the night. Picture windows were colored with flickering TV light.

At the end of the block stood number 715.

I cut the engine and set off on foot toward the old abode. From a distance I could see the kitchen light was on. But that didn't necessarily mean anyone was home. Sometimes Debra left the light on for protection. Intruders, she was convinced, did their marauding only under cover of darkness. So much as a little lamplight sent them fleeing into the shadows like vampires, she believed.

Approaching, I noticed a silver sedan parked on the street out front. A Lexus, maybe. I couldn't tell in the dark. Probably it was one of Debra's recent acquisitions, but I couldn't be sure, so I dropped into a crouch, moving crabwise across the lawn, hoping to better assess the situation before anyone happened to notice me.

I reached the front window and turned my back to the wall and slinked down out of view. At the right moment I would pop up and brave one look inside, see whether she was home, gauge the climate. I didn't want to come knocking, putting myself out in the open, without a sense of the mood.

I counted to three and then ventured a peek. There was a new leather sofa in the living room, shiny and tan. There was a new flat-screen TV on the wall. And on the opposite wall, across the room, there was a six-by-ten-foot framed print of the photograph that had graced the cover of *The Widower's Wife*.

I looked over my shoulder to see whether any of the neighbors were out, whether there was anyone who might be suspicious of a middle-aged man in khakis and tweed peeping into windows like the shadowy figure on a neighborhood watch sign. Believing I was safe, I reached for the door handle, but it was locked. I lifted the corner of the planter by the front door, looking for the hide-a-key, but it wasn't there. I gave the handle another little shake—I knew it had a tendency to stick—but it wouldn't budge. Inside, across the room, I spotted Ernie resting peacefully on his flannel bed in the corner. He raised his head. When I looked inside again I saw him staring, shell-shocked, at his old master's bedraggled face. I could see his canine eyes glowing in the darkness. I raised my finger to my lips—*shhh*—but the dog came running toward me anyway, paws skating on the hardwood like a cow on ice. *Shh, shh, shh*, I kept telling him, but by now he was doing figure eights, stopping every few laps to look back up at me, remembering me as the source of his mania, then launching into another set of turns.

I backed down the steps and went around the side of the house. When I looked in the side window again, Ernie had thankfully forgotten all about me and returned to his bed—so much for my significance.

I sidestepped toward the back, where the kitchen light was still shining. At every window I pressed my hands and face binocular-wise to the glass, looking in at the remnants of my old life. The newel post where I used to hang my satchel after class. The dining table where I wrote whenever Debra was gone and I could have the house to myself. The scratches on the pinewood flooring from when Debra and I first moved in and couldn't decide where the sofa should go. The grayish blotch peeking out from beneath the Persian rug where Debra's sister spilled wine once when we were hosting a faculty party.

I turned away and continued in the direction of the kitchen's tremulous glow. As I came closer, stepping over an uncoiled hose and a rake, I saw shadows on the wall inside. So Debra was home after all. I saw movement, shapes coming together and pulling apart, shifting like dancers behind a scrim.

I moved tentatively toward the light. As I approached, I heard the sizzling of a sauté pan, the whir of the exhaust fan, and smooth jazz. She had company. I came closer, crouching below the lip of the window, listening.

Finally I raised myself up, fingers curled over the windowsill, eyes barely above the perimeter of the glass. And that's when I gained witness to what the astute reader will have guessed long ago. In an apron and tennis shorts, head gleaming in candle-light like a marble garden statue, slurping tomato sauce from a wooden spoon presented for his approval by my former wife, the author Debra Crawford, was none other than Chair of English at Eastern College, Chet Bland. And there was Debra, standing before him with the wooden spoon in one hand, wiping sauce from his lip with the other.

My bowels sank. I gagged. The scene playing out inside this diorama was as gruesome as bloodshed. It was as unholy as the mating of different animal species. I wondered how long this had been going on. Maybe Debra sent me off knowing that as soon as I was away she'd be calling on Chet to fill my role. I envisioned one of those cartoon images of the guy running through a wall and leaving his shape behind him in the plaster. It dawned on me that maybe the thing with Chet had started long before I was gone, as far back as when I left for France. Maybe Debra had been the one cheating from the start.

I watched for several seconds—maybe a minute—as she stirred the sauce. Chet sat across from her, the two of them talking. I could faintly hear their conversation through the single-pane glass. Chet suggested it might almost be time for Debra to take over as department chairperson. He had designs on the dean's office and would be vacating his post soon, he hoped. Maybe it wouldn't happen overnight, he was saying, but an eighteen-month timeline wasn't unreasonable. Debra chopped parsley, listening. She turned around every once in a while to throw in her two cents. I heard more muffled conversation. If news of the two of them got out too soon, Debra worried—if they didn't get ahead of it themselves—then her taking over the chair position might look like rank nepotism. And Chet's ascension to the dean's office might seem like a power grab aided by Debra's own promotion. Somehow they'd have to finesse this, they agreed. Yes, that would be the plan. "Easy does it," said Chet. "But we'll get there."

Debra opened the refrigerator and pulled out a bottle of champagne. She came around with it and handed it to Chet. Standing back with a large chef's knife like the samurai sword he'd wielded in my nightmare, holding the bottle neck at a diagonal, Chet whipped the blade through the air and sliced the champagne in one clean cut, foam spilling from the end of the masterfully sabered bottle like on a television commercial. Then he poured two flutes and handed one to Debra. And as they held the glasses up—cheers!—I realized something. Those flutes had come from John and Sophie! They'd given them to us years before as a wedding gift. Now Chet and Debra were celebrating with them. The whole thing was disgusting. And perhaps that's why, as Debra took Chet's chin between her thumb and forefinger in a *don't-you-worry-sweetums* kind of way, I lost myself and let my forehead smack loudly against the window, causing both of them to turn suddenly toward the sound.

In a fleet display, Debra grabbed the chef's knife without looking and came toward the window with the steel blade thrust out like a bayonet. I had already seen what violence Chet could wield with it.

I made to dart away, but my body stood motionless. Debra and I locked eyes in a brief second of frozen astonishment. The knife blade glinted in the kitchen light. Then she came forward and reached to open the window. I dropped away, launching into a frantic sprint through the neighbor's bushes. By the time Debra got the window open, all that was left of me was a gray shapeless outline zigzagging through the trees for cover.

10

I SPED BACK TO INWOOD THROUGH EMPTY ROADS, MY thoughts coming into focus. The bare poplars whizzed by on the right, the headlights cutting a path through the black tunnel of night, guardrails making a steady trail toward home like the inner ring of a horse track. I felt myself careening toward one inevitable destination, one ineluctable conclusion. I would tell Sophie about Debra and Chet and the cabal they'd concocted. She would have no choice but to sympathize. Who could blame me now, knowing Debra and Chet had been pulling the strings all along? It made so much sense, I couldn't believe I hadn't seen it earlier. Probably the entire thing had been a rig-up from the start, I thought. Tomorrow I'd have to call John again, too. Maybe I could sue the department for wrongful termination. Somewhere in all this there was a bounty to be had. And it would help me restore things with Sophie, too. Explaining that I now understood why I'd lost my job—how it had been Chet and Debra's plan all along—she would have to forgive me, and we could get back to planning our escape from these people once and for all. Maybe we'd have to stay on at the apartment until a settlement came through, and Sophie might have to hold on just a little longer to her marketing job at Creative Industries, but that wouldn't be so bad, would it? What was a couple of months more if it meant getting away forever? And maybe Carlos would pull through in the end, too. The possibilities were endless; we had reason to hope!

I went up the stairs an hour later full of eagerness and brio. I charged down the hallway with an idiot's optimism. I couldn't wait to share the news. But I should have known not to trust myself. I should have known I was already too late.

I was halfway down the hall when the overhead light blinked and sputtered and then went dark. I moved cautiously, feeling my way along the walls toward the door at the end of the hall. When I finally reached the apartment I pressed my ear to the door. It was strangely quiet on the other side. I took a deep breath, readying myself. Then I fit the key in the lock and started to turn it, but I realized the door was already unlocked. I paused. Then, reluctantly, I pushed the door open and stepped across the threshold.

I felt a light breeze from a cracked window, but I couldn't see anything. I patted around for the light switch. And when I finally got it on I saw the apartment in disarray. There were papers and pens and trash bags strewn everywhere. The sofa was knocked eight or ten inches out of place. There were glasses and bowls and silverware all over the counter. The fire escape window was open and the cold was blowing in. I went and shut it, and I called out to Sophie. "Hello? Sophie? Sweetie?" But I knew I was talking to myself. I went to the bedroom, calling out to her again like a fool. "Hello?" But there was no answer.

Then I saw the dresser drawers. They were hanging open like wagging tongues, as if to taunt me. And the closet hangers were dangling empty on the rail. I crouched down and looked in the back. The suitcase that usually sat in the corner was gone.

I stood up, backing away. I turned around, dizzy. On the nightstand I noticed a bottle of Jameson. I went to it and took a swig. The bottle tasted of Sophie's lips. I sat down on the edge of the bed. I hung my head in my hands, and a scene played out in my mind. I saw Sophie sitting there on the edge of the bed, where I was sitting now, holding her head like I was holding mine, drinking from the bottle as she convinced herself to go through with it—to leave before things got worse, telling herself she had to do it, she had no choice, we'd both be better off for it. The evidence was all over the apartment. The drawers left open. The window. She'd fled in a hurry, before something could change her mind, before I returned. I thought I could feel her warmth still on the duvet. I put my palm down on the fabric, touching, feeling for her. My breath drew up short. I felt palpitations in my chest like a drum played by a child—too hard, too fast, out of time.

I looked up and out the window at the black night sky smudged with clouds. How long had she been gone? The fire escape window couldn't have been open very long; the apartment wasn't that cold yet. Perhaps she'd only left a few minutes ago, just moments before I came inside. Maybe I could catch her if I hurried down to the C train right this second. Find her on the platform with her suitcase. But where was she going? Back to John? To her mother's house in Ohio? To the Washington Square Hotel, alone? I thought about our first night together last summer. Our entire story had only lasted seven months. This was already the end of it. I remembered riding the train back to Halbrook with the taste of her cigarettes on my tongue, feeling sick in my spleen, fearing the taste would fade. I swallowed hard and felt a lozenge of air travel down my throat. I felt nauseous with helplessness.

I called John's number, but he didn't answer. I left a message. "Did she tell you anything? Call me back." Then I sat waiting for a response, but nothing came.

I grabbed the Jameson bottle and brought it into the living room, where I figured I'd sit with it until I passed out or Sophie returned. I was entirely de-animated. I felt heavy and immobilized. I tried breathing—counting, in through the nose, out through the mouth, trying to find some kind of focus—but my breath was shallow and erratic. I couldn't take in a full gulp of air. It was as if my throat had contracted, or the air itself had grown too thick to swallow. My head felt light, and I stood up and bent over the counter and retched. I stood back up, panting, and that's when I saw my laptop sitting open on the counter. I bent over it and looked at the screen. My email was open. There was a note from Carlos Cross, who had forwarded a note from his agent. She loved Sophie's pages. The treatment of the mother, she wrote, was unsentimental and spare, and she couldn't look away. The scene of her climbing out of her husband's coffin had brought her to tears. Was there a time when we could talk?

I stepped away.

So that was it.

Sophie had seen it, and that's why she'd left.

I shut the computer and went to the bedroom and looked in the closet. And there, up high, where she'd been keeping all the banker's boxes full of her old notebooks, was nothing but an empty shelf. I reached up to the dusty space where the boxes had been and felt around—was there anything remaining?— when my hand landed on a piece of paper. I pulled it down. Sophie had left me a note.

You can take me out of my life.
You can even take my life.
But you can't take my story.

11

I LOOKED OUT PAST THE GRAY PENUMBRA OF MY VISION AND saw highway reflectors flashing by on the asphalt, a pale night sky hanging heavy and low. I was driving back up to Eastern College, drunk and desperate and headlong into another fugue. Sophie had left, and while I understood the facts, I didn't know what to do with them. At some point I had gotten it in my head that if I could somehow prove that Debra and Chet had set me up, then maybe I could convince Sophie to come back. Maybe she'd see that I wasn't a thief, like Debra, but a patsy. I was only trying to help her out.

I got in around two, stepped shakily out onto the street, and crossed the quad toward the English Department. When I got to the Humanities Bloc all the windows were dark and the doors were locked. I tried my ID badge at the main entrance but the college had already cut off my access. I went around back and found a hallway window open (the heaters were acting up again and several windows were slightly cracked) and I climbed inside. I found my way through shadow to Chet Bland's office in the corner of the building and tugged on the door handle, but it was locked, too. Then I remembered a master key in the department secretary's desk, which was in an open lounge area and accessible anytime. I jimmied the desk drawer open with the use of a yardstick that was lying across the room and found the key ring.

I got into Chet's office and felt my way to the metal file drawers along the wall. I couldn't see anything, and I didn't want to risk turning on the light and being caught (apparently Debra was right about burglars), so I scrabbled around in Chet's desk drawers for a flashlight or a lighter. Eventually I found a book of matches by some incense and lit one, using it to light the way as I wiggled a paper clip in the keyhole of the file cabinet. That didn't work, so I got a pair of scissors and forced the drawer open with brute strength. I had to get hold of something—anything—to prove my innocence. I felt in my pocket for my phone. I would take photos of whatever I found. That way I could leave the office intact—not taking anything— and still get out of there with the documentation I needed.

I started flipping through the files, browsing tabs and headers, but the match went out and I couldn't see anymore. I tossed it on the ground and lit another one to read by and kept flipping through. My head was spinning, the air felt heavy and dense. Several times I thought I heard someone coming from the hall and I hurried to shut the drawer, then it would grow quiet again and I'd light another match and keep sifting. Eventually I found a tab with my name on it toward the back of the third drawer. I pulled it out and held it up to the flame to read. Contained inside of it were my application materials from four years earlier. There was the excerpt from *The Last Resort* that had helped me get the job. There was my CV. There were recommendation letters from my chair and associate chair in Chicago. And there was my offer letter from Chet. *With the support of the faculty, I am pleased to offer you a tenure-track appointment at the rank of assistant professor. We trust that here at Eastern College you'll discover professional success and personal satisfaction. We look forward to welcoming you to our happy community.*

I remembered receiving that letter with the hopefulness of a lottery winner. Holding the paper in my hand in the living room of our apartment in Chicago, I felt in the vaguely optimistic way of a matriculating college student like everything was about to change. I remembered smiling, and then just sitting there for several minutes, looking down at the page and shaking my head in awe. Now the page was slightly creased and yellow. The ink on my name was a little smeared. A lot could happen in four years.

I slipped the letter back in the file and flipped through to the next item in the dossier. There were diversity statements, student evaluations, annual reviews, travel reimbursement requests—and then, there in the back, was the document I'd been hoping not to find. A letter addressed to "Professor Bland," with the dean's office cc'd underneath the heading.

The match went out again as I started to read, and I tossed it on the ground and struck another one and continued.

Dear Dr. Bland,

I hope I'm addressing this to the right person. I'm not sure how to go forward. If you could keep this exchange private, I'd appreciate it. I'm an English major here at Eastern College, focusing on creative writing. Last semester my instructor abandoned our class and left me in charge and I feel it caused me post-traumatic stress. I have notes from my physician and my therapist. My father is a lawyer. (He told me to tell you that.) Please respond as soon as you can. That's all I want to say for now.

And there at the bottom of the letter was not the name of one of my class's wilting lilies, the silent, anonymous majority that hid behind drawn wool caps and headphones, but Winston Armstrong himself, my star pupil, mock disciple, and evident Brutus.

I flipped through the remaining documents, tossing matches and lighting new ones to read by. In a dozen email exchanges printed out for Chet's records, Winston recounts a narrative of total chaos. Students are going at each other in workshop like Bolsheviks, hurling insults, spewing hateful invective. In one episode Maud Darcey calls Poppy Hartwell a "rich cunt" and Brian Tallis has to physically restrain Poppy after she throws her Nalgene bottle across the room at Maud. Winston gets hit in the cheek with it, trying to bring order to the mob. In the final email from Winston, he tells Chet that he's decided to withdraw from English and focus on prelaw for the rest of his time in school. Chet wishes him good luck.

I shoved the drawer closed and stepped back. There was no end to the betrayal, I thought. I had a mind to overturn the entire filing cabinet and trash the place. If I couldn't prove Chet sabotaged me, then at least I could get a different kind of revenge.

But it was already too late. I felt a warmth rising up my back, getting hotter, and when I turned around, there were flames whirling around in the trash bin where I'd been tossing the matches.

I tried stomping the fire out, but every time I stomped down the flames fanned up. I pulled my shoe out in a hurry, waggling it in the air to stop the toe from smoking, and then looked up at the ceiling. I sensed what felt like rain. Then I heard a click, and all of a sudden there was water spraying down on me from the emergency sprinkler, gushing like a broken shower head. Then the alarm started bleating loudly throughout the Humanities Bloc, and the emergency lights started flashing. I threw my coat over the trash can and it seemed to tamp the flames, but the sprinklers were already shooting off up and down the halls, and the lights were shining bright.

I opened the door to the hallway, thinking to make my escape before anyone found me. I looked toward the door, ready to make a run for it. But as soon as I was about to make a dash toward the exit, I saw two campus security officers coming in with their thumbs looped through their gear belts. They stood there amid the flashing lights, swiveling their heads about curiously.

I started down the hall in the opposite direction, picking up a sprint as soon as I rounded the corner. Maybe I could make it to the stair column before they found me and exit through the loading dock off the basement. But when I made the next turn another security guard was already there, filling the corridor with his arms out in the shape of a T. I made a ridiculous dive under his outstretched arm but I hit the ground hard, didn't slide past him like I'd imagined, and stopped with a thud beside his polished boot. He grabbed me up in some kind of wrestling hold. I hung, squirming in his arms, until eventually he said, "Just quit it already and I'll let you go." I relaxed my body and he let go of me and my feet hit the ground. I gathered myself in a standing position. "Now don't move," he said.

Eventually the fire was quelled and the floor was proved safe and the alarms and the sprinklers were turned off. I stood by, watching the campus police officers make their inspections. I attempted a couple of half-hearted dashes for the door but I was detained every time. After the first few feeble efforts they didn't even bother going after me. The biggest of them—the one who'd hoisted me in a half nelson—just turned and shook his head and I stopped in my tracks.

After about an hour I was taken to a security van, which was usually used to cart coeds safely from the bars to their dorm rooms. I sat in one of the bucket seats in the back, not manacled, but with the understanding that I was to wait there until the security officers figured out what to do with me. Apparently the situation was unprecedented. The one in the passenger seat was looking through his laptop, running my faculty ID through his database, trying to determine whom to call.

"Professor?" he said, reading my campus directory page.

The other one looked over at his friend's screen. "Well, *assistant* professor," he said. "Says right there."

"What's that mean?" the other one wanted to know. "He's like a secretary or something?"

"Means he doesn't have tenure," the other one said.

"Publish or perish," the one said.

"Publish or perish," the other one agreed.

Finally I was taken to an office in the basement of the utilities building, which also happened to be where the IT equipment was stored. I was seated in a desk chair amid computer servers and printers and nests of coiled electrical cables. I sat for about an hour, swiveling and waiting, watching the room twirl dizzyingly while the security officers made more phone calls, trying to figure out what should be done with me, on whom they could unload me. They called Chet's house but he didn't answer. It was the middle of the night, after all. "You might try my wife's house instead," I told them, but when they looked at me with screwed-up brows I didn't have the heart to explain further. They went back to their business, calling Halbrook City Police, but were told there was nothing they could do to help since this was a campus incident. They discussed arresting me, or charging me—they didn't seem to know the difference—and besides, that was not something they were authorized to do, they reminded themselves, so finally they looked at their watches, determined it would be morning soon, that someone would eventually call them back tomorrow, so for now they would just leave me there to wait. "We'll be back soon," they said, turned out the light, and shut the door.

It was dark inside the windowless room, and even with my eyes open I could see nothing. Even my mind was dark. From time to time I rolled my swivel chair across the room and jiggled the door handle, but it was locked, and I was relieved to be deprived of a choice in my situation. There was almost a sick satisfaction in being abandoned to this setting, like being finally diagnosed with a fatal disease after sensing a weird pain for some months that you couldn't do anything to mitigate. There was a modest relief in being left alone with the coaxial cables and toner cartridges. Finally, I had absolutely nothing to strive for. I folded my arms over the cold metal table, laid my head down on top of them, and closed my eyes and fell into a black sleep until morning.

I couldn't tell what time it was when I woke up. It was still dark inside the IT room. Eventually I heard the door squeak open and saw the light from the hallway shine and expand across the desk in a yellow diamond. I raised my head. My face hurt from lying against the metal desktop. I touched my forehead, which was warm and throbbing. I heard a voice behind me.

"These boys treat you all right?"

I breathed in a deep, satisfying gulp of air and exhaled. It was the voice of Carlos Cross, Visiting Writer, author of *We're All Gonna Die!* I swiveled around.

"Come on, let's get you outta here," he said, standing there with a bag of croissants and two coffees in a cardboard carrier.

I stood up, faltering a little at first. Carlos put his hand under my armpit and gave me a lift, then I found my strength and came to a full stand. We proceeded out into the vestibule, toward the hallway. The campus cops stood like sentries on either side of the doorway. They nodded vaguely at Carlos as we passed.

Together we walked outside into a bright day, late winter, with the first taste of spring in the air, and swallows fluttering in the trees. We started across the quad. Carlos tore off a corner of a crusty buttered croissant and handed it to me; I chewed it and kept walking. He explained the circumstances of my release.

"They got in touch with Chet this morning," he said. "Guess

he didn't want to press charges. Thought it best if we just brushed this whole thing under the rug." He tore off another morsel of pastry and handed it to me like he was feeding a pigeon. "Matter of fact, he sounded a little sad about it all. Anyway, he sent me to fetch you. One might say you got lucky. Here, have a coffee."

We stopped at the northwest corner of the quad. I sipped the coffee and looked around. I couldn't remember whether I'd parked in the complex last night or on the emergency access road behind the Humanities Bloc, or maybe on one of the residential side streets nearby. I didn't have a clue. The whole incident was a total blur like something I'd dreamed. The whole last year was starting to seem that way. A wash of months as meaningless as a blank calendar. Where was my car?

"Come on," said Carlos, "I'll drive you around till we find it."

We went up and down the roads in Carlos's Prius, searching. All of the roads around campus were named for Eastern College presidents and deans. Needham Road. Patterson Place. Holstein Drive. Schneiderman Court. Glenn Street. Maybe Chet and Debra would get a dorm named after them before it was over with, or a dining hall, or an academic building, I thought. Bland Commons. Crawford Hall. Anything seemed possible at this point, which was a realization that didn't exactly give me comfort about the future. At any rate, I knew there would never be a building with my name etched upon it.

Finally Carlos turned onto Leggum Road and my blue Saab appeared on the corner, parked with the front right tire up on the sidewalk, a ticket flagging in the breeze on the windshield.

I got out of the Prius and went over to the Saab and grabbed the flapping yellow sheet from under the windshield wiper, balled it up, and threw it on the ground. I fiddled with the lock for a minute and then got the door open. A musty odor of stale paper and cardboard wafted forth. My entire office had been kept inside the little hatchback for more than a month now, and all the files and dirty coffee mugs and dry-erase markers were starting to permeate the upholstery with an acid scent. I stood outside with the door open, taking in the miasma, and sighed. I had a vehicle, but nowhere to go.

"You sure you're all right to drive?" Carlos called out.

I turned around. "I'm fine," I told him, and plunged myself into the driver's seat.

"We could grab breakfast if you want."

"I'm no good for company."

"Here, at least take your coffee, huh?" He got out of his car and came around the hood and handed me my cup. I nodded. "Thanks," I said, and took an obligatory sip. In truth, I appreciated the gesture. The author of *We're All Gonna Die!* was turning out to be an okay guy.

"All right," he said, patting the roof of the car. "I guess that's it, then."

"Thanks for the boost," I told him. Then I rolled the window up, got the car started, and headed out Leggum Road toward the highway.

I hit the Taconic around seven thirty, starting the usual unconscious route back to the apartment in Inwood. But at White Plains, without thinking, I cut over on 287 and crossed the Hudson into New Jersey, and then kept going, past the city, through Newark, and south down I-95. I didn't know where Sophie was, but I knew she wasn't at home—that period of my life had ended, as all of them had. And I didn't care about anything left in the apartment. The landlord could take it, or have it hauled away—whatever he wanted. All of it was meaningless now. I kept driving southward, along the highways, through the cities, on the beltways, past Philadelphia, Baltimore, Washington, and Richmond, until I realized, somewhere around Fayetteville, where I was headed.

part four

PERISH

1

IT WAS ALMOST DAWN, TWENTY-TWO HOURS LATER, BY THE time I crossed Seven Mile Bridge onto Big Pine Key. The bars and fish shacks were dark. The tackle shops, liquor stores, gun dealers, and pharmacies were all shuttered. Beyond the storefronts to the east lay an endless stretch of black ocean, a shaft of pale moonlight rippling on the water's surface. I turned off the highway, onto the macadam road leading to the Last Resort, rolling by scrub briar and sea grass, passing under familiar pines and oaks where I'd played as a child. Coming out from beneath the dark canopy, my parents' resort finally came into view: a ramshackle cinder-block structure with a flat tar-and-gravel roof laid out in an L shape, with an office that said OFFICE on the roof and a porte cochere attached to the side of it, my father's red Chrysler LeBaron parked underneath with the top down. The motel's pastel-green paint had faded to bluish gray over the years. White cement columns and a matching steel railing framed the second-floor balcony. Faded pink Bahama shutters covered the windows, and Florida silver palms stood up like alligator heads all around the parking lot. I hadn't been back in eighteen years. Nothing had changed, everything was just older.

I parked beside a white panel truck with flat tires, where an iguana was stomping past on his big webbed feet. I cut the engine and took a deep breath. I was tired from the drive. I'd stopped only twice to gas up and use the toilet, making a pact with myself to just keep moving. I'd fixed my attention on the changing scenery, on the land and space expanding upon the southern states, on the daylight shifting from afternoon hues into evening and on into the night. I'd put myself in a meditative state, just to survive. The humming of the engine, the thrum of the tires over the seams in the asphalt, the rhythmic pulse of tractor trailers going by, the smell of diesel fumes in the air—these were the things I put my focus on, throwing my attention into whatever was nearest. Now that I'd stopped, the thoughts I'd kept at bay came flooding back. I was suddenly very aware of my sorry condition. For one, I had no home to go back to. Even if I'd gone to the apartment in Inwood, I couldn't have stayed. Rent was due at the end of the month, and that was only four days from now. I could barely afford gas. I'd put forty bucks in the car somewhere around Jacksonville and then heard my phone buzzing in the cup holder twenty minutes later to let me know I'd overdrafted. I kept thinking about calling Sophie. But for what? To beg her back? For sympathy? Reassurance? A loan? Or just to find out where she was. I batted the idea back as I drove, turning the radio louder, rolling the window down to concentrate on the beating of air, trying to drown out my thoughts. It had worked, more or less, until now.

I got out and shut the car door behind me and headed for the motel office. The light was on but there was no one inside. I looked around, called out, but no one answered. I stepped around the desk and reached underneath for the key to the utility closet where all the room keys were stored, went in and flipped on the light, and reached behind the mops and broomsticks for the keys on the rack. I grabbed 2A—my old bedroom—and shut the closet door and went back outside to the parking lot.

There was nothing in the car but my office files, books, a

laptop, and a half jug of gin—no luggage, no change of clothes, no Dopp kit, toothbrush, or razor—so I grabbed the gin and the computer and climbed the stairs to the balcony.

Inside, the room smelled of dank carpet, humid salt air, and the ammonia scent of industrial carpet cleaner. In the moonlight I could make out the familiar floral-print wallpaper and a framed watercolor of a blue heron on a bollard that had been there since I was in high school. I tossed the laptop on the bed and uncapped the gin and took a swig. Looking at the old room, I felt the span of my life's accomplishments shrink to a pinpoint, folding like origami into a layered dot of memory. All at once I was in my childhood bedroom, pressing my ear to the wall, listening to the fornications of the neighbors. Then I was at home in bed with Debra the night we moved into the house in Halbrook. The furniture was being delivered the next day, I remembered. All we had was a mattress, which we'd packed in the small U-Haul trailer we'd used for essentials like sheets, towels, pillows, glassware, pots and pans, and a week's worth of clothes in case the movers were late. The rest of the house was completely empty. The slightest noise, I remembered, was clamorous—the flushing of the toilet, water through the pipes, Ernie's claws on the bare wood floor. Then I was in McCarren Park with Sophie, just back from three months in France last summer. We were walking past the running track, our hands touching for the first time. Her voice was soft. What was going to happen next? Both of us were waiting for an intervention, something to stop us, but nothing did. Then I remembered a trip to New Orleans that the four of us had taken after Debra got news that her second book was being published. I remembered John and Debra dancing to the jukebox at Cosimo's, on Burgundy Street, while Sophie and I sat with our backs to the bar, laughing at her husband and my wife doing a stumbling pas de deux while someone broke a rack of pool balls in the other room. The door was open to the street, cigarette smoke was wafting in. I remembered another afternoon at Glascott's, on Halsted in Chicago, after Sophie and John visited from New York. For some reason John had flown back a day before Sophie, so she was staying on alone with me and Debra. Debra had gone home to walk Ernie, so Sophie and I spent the rest of the afternoon drinking Malört together and playing gin rummy at the bar. I could see the hazy afternoon light coming in through the diamond window in the door. I remembered our elbows touching, a brief inexplicable excitement at being alone together, the sheer rarity of it, the strangeness. I remembered the place being empty but for the career drunks who sat hunkered in a line at the bar, and us.

But what did it mean? What was the point of all those memories? I felt as if everything I'd done since leaving the Last Resort never happened now that I was back there. Maybe I'd gone off the path, like Sophie said. And in order to make sense of the detour, I had to go back to where I started. I could see it and hear it all, but it was like the pages of a faintly remembered novel. Oysters on Berry Street with Sophie four months earlier. Her hoarse whisper as she lay in my lap, asking me to tell her about everywhere I was going to take her during my sabbatical. I remembered an afternoon spent walking around Lincoln Park with Debra three years earlier, shopping for a wedding gift for her cousin. The snow, out of nowhere, suddenly coming down in a flurry of white, like buds growing out of thin air. But none of it was real, there was nothing you could point to. There was no evidence, except in my own imagination, that any of it had ever happened.

I laid down on the bed and stared up at the popcorn ceiling and watched the shadows of palm trees wriggling gray and black on the cracked, dappled surface. What was life, I wondered, but a senseless accumulation of time. I thought about

Debra, how things between us had gone cold and hollow long before Sophie and I ever got together, how our marriage had taken on the mood of an empty apartment almost the moment we moved to Halbrook. I thought about her fingers tracing patterns on my back in the night—I felt her lips against the nape of my neck, her breath hot on my skin—and sensed her absence now like a phantom limb. When I thought of her my heart grew heavy, my breath drew up short. I lay there with half-open eyes, watching the night shapes change patterns like germs under a microscope. After a while I reached in my pocket for my phone and thumbed through and found Sophie's name and held my finger over the button, twitching, waiting for a decision, a reason, an excuse to press the button, but nothing came. I opened my laptop and checked my email. Dr. Stern had written. She was worried she hadn't heard from me in a while. She was available just to chat, she said. As friends, if I preferred. And AT&T had sent a message. My bill was past due. My service would be cut off if I didn't pay the balance by Friday. And there, beneath all of it, was the email from Carlos Cross's agent.

I shut the computer and tossed it on the ground beside the bed and lay back down. Outside, the iguanas were making their burping sounds and the palm fronds were rustling loudly. The surf was pushing in and out against the beach like the rhythmic brushing of a snare drum. I couldn't sleep. I was bone tired and desperate for unconsciousness, but my thoughts kept reeling. I thought of Fletcher Mills alone in the neurological care unit the other day, no family with him, his fingers peeling like onion skin. I thought of a booth in the back of a cigar bar on Bienville Street, and a photograph of me and Debra and John and Sophie that we'd asked someone to take for us. Who had that photo now? I wondered. We'd used Debra's Nikon, handing it to a middle-aged tourist in Bermuda shorts who said, "Chortles!" right before he snapped the picture. There was only one print.

But where was it? In a shoebox in Debra's closet? Under the bed with her family albums? Thrown away in the trash? Lost in the back of Chet Bland's sock drawer? I remembered an afternoon in grad school in Virginia when Sophie called to say she was stuck up Route 29, her car was broken down, and it would be hours before it was fixed. What was I doing? she'd wanted to know. Could I drive up there and keep her company? John was at the library working on a poem, she'd said. Debra was away, visiting her sister. She had no one else to call. So we got drinks at the bar at TGI Fridays while we waited for the tow truck. I couldn't remember what we talked about. All I remembered was Sophie ordering a Caesar salad and the two of us drinking Heinekens. I thought of another time, the four of us walking through Red Hook, trying to find a restaurant John had read about, when suddenly it started pouring, and we turned down another street, lost, soaked, and there appeared an open bar, shining and bright and dry on the next corner, alone in the midst of industrial buildings and warehouses, and Sophie said, "Don't go in! It's a trap!" and we all laughed, and we kept laughing as we waited inside the bar for the rain to pass. We never made it to dinner. I recalled another time in a hotel suite the four of us had shared once in Los Angeles. Through the wall one night, Debra and I heard John and Sophie singing "Free Fallin'" to themselves, drunk, barely coherent, and Debra rolled toward me in bed as we listened to our friends chanting in their room and said, "They're hopeless, but they're perfect for each other."

Where did all of that go now that there was no one left to share it with? And what was the use of holding on to any of those recollections? Why remember anything? I picked up my phone and scrolled through the photos. There were the four of us eating pierogis at Coney Island. Debra and Sophie on the beach in sunglasses and baseball hats. John and I smoking cigars and drinking cognac on a patio outside a Russian restaurant on the boardwalk. Our lives still mostly ahead of us. None of us having accomplished anything yet, therefore still believing that we might.

Through the window I could see the surf frothing on the shore, the whitecaps glimmering in the distance of the inky black ocean.

I stood up and went to the window. There was perhaps another hour of darkness before dawn. Even if I could have fallen asleep, the day would have come shining through the shutters in another ninety minutes, rousing the birds and the morning fishermen and the noise of the beach. There was no point in lying down again now, no point in ruminating any longer, waiting for sleep. I headed down to the beach to wait for sunrise.

A few fishermen were already out on the pier, their rods pitched over the railing like flagpoles. The surf was burbling onshore. A lone gull cawed overhead. Where were the late-night revelers? I wondered. Where was the endless parade of drunken partygoers that had flowed through my childhood? Where were the sodden lechers snapping women's swimsuit straps and snorting coke off bottle openers? Had I invented them? Misremembered them? Made them up completely? And where did *I* fit in to all this "stuff about boatyards"? I remembered it was Sophie who'd asked me once, all the way back in graduate school, "Where are *you* in these stories?"

I sat down in the cool sand and locked my arms across my knees and watched the surf push in and out for a while. Maybe Debra was right, I thought, listlessly staring out at the water. Maybe she had gotten my character exactly right when she said the man in her book simply couldn't be satisfied, that nothing was ever enough for him. And maybe I was wrong about her being a fraud and a thief. Because how was I any different? All along I had been scrabbling after the same morsels as her.

I dug my heels in, watching the waves break and the horizon begin to tremble with first light, thinking about the years I'd spent waiting for success, and about the version of myself I had fabricated in search of it—about all my intimations of notoriety, all my pretensions of authenticity. I had played the disgruntled outsider—the scamp from Florida—meanwhile letting Debra buy me a three-bedroom house to live in and earn me a job at Eastern College. I was a hypocrite, too.

I turned and looked down the beach. In the distance I could make out the burned black crater of someone's old bonfire, and I pictured the little trash can fire I'd accidentally started two nights before in Chet Bland's office, and I laughed. I should have let the office burn, I thought. Then I remembered all the files I'd been storing in my car the last two months. All the papers that were still boxed up in there. My curriculum vitae. The record of my life.

I stood up and headed back toward the motel and the parking lot. I stopped at the motel office and grabbed a hand truck from the utility closet, along with a matchbook, and rolled it over to the Saab. I opened the hatchback and took out the first box I could grab and set it on the hand truck. Then I reached in and grabbed another one. Then I grabbed another one. And I started stacking them as high as I could until soon the pile was six feet tall with tenure and promotion files, research statements, teaching evaluations, fellowship applications, grant proposals, and faculty merit reviews.

I tipped the hand truck back and secured the boxes and file folders with one hand and pushed the cart with the other, rolling it across the asphalt to the beach, where the wheels hit the sand and the boxes dumped out. I hauled the boxes one by one across the beach to the fire pit and emptied them out on the pyre. Some papers and envelopes had spilled out and somersaulted across the sand. I chased after them, crumpled them up into balls, and threw them on the pit. The cardboard lid of one of the boxes tumbled in the wind and I watched it bound toward the water and get swallowed up in the surf. Then I went back to the edge of the sand and grabbed the hand truck and rolled it back to the car for another load. I pulled out every piece of paper I could find, every scrap, every note, every aborted short story, every discarded chapter of *The Last Resort*, every edit and revision and markup, and I stuffed it into another pile of boxes and rolled it all back to the beach again. Over and over I made this trip. Stacking, rolling, dumping, rolling.

After the box lids and papers and envelopes and files were piled up knee-high in the fire pit, I scrounged around the beach for driftwood and kindling, scooping up dry grasses and twigs, building a bonfire around the papers. Once there was enough to get a flame going, I lit a match and bent down and held it to the pages at the bottom of the pyramid and watched the edges curl up and smolder. I lit another match and held it to some pages around the other side and watched the flames rise up in a burst of blue. Soon the fire was as tall as I was, and I stepped back as all my old documents—every literary journal I'd been published in, every rejection letter I'd held on to, every note card and Post-it and napkin—went up in flames.

I stood, feeling the heat on my face, watching the fire blaze, the day beginning to appear on the horizon as I reached in with a stick to prod the kindling. Soon the sky filled with light and the shoreline and the horizon took on shape, and still the fire burned. A cormorant swooped overhead, and an outboard motor rumbled to life at the end of the pier, and the fire burned, and I sat down in the sand and watched.

Then sometime later I felt a hand on my shoulder, and I smelled the familiar scent of coconut oil, and heard the tinkling of puka shells and the fluttering of a linen shirt behind me, and I knew it was my mother, having seen the fire from her window. I felt her hand rubbing my back in circles as we watched the flames, saying nothing, because where would I begin? With Debra? Sophie? On an Air France flight from Bordeaux last summer? I had no idea.

Then I heard the sound of my father's shuffling gait approach from behind, his cane tapping along the boardwalk and then growing hushed as he crossed the sand to join us. I felt his body warm the cool air on the other side of me, and I heard him groan as he lowered himself onto the sand.

Eventually the fire started settling down. The papers had all burned. Now the driftwood smoldered slowly. The sky was blue and the sun was above the horizon. A biplane flew overhead dragging a kite-tail advertisement for used cars.

No one said anything for quite some time. I looked back up the beach at the Last Resort, its faded paint and chipped stucco, the broken railing around the pool, the folding chairs with their slats missing, all its aborted promise. I said to my father, "When did you know you didn't make it?" seeking some kind of guidance or reassurance.

He looked at me with narrow eyes. I could see his laugh lines pinch like accordion bellows as he squinted, puzzled. "What do you mean?" he said. "We *did* make it." He passed his hand across the vista of ocean. "Look at all this." Back up at the motel, a car with a bike rack on the roof, hauling a trailer, pulled into the parking lot. My father stood up and, with the aid of his cane, tottered back up to the office to check in his new guests.

My mother was about to follow after him when she turned back.

"You know, whatever you did," she said, "I'm sure they'll forgive you."

I wasn't so confident, but I nodded anyway. "I'm sure you're right."

Then she followed about twenty yards behind my father's shaky steps, her puka shells rattling like bones down the boardwalk.

I stood alone and watched until the fire died, thinking that Sophie had understood something all along, and it was the reason she couldn't let go of her old journals, the reason she could never be done with her stories—the thing we had in common, in the end: we could never really get away from the people and places we used to know.

I went back to my room and opened my laptop and wrote two emails. The first was to Carlos Cross's agent.

I'm not the person you're looking for, but I know who is, I wrote, and I gave her Sophie Schiller's name and phone number.

Then I wrote to Chet Bland.

If it isn't too late, I wouldn't mind you putting me in touch with your friends at the community college. A few sections of composition can't be the absolute end of the world, can it? After all, there are worse places on Earth than Halbrook, New York.

2

THE FOLLOWING DAY I GOT A PHONE CALL FROM THE CHAIR of the Halbrook Community College Department of English, Communications, and Digital Rhetoric while lying in a hammock, drinking a Corona. After talking for about an hour, we agreed that for $36,000 I would teach eight sections of freshman composition next year, advise a cohort of twenty-five students, and work ten hours a week as a tutor in the writing center. It was an exploitative wage—a serious demotion from my post at Eastern—but I had no other choice.

I moved into a studio apartment in downtown Halbrook three days later. In a surprise twist my father had sent me off with an envelope full of twenty-dollar bills to help cover gas and a deposit on the apartment.

The apartment was on the top floor of a building full of lawyer's offices, with wall-to-wall carpeting and mahogany molding. There was a sloped ceiling and a dormer window overlooking the town square. You could see the clock on the bank across the street and, in the distance, the rooftops of my old road.

With my first paycheck I bought a bed off Craigslist, and a dresser and a desk from IKEA in Paramus. I bought new clothes at the Halbrook County shopping mall, as well as sheets, pillows, bedspreads, and a Teflon pan. I bought shower curtains, hand towels, countertop spray, socks, and pantry spices, and slowly the apartment came together as I checked off one item after another on my list, building a new life from the ground up.

Nights were quiet in downtown Halbrook and I found myself walking alone on the streets, which fell silent after dusk. Except for one bar and the old nickelodeon theater, there was little open after five o'clock, so my options were reassuringly limited. Most nights after I came home from my solitary wanderings I sat in bed reading, staring around the tiny room, watching the twilight shadows crawl the bare white walls, glancing at the kitchenette, and the two-burner stove and the under-counter refrigerator, remembering my house with Debra just eight blocks away, and the apartment in Inwood where Sophie and I had eked out one measly winter together, and even the old apartment in Chicago above the coffee shop, where Debra and I had lived happily before moving to Halbrook. But this was my life now, I told myself, and day by day I grew accustomed to it.

In the last week of July I attended a new-faculty orientation at the community college, then went over to the English and Composition offices and met my new colleagues for the first time. They were sincere and humorless, but I appreciated their toneless hellos and dispassionate handshakes. It was a relief to find myself in the company of people who had also lost their capacity for hoping on the little roads that led to Halbrook.

I was showed to an office at the end of the hall, which I was to share with two other faculty members. They were already seated inside, typing at their computers, when I rapped on the door. "Looks like we'll be cellmates," I said. They looked at each other quizzically. "Little joke," I said. "Anyway, nice to meet you." They both nodded, and I kept making the rounds, introducing myself to the secretary and the student assistant and the custodian and whomever else I chanced to cross paths with.

Afterward, I went back home to my apartment with a ream of sample syllabuses my new colleagues had given me and sat at the computer and started copying them in preparation for next month's classes. I had no ambition to make my mark on these courses. I was content to administer them exactly as they'd been administered by others last semester and the semester before that. Mostly my work involved changing the dates, and I felt contented by the rote process of it all. There was something satisfying about relying on a method that others had worked out on my behalf. I didn't have the energy to be original.

The semester started the first week of September. My students were weary and overworked after only the first week. You could see it in their glassy eyes and pained expressions, in the furious way they took notes, and in their frenzied sprints down the hall to whatever other classes, jobs, and family obligations they were burdened by. I sympathized. All of us were involved in one common human endeavor, I thought, which was simply to get by unscathed. So I read their outlines and thesis statements and met with them at Chick-fil-A to discuss how they might develop their ideas into essays, and I showed them where to place commas, and how to format a business letter. I gave everyone an A who demonstrated any kind of effort, and I frequently rewarded them with chewing gum and candies in class. While they suckled their Jolly Ranchers I showed them PowerPoints about deductive argumentation, participial phrases, and concluding paragraphs. After they turned in their assignments on Thursdays I took their essays to the bar near my apartment and read them with a retractable pencil, making check marks as often as I could and doing my best to ignore the run-on sentences and misplaced modifiers. Afterward I would drop in to the theater next door and watch whatever old movie was showing that night.

I kept to myself, and for the most part I didn't see anyone from Eastern College. I avoided that side of town, shopped at the Price Chopper near the community college instead of the Whole

Foods near Eastern, and I never went to Cafferty's anymore. It was as if I had moved to a completely different town from the one I had lived in with Debra. I was no one anymore—a ghost, a stranger—and I enjoyed the anonymity.

But then one afternoon after class I ran into Carlos Cross. I had stopped for gas on my way home, and there he was, standing on the other side of the pump, filling up his Prius. I tried slinking back behind the wheel and driving off before he noticed me, but it was already too late. He peered around the pump—wide-eyed and eager—and called out to me.

"I thought I heard a rumor you were back in town," he said.

I nodded. There was no use denying it. There I was.

"How long you been back?"

It was now the beginning of October, and so far I had managed to squeak by in Halbrook without running into anyone I used to know. This marked the end of that briefly successful run.

"Couple of months," I told him, pulling the handle down from the pump and fitting it into the gas tank. "And what about you?" I said. "Shouldn't you be back in Portland by now?"

"Looks like it's Halbrook from here on out," he said, then reached into his pocket and pulled out a laminated faculty ID card and held it out for me to see. *Associate Professor*, it said under his name. *Eastern College. Department of English.*

"They gave me a contract," he said. "And tenure. After you left," he explained, "they were short one fiction teacher, so . . ."

I told him there were no hard feelings. I understood completely. I was sure the department was lucky to have him.

"Anyway," he said, "I'm glad I ran into you. But I'm afraid I've got another dose of bad news. Maybe you've heard."

I already knew what he was talking about. I had read it in the *Halbrook Herald* the day before. Old Fletcher Mills had had another stroke, and this time it was fatal. Apparently he'd recovered admirably from the first one, regained his mobility, and was once again living at home. But then last week he was taken to the hospital after a fall and died.

"The funeral's tomorrow," said Carlos.

"I'm not sure I can make it," I told him. "Papers, grades, et cetera."

"I know you're not too hot on seeing everybody from the department, but it would mean something to Fletcher if you made an appearance. I'd be glad, too."

The gas pump clicked to a stop. I hung the handle back up and printed my receipt and stuffed it in my shirt pocket. Then I heard a commotion coming from inside Carlos's car. I looked through the window. His kids were pummeling each other in the backseat. The one had the other in a headlock. Then the little boy got free of his sister's stranglehold only to find his face being pressed against the glass like dough. Carlos's wife was nowhere to be seen.

"I'll see what I can do," I told him.

He nodded. "And if you ever want to stop by for a drink, you're welcome anytime." His son and daughter rolled over each other in the backseat, crashing into the door, squealing. Carlos shrugged. "Tell you the truth, I could use the company. It's just me and the kids right now," he said. "Gina's settling things in Portland still. Won't be here full-time till January."

"I might actually do that," I said. "Give you a call next week?"

"It's a plan."

3

THE SERVICE WAS HELD AT FIVE O'CLOCK THE NEXT DAY AT the Eastern College chapel. It was the first time I'd been back on campus since returning to Halbrook. In the vestibule I shook hands with several of my old colleagues, then took a seat near the back where I could hide in relative obscurity the rest of the service. Debra and Chet sat together in the front pew. Chet kept scratching the padded shoulder of his suit jacket. Debra kept tapping him to make him stop.

After a while Debra got up to say a few words about Fletcher, reading from a prepared script that echoed much of what had been printed in the obituary and on the funeral program. His years of service to the department. His one monograph on Milton. A few testimonials from former students. I couldn't help noticing that Debra looked gaunt. That could happen when she was running too much. I wanted to tell her she didn't have to try so hard. There was no one left to impress. She had already gotten everything she wanted. Soon Chet would be dean. The chair was practically hers. Time to relax a little. But it wasn't in her nature. And it wasn't my place to say anything.

After Debra, Chet got up to say a few words about raising donations to get the department break room renamed in Fletcher's honor. "Any amount helps. Even if it's just a couple of bucks," he said. Then as he was leaving the podium, he locked eyes with me across the room. I averted my gaze, but he stepped back up and spoke my name into the microphone. "Care to say a remembrance?" he said. "I know you and Fletcher were friendly. How about an anecdote or two?"

I sighed. Then I trudged up to the chancel and took the mike from Chet's sweaty hand and tapped it loudly a few times. I tried speaking, but my voice came out booming and sibilant, and I heard it through the PA like a stranger's. I hung the mike on the stand and backed away a few inches and tried again. "Hey there," I said. Everyone was quiet. I didn't know what to say. So I just spoke to Fletcher. "I'm not sure where you are now," I said, "or where any of us goes in the end, or even what most of us are doing here in *this* life, much less the next one. But I hope you're all right, wherever you are, and I hope you have something to laugh about. And if in the end we're all just on our own, which is how it's looking lately, and if you're hearing this from some lonely perch, then I hope you'll remember what your old pal Milton liked to say. 'Solitude, sometimes, is best society.'"

I stepped down and proceeded through the aisle, passing by Debra without making eye contact.

Afterward, everyone repaired to the rectory behind the chapel for finger sandwiches and cocktails. I couldn't bring myself to join them. I thought I'd been managing capably these last few months, keeping my head down, teaching my classes, trying to balance my hopes and expectations against the probabilities, but as soon as I heard Jill Talleggio talking about her book that was coming out from Oxford next week, and I heard people congratulating Carlos on his tenure, and I saw Debra step away from the crowd to take a call from her publicist, scribbling down speaking dates in the calendar she kept in her purse, I had to get out of there.

I left the chapel and got a beer by myself at the student bar down the block. I sat there drinking alone until dusk, feeling the tenuous fabric of these last few months begin to unravel. I had several more beers by nightfall, when I finally settled my tab and headed out with no direction in mind. I was feeling stiff from the bar stool. My head was spinning. What I needed was to just keep moving. So I walked, first through campus, then past the commercial district, and on into the residential neighborhood where all the faculty lived. I strode languidly past bushy rhododendrons and loamy garden beds, the sky darkening with night, until eventually I found myself at the end of Poplar Street.

I could see the southeastern corner of my old house at the end of the block, and I stood for a while in the darkness beside a yellow pennant of lamplight, ruminating on my time there, on my ignominious homecoming, on my nights on the sofa with Ernie twitching in his sleep at my feet, on wine tastings with Chet and Bonnie Bland, and nightcaps on the sofa with Debra after dinner at Cafferty's. No doubt Debra and Chet were inside there now, asleep on my old bed, or watching a movie on the couch, congratulating themselves on having organized a decent send-off for old Fletcher Mills.

What had I done to make myself so dispensable? I wondered. Between Carlos Cross and Chet Bland, I had been completely replaced. No wonder I felt a kinship with Fletcher Mills, who had so long outlived his utility, and whose greatest legacy would be his name emblazoned on the portico of a faculty lounge where second-rate college professors gathered weekdays to eat donuts and make photocopies.

I had tried telling myself there was a kind of noble dignity in disappearing your ego, in living monastically in your little apartment, in teaching classes to students who'll forget your name the moment the semester's over, but who was I kidding?

Looking at my old house, I felt a raging jealousy for the two people living inside of it. Not for the things they possessed,

or for their wealthy retirement accounts and administrative titles, but for the fact that they had known all along that it was
precisely the retirement accounts and administrative titles that
mattered. I had no career to speak of, no marriage to save, no
love affair to kindle, no children to raise. What purpose was
left for me? All I had were memories, doubts, and uncertainties.
And no place to put it all.

But at least they were *my* memories, I thought. *My* doubts
and uncertainties. They were mine, and I could do whatever I
wanted with them. Even if Debra had done her best to take my
life, and Chet had stepped in to fill my empty space, she had left
me with what had happened, and as I looked at my old house, I
could feel my past begin to stiffen like a damp rope that's finally
dried. Now it was something I could get a grip on.

I headed back home through the barren Halbrook streets,
past cricket sounds and twittering birds, and headed up the
stairs to my apartment, and I sat down at my desk and opened
my laptop, and I started writing.

I began at the end of last summer with a scene on an airplane. I had fallen asleep and dreamed of a childhood memory
of floating off the shore of the Last Resort, seeing the beach
and the people getting smaller and smaller, wondering whether
anyone noticed me, or whether they cared where I'd gone. Then
I woke to the bleep of airplane sounds and the swishing of
flight attendants' pantsuits. Soon enough I was having dinner in
Brooklyn with John and Sophie. Then I was crossing McCarren
Park in the middle of the night, holding Sophie's hand, feeling
my heart beat hard and my throat grow tight with the anticipation of kissing her again. And all of it was coming on like
summer heat, forcing its way into the room with me, pressing
on, and I kept typing and typing, for hours and hours.

It was past sunrise by the time I looked up. I didn't bother
checking the page count, but I figured there had to be at least

thirty, maybe forty pages so far, and there was plenty more to come—I could feel it.

I sat back. Outside on the street the first office workers of the day were pulling into parking spaces, feeding the meters, stepping into the coffee shop and the bakery downstairs. Soon my building started filling in with the lawyers and paralegals who worked in the offices below. I could hear their telephones start ringing, their days starting, and I went to the kitchenette and filled the coffee machine with water and grounds and turned it on. Then I went back to the desk and kept going.

4

THE SCHOOL YEAR ENDED ON MAY 9. I LOOKED DOWN AT the calendar, astonished to realize more than a year had passed since I'd broken into Chet Bland's office and absconded from Halbrook to my childhood home. In that time I had earned a second contract at the community college and signed on for another year. Just the other day I had gotten a farewell card from one of my students. *Dear Punctuation*, it read. *I want you inside of me. Love, Quotation Marks.* It was meant to be some kind of joke. I said thanks and wished her good luck in life. Overall, I'd say my year of loneliness had been a success. Plus, I had written almost the entirety of a new novel. I had gotten the characters down credibly. I had worked through the details, found a narrative arc, and I was almost ready to send it out.

But the ending was giving me trouble. I just couldn't see the right way to finish it.

I left the community college for the last time that semester and decided to give myself a break from writing and take the night off. It had become my habit to head home each afternoon and write till about eight, then head out for a sandwich and a drink at the pub downstairs, and then go back home to sleep, starting over again the next day. But tonight I went to the steakhouse downtown for a congratulatory martini. I figured I'd have one or two—a private celebration for finishing the semester—and then maybe catch a movie at the theater next door. It would be my one indulgence.

But as I turned the corner, I walked past the bookstore window and did a double take. There on the inside of the glass was a poster with Sophie Schiller's face on it. She'd cut her hair into a bob, but there was no mistaking her—her neck that I'd kissed, her collarbone, her chin, her lips. And underneath her photo there was a list of reading dates. I'd thought I was doing her a favor by packaging her journal entries and sending them off to Carlos's agent, but apparently she'd had much more to show than that. She had had a memoir mostly written already. All those mornings when I thought she was just taking notes in her journal, she must have been working on a final draft of a book, almost ready to send it out herself. And when Carlos's agent got in touch with her, she was already prepared with a full manuscript. Today was the publication date. She was kicking things off with a reading tonight at North Broadway Books in Saratoga Springs at eight o'clock.

I checked my watch. It was not yet six. If I left now, I'd have just enough time to make it.

I got to Saratoga by quarter to eight, parked, and found the bookstore. I stood outside, nervous, until just before the reading was about to start. The last time I was in Saratoga I had spent the afternoon waiting for Sophie's train. That was the night I wound up driving all the way to Brooklyn, finding her at a bar on Union Avenue, drinking a Manhattan. Now, through the glass, I could faintly make out her shape, her back turned, the nape of her neck showing beneath her new short hair, her calves bare beneath the hem of a black dress. I flashed to the train station almost two years earlier, the passengers debarking, and Sophie inexplicably missing. Even now it was possible this person with her back turned, clasping her hands behind her

239

back, might turn out to be someone else. But then she turned around, crossing the room, and I saw her clearly.

I looked away. I didn't know what I was doing there, or what I should say if we saw each other. A year had passed since she left. We hadn't spoken in all that time. I had heard from John that she'd gone home to live with her mother in Ohio, but that was all. I figured that was where she must have finished editing the book. I didn't want to talk to her. The best I could do was to leave now and stay out of the way. Yet she had to know there was a chance I'd find out about this reading, there was a chance I'd show up at it, there was a chance—maybe she was hoping—that we'd see each other here and make up for the last time we'd tried to meet in Saratoga.

I opened the door slowly so the bells wouldn't rattle and slipped inside. There were a dozen or so people milling about. I kept my head down and took a seat in one of the folding chairs near the door in case I had to make a hasty exit. Soon everyone else found their seats, and Sophie stepped up to the lectern. The clerk introduced her, read some accolades, and then sat down in the front row.

Sophie looked out. Her chest rose and fell. I could tell she was nervous. She scratched the side of her face, tucking a strand of hair behind her ear. I slunk down in my chair, trying not to be noticed. Then she opened a dog-eared copy of her book and began to read in a low but confident voice. She leaned forward and talked closer to the mike. I closed my eyes and heard her voice rise above the din of the small crowd. For a moment I could make believe there was only the two of us there, that we were back in Inwood, sitting on the fire escape in the snow, resting our heads on each other's shoulders. But soon I heard the rustling of shirtsleeves and the squeaking of chair hinges, people coughing, clearing their throats, tapping their feet, and the room and the people returned.

She read to them about her childhood, her siblings, her mother, the man who came to live with them after their father died, the aunts' and uncles' houses where they were all dispatched after their mother went to the asylum. The audience sat at attention, hearing this person's confessions and disclosures, understanding these were things this person needed to say. Spoken aloud—shared with this small band of strangers—Sophie's story took on an additional kind of weight. And as she continued reading, turning the pages, I saw that it was a weight she could finally unload from herself. Her story had become something she could hold, and then finally put down.

Afterward a few people asked questions. Did Sophie write on a computer or in a notebook, with a pen or a pencil? What time of day? Morning or night? Every day, or only in bursts? With music playing or in the quiet?

Then a few people stood in line to have their books signed, and Sophie sat shyly at the collapsible table, shaking hands and signing her name.

I stood in the back as the clerks collected the folding chairs from all around the room and carried them back to the closet.

Eventually the line grew shorter and the last of the audience departed. Sophie was still at the table, talking with a couple of stragglers. I thought of going up to her. But what would I say? And what did I want? I had my life in Halbrook, my studio apartment overlooking the square, my little desk against the window where I'd spent most evenings this past year, writing my story to the best of my memory. Of course I'd had to change everyone's names and distinguishing traits. I'd had to make Chet Bland as bald as a bowling pin instead of blessed, as he was, with a mane of curly golden locks. I'd had to make Debra an obsessive exerciser and not tending to plump, as she was wont. Of course I'd had to keep her a novelist. That part was unavoidable. But for drama's sake I'd let her be more successful than she really was. And Eastern College? I'd had to conceal the name of the real place, and move it to a fictional town, but otherwise it was exactly as depicted. For Carlos Cross I had made up some catchy book titles and given him snazzy tennis shoes and a wife and kids. And John—well, there were already too many fiction writers in this story, so he had to become a poet.

But what to make of myself?

And what to do about Sophie?

I stood there as the stragglers finally dispersed. Sophie was putting the leftover hardcovers back in a cardboard box and helping the clerks clean up. Her head was down, working, and she didn't see me.

Eventually the room was empty but for the two of us and the cashier, who was closing down the register. The overhead lights had dimmed, and I stood there among the stacks in half darkness. I could see the pink of Sophie's ear between the parted strands of her hair as she folded the flaps of a cardboard box one over the other and carried the box to the bookstore manager and set it on the counter. They exchanged some words, shook hands. Her back was to me still. Then she turned around, and her chin rose and she caught sight of me in her big, dark eyes.

There were about twenty feet between us, but it seemed an impossible distance. The room was silent. I could hear my heels against the carpeting as I attempted a first step, then stopped. She raised her hand slightly to wave, but dropped it to her side. I nodded. And for several seconds we just stood there, unsure of what to do next. I was hesitant to make an ending. But we had gotten this far. And so I started toward her.

Acknowledgments

The author would like to thank Anna Shearer, Benjamin Warner, Alex Kane, Tim O'Connell, and the Corporation of Yaddo for their support in the completion and publication of this book.

About the Type

The body text of this book is set in Sabon. Sabon, designed by Jan Tschichold (1902–1974), is an interpretation of Garamond originally released in 1967. Sabon was designed to create an identical form on both Linotype and Monotype machines. The width requirements for Linotype's casting machines give Sabon its uniquely narrow *f*.

About the Author

ANDREW EWELL is the recipient of fellowships from the Corporation of Yaddo, the Virginia Center for the Creative Arts, and Le Moulin à Nef, in Auvillar, France. He holds an MFA from Boston University and has taught creative writing at numerous institutions. This is his first novel.